The Darling Undesirables

by

Blythe Ayne

DEDICATION

To all my readers

With Heart

The Darling Undesirables
Blythe Ayne

Emerson & Tilman, Publishers
129 Pendleton Way #55
Washougal, WA 98671

All Rights Reserved
No part of this publication may be reproduced, distributed,
or transmitted in any form, or by any means, including
photocopying, recording, or other electronic or mechanical
methods, without the prior written permission of the author,
except brief quotations in critical reviews and other
noncommercial uses permitted by copyright law.
This is a work of fiction.
Names, characters, places, and incidents are fictional.

Art Nouveau graphics are in the public domain.
Book and cover design and a few of the interior graphics
by Blythe Ayne

The Darling Undesirables
Copyright © Blythe Ayne

www.BlytheAyne.com/books/fiction/genre-fiction

Paperback ISBN: 978-0-9827835-1-1

[1. FICTION/Science Fiction/Genetic Engineering
2. FICTION/Science Fiction/Steampunk
3. FICTION/Magical Realism] I. Title.
BIC: FM

First Edition

The Darling Undesirables
by
Blythe Ayne

Chapter 1

Heart stood in front of The Museum of Scientific Improbabilities and Unpredictable Oddities. She looked up at the sable brownstone building, up and up she peered, until her eyes came to the lights of the Mechanical Aurora Borealis, pouring extraordinary, revolving images into the sky.

"My Darling Undesirables," Keeper D said, "this is a great and glorious privilege you've been given by Father Inventor. Please show your appreciation."

The small band of Darling Undesirables stood at quiet attention, without a clue what was expected of them. All of them, that is, except Heart, peeved by Keeper D's pseudo-pious act for the benefit of people streaming past them into the museum.

Keeper D folded her hands as if in silent prayer. The Darling Undesirables imitated her gesture. But Eye didn't and Heart didn't. Eye didn't because he couldn't see. Heart didn't because whatever she believed, it was private.

People poured around them on both sides, keeping a respectful distance while sneaking sidelong glances at Heart.

Her fury rose. She had eyes. She had ears. She had hands and arms and legs and feet. She had hair and a mouth. In short, she looked like an ordinary girl of eleven or twelve, although she'd recently turned fifteen.

There was the staring with sidelong glances at her, and the blatant staring when they saw Eye. He'd become the most famous Darling Undesirable. He had no eyes. No residual eyes. No eye sockets. No suggestion of eyes. His face was soft skin from forehead to cheek to chin, with a beautifully formed nose and mouth.

Heart saw Keeper D glimpse at her out of the corner of her eye. Quick as snake tongues, she reached out and grabbed Heart's hands, clasped them together to her chest, then returned to her own position.

Heart tried to move her hands, but, strangely, a magnetic force held them gripped to her chest. As she gazed at the roiling lights in the sky above, the delicate pastel colors spun into a ball and became an intense, heavenly purple, forming an arch. Filmy pale green haloed out from the purple arch. Heart sensed a tugging at her entire body, as if she would pull up and soar right through that arch, five hundred feet above the ground.

Everyone around her stopped, stunned and mesmerized, watching the path that formed in the sky. Heart's feet tingled, she felt light, certain she was about to leave the ground. Keeper D grabbed her hands and pulled them apart.

"That's enough from you, Little Miss!" she hissed.

The lights of the Mechanical Aurora Borealis coalesced back to their calm patterns. Slowly people came out of their spellbound state and continued to file into the museum.

Stunned, shaken, weak, Heart stumbled. Keeper D caught her. "Whoopsie!" she said loud enough for those nearby to hear, grabbing Heart's collar. "A little dizzy from all that looking up, are we?" She grabbed Eye's forearm with her other hand, then shuffled all the Darling Undesirables forward. "Let us see the wonders within," she exclaimed, a smile glued onto her features.

"What happened?" Eye whispered to Heart.

"I … I'm not sure."

"Hush," Keeper D warned.

"I'll tell you later."

"There's nothing to tell," Keeper D said under her breath, "except more attention-getting from our little heartless wonder."

"Oh!" Heart exclaimed, but kept her retort to herself.

Keeper D's sad band of young charges came up to a jovial man at the middle entrance, while everyone else flowed through large doors on either side. Although the Darling Undesirables never paid for anything, they must always have their identity chips scanned.

"Wasn't that amazing?" The cheerful doorman said to Keeper D as he clicked each child's wrist implant—except, of course, Arms, whose identity chip was in his neck.

Heart watched Keeper D's smile fade, knowing how she loathed entering into conversation, especially pleasant chat. "What?" she replied brusquely.

"The Mechanical Aurora Borealis. I've never seen it do that. I've been here since The Museum of Scientific Improbabilities and Unpredictable Oddities opened, and I've never seen that."

Keeper D shrugged. "I didn't notice anything—I was attending to my Darling Undesirables."

The doorman nodded, subdued by Keeper D's unpleasantness.

"Where do the lights come from?" Heart asked.

Keeper D gave her a warning look. Heart ignored her.

"Well, my little Darling, we do not know."

"What are you trying to tell her?" Keeper D argued. "They come from the museum."

"No, Miss Keeper, indeed, they do not. As I say, we don't know where they come from. In the sky. Somewhere. Somehow. There is a mechanism that produces the aurora. I've watched the lights for years. Sometimes I've been fortunate enough to see truly beauteous forms—but I've never seen them do anything like what they just did. Opening up like that, making an arch, showing a path. Amazing! I wanted to walk on that path ...."

"Me too," Heart said, nodding. "I felt ...."

"You were not addressed," Keeper D extended Heart's wrist under the identity device.

The jovial man clicked Heart's wrist, lowered his head and looked at her from under his brows, then winked at her. She felt herself grinning—as if her mouth would stretch right off her face. No one had ever winked at her!

"Have fun in The Museum of Scientific Improbabilities and Unpredictable Oddities," he said, turning her hand over and giving it a pat.

Keeper D's hand went from Heart's collar to the back of her neck, giving it a squeeze, not quite painful, but definitely an unspoken, "Don't speak!"

Heart tried to wink back at the doorman, but having never seen anyone wink before, she blinked both eyes. The doorman chuckled. Keeper D's grip increased. Heart didn't care. She and the doorman shared a secret moment. Keeper D could do nothing about it.

Heart would never, never forget this moment.

Something continued to shift in her. It had started with the light path that opened in the sky and continued through to this moment when a gentle man had really, truly looked at her. Had really, truly seen her. Not staring at her because she was a Darling Undesirable, but looked at her because—because she was herself.

She'd be content to go home right now, having seen and felt more joy and happiness in ten minutes than altogether before in her life—other than, of course, her time with Eye.

Inside, the Darling Undesirables had gathered in a tight knot, waiting for Keeper D. Heart saw a round little woman with a round face, big round eyes, a little round button of a nose and a round happy smile hurrying up to them, moving gracefully as if her feet were on rollers.

"Sorry, sorry to be late, sorry. The change in the Mechanical Aurora Borealis has everyone aflutter. A group in the stargazer room was completely agog. Such a unique display! Did you see it?" The round woman nodded cheerily at each of the children in turn.

"Some did, and some didn't." Keeper D's frown deepened. "However, I fail to understand this big fuss over a mechanical light show."

"Oh!" The round woman's round smile turned to puzzlement. "It's a very big deal. It's a very big deal," she repeated, as if she couldn't believe she'd had to say it the first time. "I mean—do you not know your prophecy?"

"Prophecy? Oh no. No. Stop right there. The children are not to hear that. We at the Darling Undesirables Facility at Long Prairie do not believe in such things. And—and," Keeper D was clearly brought to her absolute wit's end, "and this is a science museum. This is *science*."

"Oh dear," the little museum docent said, distressed. "I'm sorry to have upset you. I shall rephrase my talk." The round "O" of her smile returned to her face. "I'm so fortunate to be the docent chosen to show you around today. I'm pleased to meet our special little Darlings, Heart, and Eye." Her eyes squinted down into half moons of delight.

Heart looked up at Keeper D, who rolled her eyes as if the docent's sweetness was too saccharine to endure. "Let us move forward, shall we?" she said flatly.

"Yes, yes, of course. We're going to have so much fun today!" The docent took Heart's hand, pulling her away from Keeper D's grip.

Heart reached out and grabbed Eye's hand, and the three of them led the Darling Undesirables from the Facility at Long Prairie on their tour of The Museum of Scientific Improbabilities and Unpredictable Oddities.

This day just gets more and more remarkable, Heart thought, giving Eye's hand a squeeze.

"You happy?" he whispered.

"More than ever."

"*Wow!*" he breathed.

"I wish you could see … well, everything. But most especially, the lights in the sky."

"The lights in the sky," he repeated. "You'll show me—later. Tonight."

"Oh yes. I'll show you tonight. And tomorrow and tomorrow and tomorrow, until you beg me to stop." She would show him the amazing Mechanical Aurora Borealis when they were alone tonight, just like she showed him everything in the world, and all the things she made up not in the world. With words, words, words. All the pent up words she stored every day from the Keepers "shushing" her.

She would relive the lights, she would relive her feeling. She would relive how her feet tingled, and her body became light and pulled toward the Mechanical Aurora Borealis. She would tell him, and she would tell herself again and again, too, so that she'd never forget, how the Mechanical Aurora Borealis had surely responded when she clasped her hands over her chest. Strange coincidence.

But wait!

"Eye, you had your hands clasped, did you feel it?"

"Feel what?"

"The lights—the pull of the lights."

"Lights can pull? You've never said that lights can pull."

"They can't. I mean, they don't, usually. But, did you feel a pull?"

"No. I don't think so. I'm not sure I understand."

For a fleeting moment, Heart let herself feel a thrill of selfish exuberance. The strange pull must have been for her. If anyone was going to feel something, it would be Eye, whose sense of feeling substituted for vision. "Don't worry. I'll explain—tonight."

"Be quiet!" Keeper D hissed, coming up to Heart, Eye, and the docent, herding the rest of the Darling Undesirables, each clinging to a fat golden rope strung along the aisles of the museum for them to hold onto.

The docent, who had begun a brief overview of the hall they were about to explore, clapped her mouth shut at Keeper D's command.

"Not you," Keeper D said, only marginally civil. "I mean that one." She pointed at Heart.

"Oh!" The docent exclaimed. "I didn't hear her. Was she talking?"

"All the time."

"I'm telling Eye what I'm seeing." Heart dared to speak. They were in public. Keeper D was the only Keeper here. Heart thrilled at the opportunity to say what she always wanted to say. It wasn't precisely accurate that she was describing the surroundings to Eye at that moment, but she was about to, and she wanted to be able to tell him what she saw without Keeper D constantly shushing her.

"I think it's truly sweet of you to share with him what you see." The little round woman gave Keeper D a disapproving look, which Keeper D returned with double interest upon it. The docent shrank back a step.

"It would be *truly sweet*," Keeper D said with an edge of sarcasm, "if she'd stay in the realm of the real world. It's tiresome having to reteach the poor little guy after she's filled his head with ridiculous untruths."

The docent raised her eyebrows almost into her hairline. "I can't believe it! Look how sweet she is. And she holds onto Eye's hand most conscientiously."

"All an act." Keeper D leveled her gaze at Heart, daring her to speak.

Heart felt tight in her head like she did when she became extremely upset. She returned a defiant look. "It. Is. Not. An. Act. And you know it. You know Eye is my only friend. You're the actor. The First Directive is that Keepers love us—and you do not even like us!"

Almost all of the Darling Undesirables gasped, even the ones who had a hard time understanding anything.

The docent's hand became sweaty in Heart's hand. "Oh dear," she muttered. "And I was so looking forward to today."

Heart broke her stare-down with Keeper D. She knew she'd pay for her outburst forever as long as she lived at the Darling Undesirables Facility at Long Prairie. Eye held her hand tightly, not making a sound nor moving a muscle. Heart let her gaze fall to the plaid of her shirt sleeve. Brown-over, beige-under, dark green over-over, pale green under-over-under. She could hear Keeper D's voice, but only as a far away buzzing.

"Great. Just go into a fugue state. Fine, while the rest of us have some fun." Her voice faded as she and the Darling Undesirables—all but Heart and Eye—went down the hall.

Seconds later the cheery little docent's face blocked her view of the plaid. She had kneeled down on the floor in front of Heart. She stroked Heart's arm, where she tried to stay with the traveling plaid. "Are you all right, honey? Are you okay?"

Heart wanted to answer, but she couldn't talk while she was in the plaid.

"She follows the map in the plaid," she heard Eye say. She wanted to smile. He made a good student. He couldn't even see, had no idea what "plaid" was, but he understood what it was like for her when she went there.

"I see," The docent said. "So—she's all right?"

"Sure. She'll come back out in a minute. You're sure nice. What do you look like?"

The docent giggled. "Oh my goodness! How does one describe oneself? I'm round. I have a round face. I smile a lot. I have a tiny little nose and big round eyes. People think—because I'm very friendly and because I'm sweet and caring—that I'm kind of slow. There seems to be a weird idea that if you're smart, you must be snotty and rude. But I'm actually quite intelligent and nice. I know a lot more than I let on.

"For instance, and I suppose I shouldn't tell you this—I researched your group, and I knew who was coming. I know quite a lot about each of you little Darlings. I also researched your Keepers C and D and E. I know Keepers C and D are not very nice, and Keeper E is not very attentive. I was sort of prepared for anything to happen today. But not what the Mechanical Aurora Borealis did. No, I wasn't prepared for that. Someone in your group has some kind of powerful energy.

"I only saw the lights change and do something unusual once before, and that was when ...."

"I felt it pulling on me," Heart said, finally unweaving from the plaid.

"Did you?" The docent turned to Eye. "Did you feel it pulling on you, too?" The docent asked Eye.

"No. I don't understand what Heart means when she says she felt it pull."

"Magnetic," Heart said. "Like I was a magnet, and it was a magnet. Strong, I thought my feet would leave the ground."

"Very, very interesting." The docent nodded, then stood. "I supposed we'd better catch up with your group. Try to stay out from under Keeper D's radar, okay, my darling Heart?"

Heart nodded. "Okay. I don't know what's gotten into me! And I'm sorry I made you sad. I like your round smile very much."

"Thank you, sweet thing. But you didn't actually make me unhappy. It was a bit of an act on my part."

"Oh!" Heart exclaimed. "Why?"

"For this very reason. I had hoped to be able to chat with the two of you without her big ears."

Eye giggled. "Keeper Big Ears!" He whispered.

Heart and the docent giggled too. "Shush! Shush! You two, you'll get me in trouble if you repeat that!"

"It's our secret," Heart said, kissing her index and middle fingers audibly and raising them.

"Our secret," Eye said, kissing his fingers and raising them. They locked fingers. "Miss Round Face is our particular excellent friend."

"Yes. All words between us remain secret."

"All words secret," Eye intoned.

"Well, I'm flattered. That's a fascinating ritual you have."

"Thank you," Heart said shyly. "We have a book's worth of 'secret rituals.' We have to at that crazy place we live."

"Hmmm…" the docent took Heart's hand.

They wandered down the empty hall completely by themselves. As the Darling Undesirables explored, museum guards went ahead, clearing out other patrons and roping off each wing in turn with fat golden ropes.

Their footsteps clicked against the marble floors, echoing off the glass cases.

"Marble," Eye said. "Different kinds. Are there mosaics in the floor?"

"Yes! There are beautiful mosaics in the floor. You can 'see' the floor by the sound?" The docent asked.

"Sort of. But I can't see the images."

"Clever, clever child. Ah, here we are."

The three of them came up to the Darling Undesirables, who stood, not moving, gathered around Keeper D.

"Here we are," the docent said again, gaily. "Eye asked an important question. He could hear the different types of marble as we walked on them, and, clever boy that he is, asked if there are mosaics. He's right, the museum has beautiful marble art embedded in the floors in every wing, made of the finest marble to be found anywhere."

The docent moved to the middle of the group. "Each wing of The Museum of Scientific Improbabilities and Unpredictable Oddities has marble mosaics in the floor that depict the types of items housed in that wing." She gestured to the floor where they stood, "We are in the wing that explores what life would be like if the inventions using electricity had become our main means of energy. In the floor in this wing are the images of gigantic poles stuck in the ground, with wires strung from pole to pole." She swept her hand in arcs, imitating the marble electric lines in the artwork under their feet.

Then she shuffled the group over to a showcase. "In these showcases, you will see many examples of numerous failed experiments attempting to get electricity to work universally.

"Inventors had come up with devices that they called "telephones" for communication, fragile glass bulbs that sparked electricity to make lights, and heaters that used electricity to blow heat through homes." As she talked, the docent led the children from glass case to glass case, pointing to examples of the curious inventions.

"Even Father Inventor dabbled in electricity for a while. The biggest problem with electricity was that everyone shared this means of power. Everyone had to be on what was proposed as a 'grid.' So, if there was a problem with the grid, everyone would be without power—no lights, no heat, no communication, no cooking."

A couple of the children who were following the docent's talk gasped. Keeper D "tsked" as though the mere thought of the system was ridiculous.

"But everyone would have power most of the time?" Heart asked, her attention drawn to a charming little house, not quite as tall as she, demonstrating what a household run by electricity would be like. A little girl sitting in a rocking chair read by a yellow light. It looked cozy.

"That was the theory," the docent said.

Heart had heard of electricity, but she hadn't known of its many useful inventions. She thought about the people in The Periphery, living without power, in poverty and darkness. "But—couldn't the people who live in The Periphery use these inventions? This 'grid' of power, even if it quit sometimes, would be better than the way they're living now, with no power, wouldn't it?"

The docent exchanged a quick glance with Keeper D. Heart saw Keeper D frown and shake her head with a small, but extremely emphatic "No!"

"Well," the docent said slowly, thoughtfully, nodding at Heart, "I guess I've never really thought about it in that way. It's certainly an interesting idea. A very interesting idea," she mused, moving down the hall. Heart could see that the docent utterly wished she could get away from Keeper D. But that would not happen until the tour of the Darling Undesirables in The Museum of Scientific Improbabilities and Unpredictable Oddities was over.

Heart scurried ahead to come alongside the docent, even abandoning Eye. "But what …?"

She glanced at Heart out of the corner of her eye with a look that said, "not now!" And then she winked at her. Too! Just like the doorman. Heart wished and wished she could share this remarkable secret code with Eye.

But, it could never be.

Keeper D came up to them with the rest of the Darling Undesirables in tow. "We don't even need to think about electricity," she exclaimed as if there was a raging argument. "Ever since Father Inventor harnessed Dark Energy, we have more power than we can use. Electricity—*pah!*"

"If that's true," Heart argued, "why don't the people in The Periphery have power? Why do they live in darkness and cold? Dark Energy must not be enough for everyone."

"Oh—you are so exasperating!" Keeper D said, her voice grinding in a quiet, simmering anger.

"I don't care if I am. I just don't want those people to be in the cold and dark, and hungry too. I saw the children, huddling together at night in darkness on my 3-D. That's wrong!"

Keeper D sighed, clearly resigned. "I will tell you. Those people are being punished."

"Bun-ished?" Heart asked. She looked at the docent, who looked away.

"Punished," Keeper D corrected. "P-u-n-i-s-h-e-d," she spelled.

"What is 'punished?'" Heart looked at the other Darling Undesirables. They were getting bored. Some had wandered a few feet away. Some were putting their hands on the glass of the showcases, which Heart knew Keeper D would never permit. So this subject was very big, to completely take Keeper D's mind.

"When you do wrong, you get punished. The people in The Periphery have been sent out of the cities. They are exiled from our Dark Energy advantages. They have a difficult life because they have hurt society. They have hurt others, and they cannot live with those of us who live in harmony, and who care for one another."

Heart, who had just said that Keeper D did not care about the Darling Undesirables, wondered what things the people living in The Periphery could possibly have done that were even worse than how Keeper D was all the time. "But there are children! That's not right! Why are there children in The Periphery?"

"People make children, Heart. The people in The Periphery are free to live their lives as they choose. People used to be put in prisons. That punishment was so much worse than now. These days, we are humane. People who act against society are simply removed from society and its advantages," Keeper D preached. "The Wall keeps them from entering where we live, and from having the numerous advantages of harnessed Dark Energy.

"You wouldn't have us take the children from their mothers and fathers, would you? If they choose to have children, those children, too, live in The Periphery. It's not so bad for them. They don't know what they've never had." Keeper D moved pointedly away from Heart, taking up the hands of two of the other Darling Undesirables. "Let's continue our tour, shall we? Our docent had been very patient with us."

"Oh, that's all right," the docent began, "I don't m …."

"Still," Keeper D interrupted, "I think it best that we keep moving. The children are restless. Other people are here as well, wanting to see the exhibits. I'm sure we've kept this wing closed more than long enough." She moved down the hall swiftly, with the feet of the two Darling Undesirables in her grip pedaling rapidly to try to match her long stride.

"We'd better keep up with her," the docent said, herding the rest of the group, while Heart took Eye's hand in her own.

"Such a lot …." he said.

"Going on," she completed.

"Yes."

Heart thought she would never have anything as big and terrible to think about as those children in The Periphery. Not like she was, and Eye, and all the other Darling Undesirables, who had no parents, who were just faulty test tube experiments, but lived a life of luxury. Those sad, real, young people living in darkness and cold and hunger, hurt her in a deep, sacred place.

But she didn't know what would soon befall her.

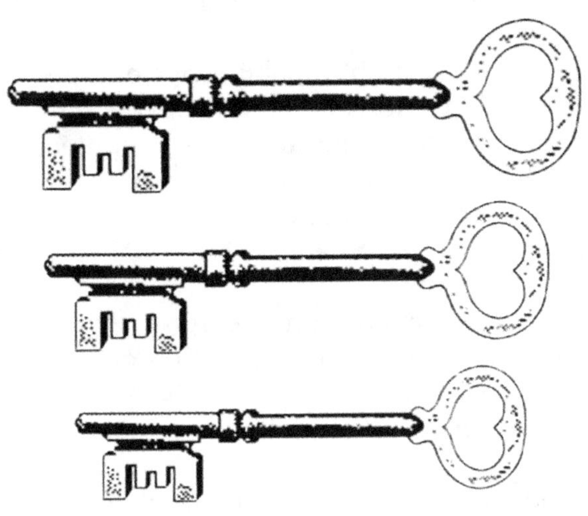

Chapter 2

The docent took them through all the wings of The Museum of Scientific Improbabilities and Unpredictable Oddities, providing a steady chat of information.

But Heart heard and saw little of it. Her thoughts of the Mechanical Aurora Borealis made her happier than she'd ever known happiness in her life, while thinking about the children in the cold and dark Periphery that she learned could have light and heat, brought upon her a sadness greater than she could ever have imagined her thin little, no-heart body could hold.

Finally, the Darling Undesirables wended their way through the maze of the entire museum, returning to the front entrance from the opposite side. As they came around the corner to the front foyer, Heart stopped short. Before her, alone in a large, beautifully lighted showcase, stood a breathtaking creature: a horse made entirely of gears.

The Darling Undesirables behind her bumped into her, then flowed around her. In the foyer, hundreds of people and dozens of newshounds mounted with cameras, sniffing out the news, waited to see the Darling Undesirables. Word had gotten out that they were visiting The Museum of Scientific Improbabilities and Unpredictable Oddities.

Keeper D, preoccupied with attempting to keep the children together, ignored the commotion on the other side of the golden rope.

"Heart," Keeper D called back to her, "stay with the group."

Heart nodded, but instead, she crept toward the glass case. As she moved from the side to the end of the case, face to face with the creature, she felt a pull in her chest—again—like she'd felt with the Mechanical Aurora Borealis! She moved around to the front of the glass case where she had a clear view of the magnificent Gear Horse, standing proudly, with a beautiful, noble head, neck arched. But his eyes were glazed—no spark of life.

Heart moved to the front of the showcase, feeling the magnetic turn in her chest where her heart would be if she had one, as she moved around the clockwork horse. Then she noticed a red light flash deep in the Gear Horse's chest. Flash. Pause. Flash-flash. The flash in the Gear Horse's chest and the tug inside her chest beat together.

She touched the glass. She thought the horse might look at her, might even wink as others had done today, but there was nothing to suggest animation about the beautiful arrangement of gears, other than the strange red light.

Heart stepped back. Wait a minute, she thought, the light was simply another security measure. The docent had pointed out several.

She looked at Keeper D and the children. Eye, wondering where she was, stood to the side.

She stole over to him. "I have to stay here," she whispered.

"Stay here? Why?"

"I can't tell you right now. I'll tell you later."

"But—how will you get back?"

"I don't know. I'll think about that later. But right now ..." she watched Keeper D try to get the children to line up, while the docent chatted, oblivious of Keeper D's frustration. "Right now, I have to stay here. When she counts you, move back so she counts you twice. She's so overwhelmed by everything, she won't notice. Will you do that?"

"Sure, Heart, sure. I'll do it."

"Thanks." She made their sign for "love you," in his palm, then stepped to the wall, putting to use one of her best talents—shapeshifting into the color and texture of the wall.

She watched as Keeper D became more rattled, counting distracted children, being called to by the crowd, fending off the bio-machine dog-form newshounds that had crept under the gold rope, their cameras taking close-ups of her and the children. Heart knew Keepers hated having their image taken.

Heart smiled as Eye was counted by Keeper D, then he stumbled to the back of the line and she counted him again.

She knew Eye was aware she'd shapeshifted. He waved absently at the wall. The crowd would just think he'd gotten turned around, even though he had a better spacial awareness of where everyone stood than anyone with eyes.

Heart watched as Keeper D herded the Darling Undesirables to the door, head down and teeth gritted. Meanwhile, the docent basked in the limelight, answering questions from the crowd and posing for the newshounds, clearly in her element.

"Heart is the dearest little Darling," she cooed, smiling. "Very bright, sweet, full of heart. She doesn't need a physical heart, she's so sweet."

"Great headline!" A newshound said as the docent's quote appeared in the air in 3-D above his camera—and, at the same instant, in billions of homes and vehicles around the planet: M.S.I.U.O. Docent Quips: "Heart Doesn't Need a Heart to have Heart!"

Most of the crowd stepped outside to wave good-bye as the Darling Undesirable's airbus lifted onto the Dark Energy Skyway. The docent continued to regale her audience with snippets of their tour, discreetly avoiding Keeper D's unpleasant behavior.

Slowly, the onlookers drifted back to their own concerns as the excitement of the day drew to a close. As the few remaining stragglers in the museum passed through the exit, they made comments about how "grand it had been to be at The Museum of Scientific Improbabilities and Unpredictable Oddities when the Darling Undesirables were there," and "did you see Eye? Did you see Heart? What Darlings they are!"

Heart took it all in, bemused. Were people's lives so totally, utterly, and completely empty as to become this animated about herself and her friend? What was the fascination? Heart heard the odd combination of voyeurism and the urgency of guilt in their voices. Each and every one of them had their own selfish interest in allowing the illegal experiments that produced the parentless creatures, the Darling Undesirables. How hollow their lives must be!

She looked toward the case that housed the magnificent Gear Horse. She could just see the tip of his nose from her position against the wall. Soon, she thought, soon she would be able to stand before him without Keeper D hovering. Without anyone hovering. Certainly the Gear Horse and the Mechanical Aurora Borealis were linked! And, she believed, with equal certainty, she was linked to them both.

It seemed to take forever, but eventually, the docent waved goodnight to the ticket taker—Heart's two new favorite people in the world. After Eye, of course. They had both winked at her. They had both treated her like a person, they had both given her affection—and not because she was a Darling Undesirable.

The round, cheerful docent glided by in front of her with her roller-like motion, then passed down the long marble hall, and finally out of sight at the back of the museum, while the ticket taker closed up his booth and left through the front door. The door's locks clicked and shunted behind him, and all the dark energy lights winked to a pale, flickering glow.

An echoing silence fell over the cavernous museum. Heart was about to pull herself from the wall when a strange, tiny man, weighted down with keys upon keys upon keys on his vest, around his waist, and encircling his wrists, came rhythmically with clicks and clanks into the entryway. He moved to a bank of switches and keyholes on the wall, twenty feet from where chameleon Heart stood.

The locks were thrown, the lights had dimmed, what, Heart wondered, could Key Man be attending to?

She nearly fell off the wall when, with a disconcerting clatter, metal grates clanged down over the glass doors. The Key Man paused for a few moments while the clattering-clanking echoed and finally stilled. Then he inserted a long thin key into a lock.

Heart heard a whirring and shushing from the hall to her right, the hall that housed the captivating clockwork inventions. As much as she desired to turn her head to see what approached, she dared not move. The Key

Man stood facing her, watching the hall. Delight slowly spread across his features. Well, then, at least the weird approaching sound was not attached to something terrible.

The whirring augmented in volume and pitch, as a gigantic clockwork moon floated into the periphery of Heart's vision. It whined and whirred until it hung over the Key Man, and, as it found its place, the ceiling of the museum dome lit up with stars.

The Key Man inserted another key into the bank of locks, and now a rolling sound issued across the marble floors from the dark hall beyond. Soon a small piano with a tiny, exquisitely beautiful clockwork woman at the keyboard came into Heart's view, playing a gorgeous piece of music that Heart had never before heard. The piano rolled into place in the far corner of the entryway.

Then the Key Man inserted a key with dual heads into a dual keyhole, and directly she heard a peculiar gliding-stepping sound, in perfect time with the music. Glide-step, glide-step, down the hall toward her. Heart held her breath. What was about to appear before her eyes?

An impossibly tall and supernaturally beautiful pair of dancers swirled into the open space, whirling and whirling, their mechanical, yet beautifully clothed arms embracing one another, their dance steps intricate and graceful.

The clockwork woman's glorious mountain of blonde hair, studded with dark blue gems, shimmered and sparkled. Dressed in a floor-length baby blue gown from a day long gone, with low cut bodice, flowing sleeves, and cinched waist, the yards and yards of diaphanous pale blue fabric billowed and swayed around her graceful movements.

The clockwork man stood ramrod straight, his blue-black hair caught the shadows, while his partner's hair reflected the moonlight that spilled on the entire scene from the clockwork moon, slowly making its way across the museum's domed sky.

Heart had never, never, ever in her life experienced such enchantment, such a mystical moment. The beautiful clockwork couple stared into one another's eyes, filled with love and unspoken language. Who would believe they were machines?

As the diaphanous moon made its way across the synthetic sky, the tiny piano player filled the air with melody upon melody, while the dancers turned and turned and turned. The Key Man sat on a little stool he pulled from a minuscule, nearly invisible, door in the wall. He put his elbows on his knees, his chin in his palms, and with a deep smile on his features, nodded his head and swayed his body in time to the delicate music, the jingling of his keys adding a gentle percussion.

Heart longed to dance with the tall, beautiful man, to sit by the tiny piano player, to sail across the fake sky riding the alabaster-colored moon. Joy so filled her that she almost forgot about the clockwork horse.

Almost, but not quite. She looked toward the Gear Horse. He stood without movement, inside his glass case, unaware of the activities of his clockwork species.

Wouldn't the Key Man turn yet another slender key in another lock to let the lovely horse come prancing out?

No. Heart resigned herself—neither she nor the horse were to join in the dance this glorious night. But it was all right, was it not? She was witnessing something that, other than the Key Man, no one in nearly two hundred years had seen. If, indeed, anyone else had ever seen these fabulous and mystical clockwork creations performing together.

The moon came to its perigee on the opposite wall, the stars faded, the music softened. Then the whirling couple turned and swirled and swept back down the hall, soon followed by the rolling piano, the beautiful, tiny woman, and the ever-softening music. Next, the moon, clanking and clicking, floated behind them, and the great cavernous entryway fell disturbingly silent, the animation of all the clockworks still hanging in the space.

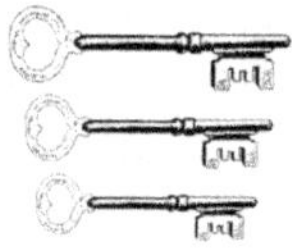

Chapter 3

The Key Man put away his very small stool through the very small door in the wall, closed the door, then closed and locked the key wall. He sighed deeply, as if he felt so very alone. He clanked softly by Heart, stopping in front of the showcase of the Gear Horse.

"Next time, my lovely. Next time, you will get to exercise your beautiful hooves and your spectacular wings. I wish I could let you all out every night, but since the collision … *Ah!*" The Key Man shook his head, grief on his features. "Ever since then, we must be careful. We must never again accidentally kill any clockwork beings."

The Key Man reached out and gently patted the glass of the horse's showcase, then turned and clanked down the long, quiet hall where all the clockworks had gone.

Killed! Heart thought. He said it as though he truly meant it. As though it was not metaphorical. How tragic. And, furthermore —

WINGS!?! The Gear Horse had wings? Where? How did he use them, how did they extend?

Heart knew she must return to the Darling Undesirables Facility at Long Prairie, because Eye needed her. But tomorrow night, the Key Man said, he would let the Gear Horse out of his showcase. She'd seen such wonders this entire day, she argued with herself, couldn't she be happy with what she'd witnessed?

In a word, no. Now that she knew the horse would prance and perhaps fly tomorrow night, she could not leave. Eye would be all right. When they were close together, they could think their thoughts to one another. She'd never been this far away from him, could she connect with him now?

She pulled herself from the wall and sat cross-legged on the floor, picturing Eye. Then she looked at the stunning Gear Horse, sending a mental picture of him to Eye. But her thought did not connect. Her mind encountered a dark wall instead of the bright colors floating in a vat of calm she knew as Eye's mind. It must be the distance that prevented contact.

Disturbed by the void, Heart switched off her efforts to communicate with Eye. She walked over to the Gear Horse, and as she moved around him, the red light, deep in his chest, began to blink, and again, something inside her throbbed in rhythm to the blinking light.

She felt breathless.

"Unlock the showcase," she heard in her head. Heart looked around.

"Unlock the showcase," she heard again.

Heart frowned. "Are you … talking to me?" she asked the Gear Horse.

"Yes. Open the showcase. Open it now."

"How? I don't have any keys."

"You are the key. Come around to the lock, use your mind to slide the locks, I will do the same on my side. The locks will open."

Heart stepped around to the side of the showcase and looked at the frame. There appeared to be a locking mechanism near the top and the bottom of the frame. She didn't have a mind picture of what they looked like, but one came to her as she stood there, putting her mind to unlocking the mechanism. She could feel it sliding, and heard a "slunk!"

She pushed sideways on the frame, and the door slid open.

"Oh!—that was easy!"

"At last!" The Gear Horse said in her mind. "You were meant to come three years ago."

"I … I could have. But Darling Undesirables have to be twelve, and Eye wasn't twelve until last year. Then he got a weird virus, and couldn't come. I didn't want to come without him."

"Yes," the Gear Horse said. "But it's been a long wait. I have much to teach you."

"Teach me?" Heart took a small step back. "What do you mean?"

"Do not be afraid. Concentrate. First, I have to teach you about flying. Please open the gear box on my chest. You see the latch?"

"Yes," Heart said, slowly reaching for the latch.

At that moment, a loud bleat of a horn sounded at the front door. Heart practically jumped out of her skin. "What is that?" she whispered.

"Your jailer," the Gear Horse answered.

Heart heard the little Key Man coming down the clockworks hall. She slid the showcase door shut, then stood by the Gear Horse, bent over, shapeshifting into his gears. She peered around the Gear Horse's chest and watched the Key Man click and clank to the front door. He opened the door over the locks and pushed buttons. As the grate over the doors slid up, the bleat of the horn sounded again.

If I had a heart, it would stop with that terrible noise, Heart thought. The Gear Horse snickered.

Oh! You can hear my thoughts, too!
Of course!

"Hold your horses," the Key Man said, disgruntled.

Heart and the Gear Horse both snickered. *Well, I am!* she thought, patting the Gear Horse.

The Key Man put three keys in three locks in the lock wall, and opened them each in turn. The front door audibly unlocked. Pushing her way through the central door came Keeper A, the Keepers' superior, a gigantic, flawlessly beautiful young woman, dressed impeccably in a pale green brocade, hour-glass fitted blouse with off-white scrollwork that accentuated her voluptuous yet wasp-waisted form. On her long, model-like legs she wore pale green leggings. She looked like she'd taken hours to get ready, but Heart knew she had to have dashed from the Darling Undesirables Facility at Long Prairie the moment Heart was not accounted for, to arrive this soon.

Heart had never seen Keeper A leave the grounds of the Darling Undesirables Facility.

She also knew that she would soon be heading home. Keeper A's bionic scent implants assured that no Darling Undesirable could go anywhere without becoming detected.

"Fool! What took you so long to simply open the door?" Keeper A looked down at the Key Man, easily two feet taller than he, her eyes flashing.

"Madame, I am not required to unlock the door after hours for anyone, even your own self-important person. You will kindly address me with good manners."

"I have a Darling Undesirable at large. Arguably the most important Darling Undesirable. I don't care about manners ..." she looked around the dark and cavernous entryway, "at—" she inhaled deeply, "this—" she moved along the wall, "moment."

She came to the place on the wall where Heart had shapeshifted and stood for a long time. Breathing deeply, Keeper A reached out and touched the wall with exquisitely long, beautiful, perfectly manicured, fingers. She held her hand, palm up, fingers toward the Key Man and blew across her palm.

"Smell that?"

"No," The Key Man said flatly, narrowing his eyes at Keeper A.

Heart had never been near this intensity of emotional conflict. She'd thought Keeper D was stressful earlier, but that was nothing compared to what she sensed now between Keeper A and the Key Man.

"If you are harboring her, you will be in the greatest of trouble."

"Harboring who? What are you going on about?"

"Heart! Heart did not come back on the Darling Undesirables' airbus. She is at large, you complete idiot. This is a crisis of the most serious degree if you do not turn her over immediately."

"If you don't stop insulting me, we will come to blows, I fear," The Key Man answered in a low, rumbling, yet terrifying voice. "I am warning you. I'm programmed to defend the museum, and, although I'm alarmed by your information, you must engage me, not alienate me."

Keeper A put down her hand, pulled back her head, squinted her eyes, and gave the Key Man an intense study, inhaling. "Are you not bio?"

"I'm about as much bio as you are dark matter, and dark matter as much as you are bio."

"Oh!" Keeper A exclaimed, "natural enemies. Well, we must calm the conflict and unite in finding Heart. I shall alter my mode of address."

"It would be wise."

"But, to clarify—you are not harboring Heart?"

"I am not."

"Then remove yourself from my immediate vicinity and remain silent while I discover her whereabouts."

Keeper A moved from the wall. She pushed her three middle fingers between her eyes. Heart knew her freedom would soon come to an end, now that Keeper A had fully activated her bionic scent implants.

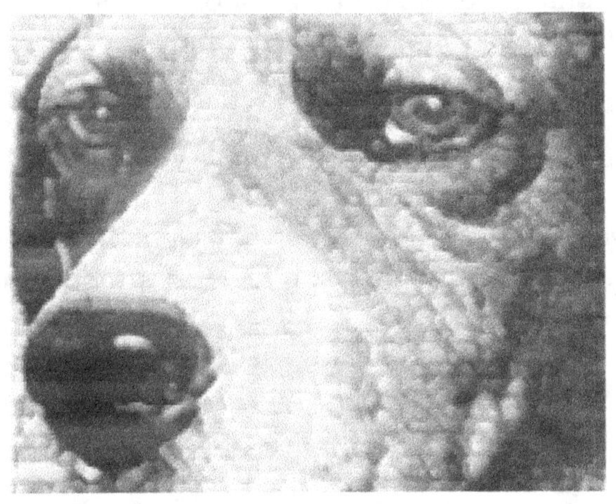

Chapter 4

But Heart held her position, hoping that the closed showcase would block her scent.

A ridiculously futile hope.

Keeper A moved directly to the showcase and slid the door open. She reached out and grabbed what looked like the side of the Gear Horse.

"No!" The Key Man shouted, rushing toward her from his station at the lock wall.

"Shut up," Keeper A hissed, pulling Heart from the Gear Horse and out of the showcase.

"Shapeshifter!" The Key Man whispered as Heart's true form appeared.

"Among other talents." Keeper A released Heart, looking down at her in exasperation. "What are you thinking? What is this about?"

Heart shrugged.

"You dare shrug at me?" Heart saw Keeper A could barely contain her fury, but she took a deep breath, then continued very calmly. "Never mind. Let us get out of this poor … whatever he is … creature's way. You've caused enough disruption for one evening. Keeper D has lost her position. I guess that'll make you happy. If you're capable of feeling anything at all."

"Oh!" Heart breathed, then fell silent. In this one day, she'd experienced more extremes of emotion than she ever had in her life.

Keeper A grabbed Heart's hand and, without another word, practically dragged her out to the Darling Undesirables Facility at Long Prairie airbus. As the airbus levitated onto the Dark Energy Skyway, Heart turned to watch out the back window as the grates slid down over the front door of The Museum of Scientific Improbabilities and Unpredictable Oddities. The little Key Man returned her gaze from inside until the grating blocked him from view.

"Do you have any idea of the trouble you've caused?" Keeper A asked, voice low but grinding.

Heart turned to face forward. "No," she answered truthfully, curious at the idea that anyone—besides Eye—cared enough about her to be troubled by her absence. Keeper D losing her position was trouble, true. But that wasn't because anyone cared about her, about Heart. Sooner or later, Keeper D would have lost her position because she was not good at her job.

"What trouble did I cause?"

"You'll see. I don't even want to waste my energy talking about it. You did this on purpose. You didn't just wander off. You intentionally caused mayhem."

"I did stay behind on purpose, and I thought about consequence. But not to cause mayhem. I …" Heart stopped. She would never tell Keeper A about how the Gear Horse had captivated her.

"There were displays I wanted to look at more. I didn't know The Museum of Scientific Improbabilities and Unpredictable Oddities would be so …" Heart leaned over to look at the lights below. The captured flow of dark energy trailed translucently below them, and the lights winked and waved from the warm, cozy homes. "Enchanting. I didn't know The Museum of Scientific Improbabilities and Unpredictable Oddities would be so enchanting. The docent made it extremely interesting. I've never seen Eye enjoy himself so much."

Keeper A didn't bother to glance at Heart. "I certainly hope that Eye enjoyed the day. I trust that your behavior is worth it in the long run. Because of your antics, I've had Eye placed in the sensory deprivation tank."

Shocked wordless, Heart turned to stare at Keeper A. Her beautiful, flawless profile showed not the least blip of emotion. Her chiseled cheekbones, her perfectly straight nose, her large, intelligent eyes, her exquisitely shaped mouth—all implacable. Like looking at a painting of flatly emotionless beauty.

But Heart knew Keeper A was filled with feelings—angry feelings. How could she be so horrible to Eye? Sweet, gentle Eye. Everyone knew he had only one thing he could not bear—not being able to hear. "You put … Eye … in …."

"The sensory deprivation tank. For punishment."

There was that word again! Twice in one day.

"But—why? He didn't do anything wrong. Why?"

"Perhaps you'll think twice before causing me so much trouble again. There's nothing I can do to you that gives you pain, other than give Eye pain," Keeper A said with calm resignation.

True! Heart was silenced.

She spent the rest of the ride quietly looking through the clear dome at the two visible synthetic moons. They were lovely, one pale pink, and the other, pale yellow, unimaginatively named Pink and Yellow. Endless rumors promised a contest to name the synthetic moons, which now, with the two blue ones in the far hemisphere, numbered four. But the naming contest never materialized.

Heart loved little Pink. She wanted badly to ask if it was habitable. But she wouldn't ask Keeper A, of course.

Finally, the airbus made a great circle in the sky as they approached The Darling Undesirables Residence of Long Prairie. Heart couldn't wait to get distance between herself and Keeper A. She dared to make one last, quiet statement. "You are not following the First Directive. You're cruel to the gentlest of creatures, the sweetest of the Darling Undesirables. It cannot come out well for you."

Keeper A didn't even glance at Heart. "If I can't control you with kindness, I must change my approach. Furthermore little deformed one, do not dare to threaten me. Or it will not come out well for you!"

The airbus thumped to the ground with the final word.

Heart exited the airbus, surprised to see the Darling Undesirables who had been with her at The Museum of Scientific Improbabilities and Unpredictable Oddities— with the conspicuous exception of Eye—lining the walkway to her residence.

Heart ignored them and she ignored Keeper A, too, who walked behind her all the way to the door of her room.

Were they also being "punished?" Was she supposed to feel humiliated? She knew that any Darling Undesirables capable of understanding what was going on would side with her, if sides need to be taken. The rest of them had no idea why they were standing in a tidy row, outside, in the night.

Heart opened the door to her room, stepped inside and shut the door in Keeper A's face. She listened at the door until Keeper A's steps quietly receded down the stairs. At least she didn't attempt to violate the Directive of Right to Privacy for all Darling Undesirables who were able to attend to self-care after the age of ten.

Then Heart heard the Darling Undesirables file in and go to their rooms. Clearly subdued, not a word passed among them. The soft shuffle of their feet touched Heart to her depths.

*   *

Heart sat on the edge of her narrow bed, studying the night sky through her star window skylight. When she was seven, a newshound had rushed up to her, asking her what was her favorite thing, and she'd said, "Stars!"

Her little chirp of "stars!" instantly rang out around the world. Gifts of star wallpaper, star-shaped toys, a star-studded tridimensional info-tainment center, clothes with stars that lit up, two dozen pair of shoes with lights of sparkling stars in sizes ranging from her little seven-year-old feet to certainly larger than her feet could ever become, immediately poured in to the Darling Undesirables Residence of Long Prairie, addressed to "Heart."

She gave away the clothes and the shoes. Keeper G and Keeper J were delighted with the star-studded shoes, even though Keeper A insisted the shoes be returned to Heart. But Heart snuck the shoes back to them. It was much more fun to see the stars flashing by in the night on other feet— which was quite a sight!—than to have them for herself.

Besides, anyone who knew Heart at all knew she only wore plaids and paisleys.

Among the gifts she'd received, the most treasured was her star-window, where she spent many hours in the night studying myriad off-planet realms.

The entire window, a geodesic dome inset in the ceiling of her second-floor room, was a three-dimensional super-telescope. The geodesic shapes of the window functioned as guides to the constellations. The window, connected to a satellite external to Earth's atmosphere, ran on dark energy. Every night, Heart contemplated a different celestial sector of the sky, regardless of terrestrial weather.

Leaning back against her pillow, looking up at the bright and companionable stars, Heart could think of nothing but Eye, frightened and alone in the deprivation tank.

She reached her mind out to him and felt his agony—he'd gotten into such a state that she discovered he couldn't even sense her. Could the deprivation tank stress him so much that it damaged his mind?

Unbearable!

Heart moved to her closet and brought out a black jacket she rarely wore as it was neither plaid nor paisley, and pulled it on. It would make her less visible. Then she tip-toed out of her room and down the hall to the back of the building, where almost no one ever went. She crept down the back stairs, and, rather than going out the door which had a 3-D receiver trained on it, she went into the bathroom, climbed onto the narrow window ledge, then slipped out through the window.

She stole across the yard to the back fence, partially shapeshifting into the trees and flowers she passed, though she found it more difficult to shapeshift while moving. The back fence, an eight-foot tall solid wall of wood, was designed to keep newshounds and curious people out and wandering, confused Darling Undesirables in.

If she crept along inside the fence, she reasoned, even shapeshifting, her movement might be detected. Perhaps, she thought, she could pull something over to the fence, climb up, then drop to the other side, although the tops of the boards were pointed pickets. And how would she get back in? The only gate in the perimeter of the fence was in front of the Keepers' residence.

She looked around for something to climb up on. She spied the tiny table and chair that Butterfly, the Darling Undesirable rock garden attendant, had placed in her garden. Heart slipped among the shadows to the rock garden, and, reaching out from the shadows, snatched the chair, paused, then grabbed the table. Even though they were small, she hoped they'd provide enough height so she could hoist herself to the top of the fence and swing over.

The creepy-skin feeling of Eye's misery grew, urging Heart to move faster. Returning to the fence with her makeshift ladder she took the time to carefully stack the chair on the table, then stepped up on the table. It held her weight! Then onto the little chair. It wobbled fiercely and threatened to topple, as she wrapped her hands on two sides of a picket.

As she pulled herself up to the top edge of the fence, a voice on the other side whispered, "Hey, hold on a sec, if you can. I'll stand up against the fence, and you can step on my shoulders."

"*Who—are—you?*" Heart whispered back, scared half witness, almost losing her grip, terrified of the gigantic clatter she'd make, falling on the table and chair.

"Come over and I'll introduce myself. But do it quick. You can't hang for long."

"Painfully true." Heart hoisted herself over the wall. As her feet dangled, one of them was guided to something rather soft but muscular. Her other foot found a similar spot, and whoever or whatever she stood on slid down the wall slowly until Heart could step onto the ground.

In the yellow-y, subdued light of a Dark Energy street lamp, Heart made out the shape of a newshound.

"*Oh!*"

"Sorry to startle you. But it worked out, eh?"

"Why are you here?"

"I'm usually here unless there's some huge event nearby."

"Here? Boring!"

"In a word, yes. But this moment, meeting you in person, makes all those boring moments worth it."

"Are you broadcasting?" Heart asked in horror.

"Of course not. I'm a bit more clever than that. I want a really good story. If I broadcast now, I'd be missing a huge story, wouldn't I?"

"Perhaps," Heart said. "All right. One, you helped me over the wall, and, by the way, thank you for that. And two, you're not broadcasting. Again, thank you. But what's your angle?"

The lanky dog sat back on his haunches, a look of incredulity on his hound dog face. "Are you serious? Just getting to meet you is the lottery winning angle of all angles!"

Heart nodded, a thousand thoughts racing through her mind. The primary one being that he could start broadcasting at any minute. But Eye's darkness crashed in on her thoughts, and the urgency of his plight outweighed all else. "I don't have time to discuss it right now, I need help."

"At your service." The hound bowed deeply.

"Hmmmm ...." Heart didn't say what she was thinking—that the hound's programming seemed a bit over the top. "What are you called?"

"My name is Swen." He bowed again.

Heart wrinkled her brow, thinking. "Ahm, 'news' spelled backwards."

The hound snapped to attention. "Clever girl! No one—whether bio, machine, dark matter, or combination—has ever immediately noticed that."

Heart shrugged. "I often see words in reverse. It can be distracting."

Swen nodded agreeably. "I can imagine."

The urgency of Eye's misery pressed upon Heart. "Listen, I've got to get to Eye."

"He's not in his room?"

"No. Because ...." Heart had a second thought about sharing so much with a newshound she'd just met, even if he was clearly not the usual sort. "Perhaps I'll tell you more later, but right now, I have to get to him. He's at the other end of the compound ...."

"The lab?" Swen asked.

"Yes. The lab."

"Why would a Darling Undesirable be in the lab in the middle of the night?"

"Like I said," Heart scurried along the fence line, "perhaps I'll tell you more later."

"All right, all right," Swen muttered, slinking along beside Heart. "When we get to where you're going to cross over the fence, you can stand on my shoulders. But I don't know how you're going to handle the other side."

"I'll just drop down. Climbing up is a bigger problem than dropping down."

"True," Swen agreed.

Heart sensed they'd reached the yard behind the lab. "I'll go over here."

"Here we go, then," Swen stood up against the fence, putting his paws against it at Heart's knee level. She climbed onto his shoulders. He slowly stood up on his hind legs to his full height. She grasped the top of the fence and hoisted herself over. Dangling for a few moments, she finally let go, landing softly in the grass.

"How are you?" Swen said through a knothole.

"Fine. Just getting my bearings." Crawling to the back of the lab, she recalled the floor plan. At her own request, she'd been in the deprivation tank three times in her life. She loved it, loved being utterly and completely alone with her thoughts, as if all the keepers were millions of miles away.

But it was not the same for Eye.

Looking at the back of the unassuming little building, she wondered how best to get in. There was the side door, not an option as it was 3-D monitored. She crept along the back of the building and came to a small window just above her head that she'd never noticed before. She reached up and pulled off the screen without difficulty. The window was open a crack. She tried to slide it further open, but it came against its locking mechanism.

"Try lifting it out of its track," Swen whispered through the knothole.

"Then what?"

"If you can get it off its track, you can angle it out through the opening."

Heart grasped the bottom edge of the window with both hands and pushed up. She almost dropped it when it slipped readily out of its track. She carefully angled it out and set it on the ground. "Must not forget to replace it," she said to herself.

"I'll remind you," Swen said.

"Are you going to stay?"

"Sure, sure. I'll be right here."

"I'm likely to be inside all night."

"Do what you have to do. I'm the most patient newshound in the world."

"Good to know." Heart pulled herself through the window, her feet landing on a sink. From there she jumped to the floor. She glanced around the tiny bathroom, filled with personal items—perfume, a few items of clothing on a small clothes rack, and some other things she couldn't even guess what they were for. She stepped to the door, opened it a crack and peered out. Utter stillness and almost total darkness met her on the other side. Creeping out into the hall, she got her bearings and moved toward the deprivation chamber to her left.

She passed a lab with numerous glowing lights and scores of beakers and test tubes, many with who-knew-what, roiling and flowing inside. Shuddering at the eerie fluorescing light of the living matter trapped in their small glass prisons, Heart scurried past the lab. She then stood in front of the deprivation chamber door, feeling into the space on the other side.

Immediately she sensed Eye calm down—he knew she was there.

She opened the door a crack, wide enough to slip inside, not daring to speak for fear of being discovered. She stepped forward and placed her hands on the tank. On the other side, Eye relaxed yet more. Heart leaned her forehead against the tank. She longed to tell him about the fabulous clockwork dancers, the clockwork moon sailing across the museum sky, and the petite, beautiful pianist at her little piano, making a music that filled the whole museum foyer like a delicate, exotic sweet. She wanted to tell him about the curious little Key Man.

But most of all, she wanted to tell him about the amazing Gear Horse, who had talked with her mentally in the same way she and Eye often talked with one another. However, she moved away from those thoughts. She wanted to save the wonderful story for when they were happily alone. She would draw word pictures out loud, so he could see everything clearly, not in this furtive manner, with him locked away from her on his pillow of air.

"Horse?" Eye asked in her head.

Well, she could only cloak her thoughts so much!

"The Gear Horse," she thought to him. "But let's wait until you're out of there and I can paint the whole word picture."

"I can't wait to hear everything. Oh, Heart, I've been so frightened! But now that you're here, I'm all right."

"Yes. I'm here."

"How did you get in?"

"I crept to the back fence, jumped over it, then jumped back across behind the lab."

"Over the fence?" Even in mind-speak, Eye was able to raise his voice.

"Over the fence."

"How? It's so tall."

"I seem to have a friend—or ally at least—of a newshound." Heart showed Eye mind pictures of stacking the little table and chair and then dropping over the fence onto the shoulders of the newshound, who helped her back over the fence.

"Wow!" Eye sent back to her mind in tall, waving, bright red letters.

Heart stifled a giggle, feeling so warm and close to her friend. They mind-chatted for the rest of the night until Heart sensed the sun about to rise and knew she must leave.

"I must go now, before the sun comes up."

"Go!" Eye urged. "I'm all right. I thought it was going to be the worst night of my life, but you made it wonderful."

"If I hadn't stayed at the museum, this never would have happened to you. It's all my fault."

Heart became anxious when she sensed no response from the other side of the deprivation tank. Then Eye said in her mind with unmistakable clarity, "I just think, Heart—it seems something is coming in your future that's—that's amazing. No Darling Undesirable has ever done anything like what you did last night. And look, now, you're here with me. You're so—so brave! I know what I mean to you, but you can't let anything—not even me—interfere with what you're supposed to do. I mean, you can't let me be in the way."

"You're never in the way," Heart wanted to shout it out loud. "You're my family. What do I care about a 'grand future' if you're not in my life?"

"I'm still your family, but you have to do … I don't know, whatever it is. And, look, I can be strong! This night proves it. You don't have to worry about me so much." The thought-stream from Eye stilled. Then Heart heard, "Go, Heart. I'm all right. They'll let me out soon. I'm okay."

Heart gently patted the tank and stepped back. A sadness washed over her. Her little friend was no longer a child. She told herself it ought to make her happy to see him so strong and so wise. But it wasn't fair that his maturity blossomed because of her behavior.

And she felt sad because she knew Eye was right. Her destiny had forced her onto a path. Like it or not, the previous day propelled her into a future she'd never asked for.

But then, she'd never asked to be created in the first place.

Chapter 5

Heart stepped out of the deprivation chamber and crept back to the tiny bathroom in the back of the lab. A fulvous glow of early dawn stole along the horizon. She'd stayed too long with Eye! She climbed onto the sink and peered out the window. Curled up below, slept Swen.

"You came inside the fence! What if someone found you here?" She whispered.

"Hey," he whispered back, reaching out his forepaws in an impossibly long stretch, "I'm just an old hound without my chest pack and camera, which I left on the other side of the fence. Hurry, the morning is fast upon us."

Heart jumped through the window, then stood on Swen's back to replace the window and the screen. She stepped off his back and he appeared to vanish through the wall.

"Where are you?"

"I dug a tunnel under the fence." He waved his paw under the fence through the flowers.

Heart shoved aside the flowers then wiggled through the tunnel. As she stood, Swen rapidly pawed the dirt back into the hole, then pulled on his chest pack and camera. Their auto locks wrapped around his body, clicking into place.

"Follow me." Swen trotted back up along the fence.

Heart ran after him, and he pointed out the second tunnel he'd dug in the night while she was in the deprivation chamber, this one opposite the little table and chair. She started to jump into the tunnel, but stopped, turned, and gave the newshound a huge hug. "Thank you, Swen, I don't know when I'll see you again, but I have a feeling we'll meet in the future."

"Yeah. Me too."

She started to crawl into the tunnel, but stopped once more. "I'm curious, who named you?"

"I named me."

"You did? How can that be? I mean, your creative intellect is very impressive. But you're still a machine. Machines may not name themselves. Only if you are some part …."

"Some part bio, yes. I am. I appreciate my machine intellect and strength, but I'm driven by my bio intuition and emotions."

"Fascinating! I'd love to know more, but …" Heart turned and jumped through the tunnel. She heard Swen fill it up behind her as she crawled out into the early morning dawn. She put her cheek on the fence, "Friends?"

"Friends! Now get to your room."

Shapeshifting into the background vegetation, Heart returned the little table and chair to the rock garden, placing them as close as she could recall to where they'd been, and hoping against hope no 3-D receiver picked up the furniture appearing to float across the yard. She climbed through the bathroom window, then shapeshifted up the back stairs and down the hall to her room.

Showering the dirt off, she discovered herself smiling like she'd rarely smiled in her life. She got into her paisley night clothes, even though it was now fully daylight. She didn't care. She would wait in bed for the sound of Eye returning to his room.

Before long, she heard Keeper G talking quietly to Eye, then the door next to hers softly opened and closed. Heart got up from bed and went next door.

Keeper G and Eye were sitting on the bed. Keeper G had his arm around Eye's shoulders, and Eye leaned into him, relaxed, clearly relieved to be in his own room. Heart moved quietly across the room and sat on Eye's other side.

"You all right?"

"Yes."

Heart put her arm around Eye's shoulders too, relieved that it was Keeper G who released Eye from the deprivation tank, and the three of them sat in companionable silence for a few minutes. Of all the Keepers, Keeper G was the most gentle and, like Heart, particularly attached to Eye.

Keeper G pulled away from Eye, and gave Heart a long, intense look. He raised his eyebrows as if to say, pay attention. Heart watched as he crossed to Eye's desk and searched around for something to write with—not an object Eye had much use for. He finally found a writing pad and pen, then pulled the chair from the desk over to the bed. He sat in front of Heart and Eye, very close so that all their knees touched. He started to write, while at the same time he began a ridiculous conversation.

"I see that you're in your paisley night clothes, Heart."

"Yes."

"Are you planning to spend the day in bed?"

"I might. I'm still thinking about everything we saw yesterday."

Keeper G turned the note he'd written to Heart. She read:

I remote monitored the Deprivation
Chamber last night. You know what
I saw.

Heart gasped. "Yes," she said. "I want to talk with Eye about some of the inventions we saw, and tell him about some of the text I read in The Museum of Scientific Improbabilities and Unpredictable Oddities that explain the many applications of dark energy."

Keeper G scribbled on with his note while continuing the conversation. "Well, that sounds like a good use of your day. Plus, Eye may have noticed some things that you didn't catch, isn't that so?"

"Certainly," Heart agreed, anxiety rising in her chest, wondering what Keeper G was about to tell her in his note. "He always 'sees' things I miss."

Eye giggled. "It's true!"

Keeper G turned the note so Heart could read it.

I don't know how you got into the lab
without being seen, but, dear Heart, you
must be careful. You are very fortunate it
was me on duty last night.

"Yes," Heart continued. "I'm fortunate that Eye's senses are so keen." Heart looked into Keeper G's eyes and nodded.

"Maybe you wouldn't mind if I sat with you and Eye today while you recap yesterday," Keeper G suggested. "I'd find it highly interesting. I could tutor and we could log it as class time."

"I'd like that," Eye piped up, fully aware that both spoken and written conversations were taking place.

"I'd like it too," Heart agreed.

"All right then. I don't know if you got any sleep last night, Eye. Do you want to sleep for a while?"

"No, not right now, I'm wide awake. But if Heart is in her paisley night clothes, I want to be in mine too. I'm going to take a shower and change."

Heart had insisted that Eye have paisley night clothes, and so among their many gifts, they shared a closet full of night clothes of every kind of fabric with every sort of imaginable paisley. Heart was fond of flannel, while Eye loved silk.

"I'll go get my classroom stuff," Heart said, going to her room. She needed a few minutes to think. If Keeper G had seen her last night with Eye in the deprivation chamber, then there must be a recording of it somewhere. If Keeper G destroyed the recording and it was ever discovered that he'd done so, he would be in the biggest trouble of all time. Much worse than Keeper D.

Was he really willing to risk everything to that extent?

Heart felt confused. Before yesterday, every day was the same as the day before. She ate, she went to class, she worked in the flower beds, she hung out with Eye. Everyone avoided, at all times, Keeper A. When one succeeded, life ran smoothly. When one came to her attention, life did not run smoothly.

In one short day, Heart's life had altogether turned upside down.

*　　*

Heart and Eye recapped the trip to the museum, while Keeper G asked interesting and relevant questions. They were all giggling joyously, when a soft voice came into Eye's room.

"Keeper A requests the presence of Miss Heart at her office immediately."

The voice clicked off. Heart exchanged a troubled look with Keeper G. Could someone have found out about last night?

"I must get dressed."

"I should go with you," Keeper G said quietly.

"They might wonder why, when you've not been requested," Heart whispered.

Keeper G nodded. "Go change. Let me think about it for a minute. Stop by before you go."

Heart hurried through the door. In her room, she changed into her matching plaid shirt and pants. She rarely wore the same plaid for both shirt and pants, but this strong plaid was a shield. She stopped and studied the plaid for a moment before going back to Eye's room. Blue: over, under, under, over. Red: under, over, under, over. Green: over, over, under, under. A powerful path.

She stopped at her door. Breathing deeply, she imagined her anxiety pouring out of her body and into the floor. Then she pictured the plaid weaving through her body, making her impervious to the lion's den she was about to walk into.

As much as she wished Keeper G might come with her, she felt equally certain that it would be a disastrous move. Still, she longed to have a witness. The next best thing was to have an audio recall device on her, so she slipped her necklace of a shooting star over her head and inside her shirt. The little star was also an excellent audio recall device, capable of recording the softest sound across a large room.

She stepped back into Eye's room. "I'll return shortly," she said cheerfully as she and Keeper G exchanged a look in which they agreed that he ought not join her. "Don't talk about anything interesting until I come back."

Eye chuckled, but Heart could hear the edge of fear in his fake laugh. "We won't. I'll stop Keeper G in his tracks if he tries."

"Right." Heart closed Eye's door and headed down the stairs, then outside and across the compound to Keeper A's office. She barely paid attention to the path, which usually filled her with joy. Its pastel stones wound in long, lazy curves, inviting the walker to enjoy the moment, while a myriad of seasonal flowers lined the walk every month of the year.

The burst of colors and the intriguing shapes were some of Heart's and Eye's favorite experiences, as she drew word pictures for him of each new flower. Delicately wrought benches, also of pastel colors with beautiful metal scrollwork, no two alike, intermittently lined the walk. The benches had been made during the Clockwork Era, and, although now nearly two hundred years old, they remained like new.

But Heart didn't see the flowers, she didn't rest a few moments on one of the benches to drink in her surroundings. She hurried, making as straight a line as the path allowed to Keeper A's office. She passed the dining building, the school building, the building where the Darling Undesirables who could not move about on their own lived. Behind that was the lab.

She passed the fairly luxurious home of Keepers B through E. Behind their building were arranged the three modest homes of Keepers F through L, Keepers M through S, and Keepers T through Z.

Beyond the Keepers' homes, over a little hill, not visible from the front path, were the small-but-well-appointed cabins of all the onsite workers; the people who made and mended and cleaned the Darling Undesirables clothes, the people who bought and prepared all their food, the people who maintained the property, the people who repaired every piece of mechanical equipment.

Next, she passed the flower and herb garden with a plethora of flowers and herbs. Little wooden archways and benches sprung up like delicate surprises throughout the garden, and a charming potting shed with cupolas, a turret, shuttered windows and an exterior winding stairway leading to a small walk around the roof made the garden compelling.

However, it remained the private domain of Keeper A, entirely enclosed by a beautiful but foreboding fence and locked gate. Only Keeper A and her gardeners had access. Everyone else could only admire the garden from outside its elegant, scrolling fence.

Whether alone or with Eye, Heart always leaned against the fence of Keeper A's garden, breathing in the fragrances that welled up into a delightful single, heady, fragrance. It was the one pleasure, the one common ground, Heart imagined, that she shared with Keeper A and her bionic scent implants.

But today Heart didn't glance at the garden. It rubbed salt on her wound. Keeper A, ignoring the Principle Directives, had no right to be here at the Darling Undesirables Facility at Long Prairie at all. And yet, she had her way with everything. She made the world here completely to her liking.

Heart mounted the three steps to the front door of Keeper A's office and residence building, a small stone building, constructed of the same colorful stone as the paths. Gorgeous pastel metal scrollwork, echoing the sensual curves of the walkway benches, surrounded the wide front door and trailed to its base and down along the edges of the steps.

Heart stepped through the front door. Keeper A's receptionist, sitting at a huge, pale brown wooden desk immediately inside the door, gave her a studied look. "She's waiting for you," he said, then quickly averted his eyes to the paperwork in front of him. "Or, rather *they're* waiting for you."

They? How many "theys" were there? And who were they? Heart said nothing, turning to climb the stairs to the second-floor office, a place she'd been exactly twice before in her life. Once, when she was first found on the front doorstep, nested among the metal scrollwork like a little bird. And then two years previous, when a news team assembled from around the globe insisted on an interview with Heart, the Darling Undesirable who had become everyone's darling.

What a wonderful day that had been! Heart took to the interview as if she'd done it every week of her life. She brought the newshounds, who'd been crowded out and hanging at the edge of the room, forward and let them stand right in front of her.

Today would not be like that day, Heart thought, pausing at the top of the wide stairs, reaching for her star necklace and turning on the audio recall.

She walked up to the huge, dark, floor-to-ceiling, thick wooden double doors. Inhaling deeply and exhaling slowly, she pictured the strong plaid pattern she wore giving her strength as the doors swung inward, revealing an opulent office entirely in pale green, with touches of beige. Pale green walls, floor to ceiling windows draped in gauzy pale green fabric, delicate chairs, and sofas carved with wooden scrollwork that replicated the scrollwork of the front entrance, upholstered in pale green velvet.

Heart crossed a thick, pale green carpet, with the same scrollwork pattern cut into it, in shades of eggshell and beige.

Keeper A, sitting behind her huge, scrollwork-carved, pale green desk, varied the color scheme slightly, dressed in a pale apricot silk shift, cloaked in her stunning beauty, looking as cool as the pale green that surrounded her.

She gave Heart a calm and somewhat disinterested glance, then swiveled to face the windows, as if she preferred not to see Heart at all.

Heart suddenly understood that this was Keeper's A's strong position. Mental pictures of her profile shot through Heart's mind as she replayed all the times Keeper A decreed something that would be a challenge or hardship for the Darling Undesirables.

Years ago, Keeper A had denied the Darling Undesirables the sandbox Heart requested after seeing natural children playing in one on a 3-D. Keeper A insisted the Darling Undesirables would eat the sand. Or when Keeper A wouldn't let six-year-old Eye keep the dog someone had given him after he'd drawn a darling little floppy-eared puppy and gave it to one of the newshounds. Keeper A said it was ridiculous for Eye to have a dog when he couldn't even see it. Both Eye and the dog whimpered piteously when separated.

On and on the pictures of Keeper A's profile fled through Heart's mind, right up to last night on the airbus when Keeper A, staring straight ahead, made her vile threats.

So Heart knew Keeper A was about to say things too impossible to contemplate. She wanted to turn and run from the office, from all the Keepers, from the whole place. It was full of lies, manipulation, and abuse, curling around everything, like all the scrollwork that surrounded Keeper A. On the surface, it was beautiful. But underneath, Heart saw a convoluted, calculating, deceitful maze.

She lowered her eyes to her plaid. Straight forward. Clear map, no curling, dead-end mazes. Just a map with straight lines, and plain and simple truths.

"You're becoming a problem larger than I have patience to deal with," Keeper A said quietly.

Keeper D, who had been sitting in a large wing-backed chair with its back to the room, stood, came around the chair and faced Heart. "So much trouble!" She nodded emphatically. "You've caused me to lost my position!"

Keeper B and Keeper C came up behind Heart through the open door.

"Heart, my dearest Darling Undesirable," Keeper C began, "I've always been partial to you. Although we're not to show favoritism, or to even have any favorites, I confess, you have been mine. I've always supported you and championed your anomalous and challenging behavior. However, lately, it's gotten out of hand."

Heart remained silent. What, she wondered, besides the events of yesterday, could Keeper C be talking about? In her lifetime she'd broken a small handful of minor rules, which was still fewer than most other Daring Undesirables. True, rules were broken by them because they couldn't understand the concept of rules, let alone the rule itself. Such was not the case with Heart, who understood the rules very well. That was her frustration. When a rule was simply stupid, why ought she to follow it?

"What do you have to say for yourself?" Keeper B, a tiny, wiry man with frizzled, dull yellowish hair and minuscule features asked in his buzzing, insect-like voice.

Heart's mental image of Keeper B was of him living in Keeper A's pocket, her own pet bee. No bigger than the children himself, he was the only Keeper who loved the attention of the newshounds, grinning, giving the Darling Undesirables fake hugs and playing with them whenever the newshounds were around. But he could sting. He'd actually pinched her, years ago, when she'd stepped between him and a newshound. Although pinching was specifically forbidden in the Principle Directives, Heart kept the incident to herself.

He moved toward her on his sprightly little feet. Heart stepped back.

"Relax, Keeper B," Keeper A said softly. She gave him a sidelong glance, arresting his movements, with, literally, one foot raised. Keeper A's gaze returned to the long drapes billowing in the breeze. "But I'd like to hear your answer, Heart. What do you have to say for yourself?"

Heart took a deep breath, following the blue thread in her sleeve. "Nothing."

"Nothing?"

"Nothing."

"That's not acceptable." Keeper D moved to the desk, placing her hands flat on the desktop. Heart saw her knuckles become white with the pressure she exerted, her body quivering.

Heart began to feel decidedly unsafe.

Like lightning, Keeper A swiveled, shot from her chair, grabbed Keeper D by the shoulders and flung her into her wing-backed chair with shocking strength. Then she glided deftly back to her own lovely scrollwork chair. "Silliness. Tiresome silliness. You're all too stupid to breathe. With the exception of Heart. She's brighter than all of you put together. Which, of course, is our problem. Now then, no one is to speak unless I directly ask you a question.

"Heart, my very dearest Darling, tell me, what am I to do with this band of nitwits, and what am I to do with you?" Keeper A looked directly into Heart's eyes. "I've asked you a question, and I do expect an answer."

Heart shrugged. "They're the nitwits you have, so they're probably better for you than nitwits you're not familiar with.

"Regarding me—I don't understand why you're upset. I've rarely broken a rule. I have many times protected, overseen, redirected and cared for the most delicate Darling Undesirables. I often visit the Darling Undesirables in the Bouquet of Flowers Residence, even ones who cannot understand a single word."

"All true," Keeper A agreed. She returned her attention to the billowing drapes. "True, true and true." She steepled her fingers. "But no one, not even I, could have imagined you doing what you did yesterday."

Heart folded her arms over her thin and heartless chest. She could not have imagined her behavior either. If this time yesterday someone had told her she was about to behave the way she behaved, she'd have been stunned.

"What are you thinking?" Keeper A asked.

"Just as you say. An endlessly surprising day."

"Yes. Well. Too bad you're a Darling Undesirable, you'd make a good Keeper."

"No, thank you," Heart replied without hesitation at the chilling thought. Having to obey yet more rules, and, even worse, being paid to care for her beloved peers. Several wrongs did not make a right.

"You're right." Keeper A nodded, again turning away from Heart. "That would not be a good position for you. Now, back to our business. Let's start from the most recent of your rule-breaking, and work backwards. First of all, Keeper G's 3-D notes from last night." Keeper A waved her hand over her desk console. The diaphanous drapes slammed into a solid phalanx of shutters, banging shut against the windows and throwing the room into darkness.

A 3-D hovered above her desk. Heart saw herself, hands and forehead on the deprivation tank.

Keeper G had lied!

Pain shot through her at the betrayal of her one trusted Keeper, but Heart kept silent.

"We appreciate Keeper G's notes, even though he failed, somehow, to record audio. Apparently, you didn't have much to say aloud, mostly mind-meld, I guess. Nothing new with you and Eye. But I didn't know it was so well-developed. Eye's vitals calmed significantly, even before you arrived in the deprivation chamber.

"At present, our biggest mysteries are how you got to the lab and then how you got in the lab. If I ask you directly, will you tell me?"

"No," Heart answered simply.

"As I thought." Keeper A waved her hand over her console, the 3-D shut off, the windows sprang open, the drapes returned to billowing. "So … how to control you? We've been brainstorming," Keeper A looked at the three Keepers, each in turn. "Well, I have, with a lot of background noise from these three. A few ideas came up. Keeper D, please calmly apprise Heart of these ideas."

"Gladly." Keeper D stood but stayed by her chair. "Solution Concept One: send Heart to a different Darling

Undesirables home. Problem: not only would we appear unable to take care of our charges, we'd also lose a huge amount of revenue.

"Solution Concept Two: send Eye to a different Darling Undesirables home, with of, course, the same drawbacks. A double-edged choice. The positive edge, Heart generates more revenue than Eye. Negative: she's significantly more challenging. Second negative, it's not clear how much of the revenue generated is because of the Heart-Eye duo, and if Eye were not here, might there be the same financial complication as if Heart were removed?

"Solution Concept Three is the most viable option. Perhaps Eye needs emergency brain surgery. This has the dual advantage of generating a considerable income bump, and, because of the emergency nature of the surgery, most likely alter his personality. It is possible he will not remember his relationship with Heart after the surgery."

Heart had kept her eyes downcast during Keeper D's recitation. She gasped at this last, raising her eyes to Keeper A, who, implacable, gazed out the window.

"Do not the flowers smell enchanting? Even with your weakened sense of smell, Heart, tell me, can you sense their heady aroma?"

"*You ... cannot ... commit ... this ... crime,*" Heart whispered, breathless.

"It is not a crime to save a Darling Undesirable's life. No one will believe you if you say anything. You have no alternative but to become agreeable and less problematic. Just kindly please return to your quiet, unassuming little popular self. Stop exploring. Stop thinking for yourself. Stop doing the unpredictable.

"Just *STOP,*" Keeper A barely held onto her rage. "This is not a warning, this is not a threat. This is what will be if there are any further infractions from you. You know the rules better than this band of idiots. When you're eighteen, we'll heave a sigh of relief, you can go, and good riddance. Yes, we'll miss the revenue you generate."

"But," Keeper C said, "there may be another Darling Undesirable by then who captures the world's fancy. One can hope."

"Did I ask you a question?" Keeper A's wrathful gaze fell on Keeper C. She paled as though she might faint away.

"No," she barely whispered.

"That's right. I know Heart will not tell what has transpired here today, because she loves Eye better than herself. Why this is so, is entirely beyond me, but she does.

"However, Dear Idiot C, she will have no compunction against sharing that which does not relate to her little soulmate. Have you even been around since yesterday? What happened to Keeper D?"

"She lost her position," Keeper C said in an ever quieter, quavery whisper.

"Yes. And why?"

"Because she didn't take proper care of her charges."

"Correct. And which Principle Directive is that?"

"Number Three."

"And which Principle Directive addresses anyone who wishes there to be more Darling Undesirables for 'entertainment, fiduciary gain, or any other reason?'"

Keeper C turned paler than the off-white in the carpet. "It is not a directive. It supersedes all directives."

"Punishable by?"

Keeper C could barely move her mouth, faintly whispering the words, "punishable by removal of sensory input of eyes, ears, taste buds, nose, and, in extreme cases of repeat offenders, skin."

"That's right, you supreme idiot. Lucky for you, no matter how much she may dislike you and wish you gone, I know Heart would not be responsible for such as that to occur to you. But keep your simple-minded mouth shut." Keeper A shook her head in disgust, which Heart had never seen her do.

Heart recoiled at this information. She'd not known she lived in a society filled with so much "punishment," an idea she'd not even heard of before yesterday. Curiously, she saw that she, by herself, single-handedly, had driven several Keepers to the brink of madness. Perhaps she had even shoved them over the edge. She'd not known they were so fragile and incapable of handling situations as she now witnessed.

"You may go now." Keeper A waved her away, without so much as a glance in her direction. "I know you'll return to behaving like the sweet little Darling that you are, and not give me any more headaches."

Heart didn't wait for her to finish her sentence. She rushed through the gigantic double doors, down the stairs, outside, then hurried along the curving lane to return to Eye.

She wanted to run. But Darling Undesirables did not run. They ambled, they stumbled, they hurried when they were hungry. But they never ran unless specifically instructed to do so for exercise.

I will be the Darling Undesirable Keeper A wants me to be. I will plan for the future. I'm fifteen. I only have to act stupid and slow and not want to know anything, or do anything, not say anything original, not ask any questions—just not be myself—for three years.

Three years, three years, three years. She stopped on the path, looked down at her plaid, following the blue thread. Just follow one thread. Pick one and let the other ones go. That'll make me dull. But I'll be with Eye. When I'm eighteen, I'll steal him and we'll leave. We'll go as far as we have to, to have lives of our own.

Chapter 6

After studying the blue thread for a few moments, Heart ambled back toward Eye's room. She'd become calm. She had only one purpose in life for the next three years, and that was to protect Eye. Learning that even Keeper G was a spy had been a shock—but only for a few moments.

How could it be any other way? Keeper A hired all the current Keepers, slowly releasing the previous Keepers and replacing them with ones who suited her needs. Keeper G was particularly talented, Heart admitted to herself. She could usually read anyone accurately, but she'd seriously – and dangerously – miscalculated Keeper G.

She climbed the stairs, gathering her thoughts. When she opened Eye's door, Keeper G and Eye were facing her, sitting on the edge of the bed. Eye had heard her coming of course, and they'd clearly planned this prank while she was gone.

There Eye sat with carefully painted, beautiful blue eyes on his face where eyes would be if he had them. Both Eye and Keeper G were grinning from ear to ear. Heart had to pull at every bit of her calmness not to cry, or yell or, *scream*, even, although she'd never screamed in her life.

When she had no reaction, the smiles faded from their faces. She closed the door behind her softly.

"What?" Eye asked, getting up and coming to her. Taking her hand he led her to the bed and made her sit. *"What?"* He put his face close to hers and the blue painted eyes looked at her without sight. The incongruity almost unhinged her. She closed her eyes against his sightless ones.

"Keeper G insisted that he drew very good eyes. Of course, I can't tell because they're flat, so I can't feel them. But we thought you'd … hmmm, I'm not sure now what we were thinking. What were we thinking, Keeper G?"

"I guess not very clearly. I'm sorry, Heart. I thought it would be funny. But, of course, it's not. It's … not. It's something else sort of awful."

"No, it's not awful, if Eye thought it would be funny. It's a shock, you know. I guess you didn't think of that. But it's funny, too. In a dark, weird, droll, ironic, confusing way."

Eye nodded his head against Heart's forehead. "Yes, in a dark, weird, droll, ironic, confusing way. Oh! We really were not thinking. Very insensitive of us."

"Agreed." Keeper G put his arm around Heart's shoulders. She couldn't help it, she stiffened. He'd betrayed them worse than anyone. Of course he wanted to continue the same as ever. And she must, must, *must* not show negative emotion, or show intelligence, or even show awareness. It was a tough transition to make in the few minutes walk from Keeper A's office to Eye's room.

Keeper G removed his arm from her shoulders, but leaned over and asked very quietly in her ear, "What has happened?"

She said nothing.

"Heart, what—what happened?"

Before she could bite her tongue off, she said, *"You know."*

"I know? I do not know."

Eye devised a cover for their conversation. "Good guess, Heart. Now, Keeper G, what letter am I thinking of? We can find it on the path ...."

Heart remained silent, focused on her blue thread.

Suddenly Keeper G stood. "Oh!" He moved to the door. "Oh!" He caught Heart's look, narrowed his eyes and shook his head with the slightest motion. "Eye, is your letter 'F,' for flowers?"

"Why, yes, it really is. Wow, how did you do that?"

"Magic. It's my turn. I'm going to write a word, and you two have to guess it."

"Let's have it!" Eye crowed, voice raised in fake enthusiasm.

Keeper G wrote a word on the slate and put his hand over it. "Ready."

"I think it's 'starlight,'" Eye guessed.

"Fantastic! You're exactly right," Keeper G laughed. He showed the slate to Heart.

She read:

Betrayed?

"Right," Heart said, feigning laughter. "I never would have guessed it."

Keeper G rubbed the word off the slate and casually held onto the pendant around his neck. "Yes, starlight. That was my word. You're very clever, Eye."

Heart caught his meaning immediately. After what she'd just gone though, she had forgotten all about the audio shooting star hanging around her neck. But Keeper G saw its chain around her neck, and he'd been the one to show her how to make it record. As he could no longer to be trusted, she had to derail him.

"I was going to record the star shower we had recently, but I forgot to turn on my recorder."

"Oh, that's too bad."

"Yes. Isn't it."

A soft, lilting voice through the audio system interrupted, "Come to luncheon, my Darling Undesirables. Lunch time."

Keeper G exchanged a look with Heart. In it she saw pain, confusion, anger, resignation. Patting Eye on the back he said, "All righty, my boy, let's get your face washed off so you don't shock a whole lot of other folks like you did Heart."

"Oh, yeah, good idea. I may have eyes, but I can't see what they look like." He laughed, awkwardly. Keeper G and Heart didn't join him.

A few minutes later, they stepped from the building, joining everyone else moving toward the dining building.

All meals were formal, with expensive linen table clothes and linen napkins, and the finest silverware and china. Two helpers in identical uniforms attended every table, at each meal.

Thousands of beautiful young people applied for the rarely available positions, hoping against hope to at least get interviewed. The minimum requirements to apply were that the young person had at least started a medical education, with a psychological profile rating high in patience, interpersonal skills, ability to cope with unanticipated events and a loving disposition.

Furthermore, the applicant must be physically pretty, as Keeper A felt that the Darling Undesirables should see beauty everywhere in their lives. Last but not least, the Darling Undesirables Dining Helpers must have essentially no personal life. Most of the people who were hired were young, single, beautiful women.

Although the Dining Helpers could live anywhere they pleased, they had a residence hall just outside the wall. Each apartment, though small to discourage parties, was luxuriously appointed with every quality convenience, and beautiful furniture of their choice, all inclusive with the position. So, of course, the Dining Helpers lived in the Darling Undesirables Dining Helpers residence.

Heart adored these sweet, kind, pretty people, most especially their own Loruza. She and Eye daily engaged her in intelligent, amusing conversation.

But not today. Heart ate lunch quietly, playing over in her mind the many conversations she'd had with Loruza, trying to recall if she'd ever said anything that she would never say directly to Keeper A. She couldn't recall having discussed anything other than bits of knowledge of particular interest to the three of them, herself, Eye and Loruza.

Loruza shared Heart's love of the stars. Most of their mealtime discussions revolved around the cosmos, the nature of discovered anomalies, and which star systems they would most like to visit.

"Good afternoon, Eye, Heart," Loruza greeted formally yet warmly as they took their seats.

"Good afternoon, Loruza," Eye replied.

Heart nodded at her, but remained silent.

"I was looking forward to seeing you at breakfast this morning to hear about your wonderful day at The Museum of Scientific Improbabilities and Unpredictable Oddities yesterday, but neither of you were here."

Heart tapped Eye's thigh. He understood—don't speak.

"We missed breakfast, that's true," Heart answered. "Our trip yesterday was very nice. I recall that you've said you've not been to The Museum of Scientific Improbabilities and Unpredictable Oddities. We would recommend it to anyone, wouldn't we, Eye?"

"Yes," Eye agreed quietly, clearly puzzled by Heart's stiff manner.

Loruza took a sip of water, studying Heart. "Is something … bothering you?"

Heart realized that Loruza, even if not a spy, would mention to a Keeper that Heart did not seem her usual self, and that, alone, could cause a chain of attention drawn to her. Precisely what she was trying to avoid.

She turned to give Loruza a sweet smile. "Sorry. I'm still tired. Yesterday took it out of us, all the walking and all that information. Isn't that so, Eye?"

"Yes. Lots and lots of walking and learning. Plus, harder on Heart, you know, because she had to keep stopping and telling me things, or reading the bits of information on all the showcases to me."

"Oh, I never mind that in the least, Eye."

"Yes, I know." Eye patted Heart's hand, resting on the table.

Loruza looked from one to the other of them, with a puzzled look.

"So, what was something that impressed you, Eye?"

"Well," Eye began without hesitation, "everyone knows Father Inventor changed the world when he discovered how to harness dark matter, followed, four years later, by his accessing the power of dark energy. The two most relevant discoveries of all time.

"So it was interesting to learn more about that initial period, where his focus was on understanding how to employ the four forces and his use of gravity to develop perpetual motion machines and all the clockwork genius he displayed at one end of that time, and his great 'aha!' about dark matter at the other end.

"During that shift in focus he came up with the most amazing inventions, including bio and dark energy means to double and triple human life span."

"Very good, Eye!" Loruza exclaimed.

"Yes," Heart agreed. "You're right. You can see that clearly when you go through the museum. Eye is so much better than I am at putting together details."

"Everyone always says they don't know how old Father Inventor is," Eye went on, clearly enjoying the conversation. "But I did some calculations with the information I learned yesterday, and discovered that he is around two-hundred-and-fifty years old."

"*Wow! Eye!*" Heart exclaimed. "You didn't mention that in our studies this morning."

"I wanted to surprise you, and to share it with Loruza."

"Wow, indeed, Eye," Loruza agreed. They all fell silent. Unspoken was the common knowledge that the average life-span of a Darling Undesirable was fourteen years. Many of them did not survive even to the age of four.

"So," Loruza said cheerfully, shaking the dark mood, "what impressed you the most, Heart?"

There was one thing, and one thing only—the Gear Horse—that stuck with Heart like a burr in her plaid. But she would not say it. "There were so many things that impressed me, but the Mechanical Aurora Borealis in the sky outside the museum filled me with awe."

That, too, was true.

Chapter 7

Heart only wanted to be alone, or alone with Eye. But she made it through the rest of the day, speaking only when spoken to, while trying to reassure Eye, whose mounting anxiety at her peculiar behavior added to her own anxiety.

In the afternoon they decided to do some gardening, which always calmed Eye when he felt anxious, Heart knew. And today it was the best hope she had of calming herself.

Still, they could not seem to get off by themselves. Keepers and workers came by to ask them about their experience at The Museum of Scientific Improbabilities and Unpredictable Oddities. Most of them had never been to the museum, Heart knew. But she could not quiet her suspicion that Keeper A had advised them to try to find out things that Heart would never tell.

Never!

Finally, the lilting, ubiquitous voice called the Darling Undesirables to bed. With a sigh of relief, Heart climbed the stairs, Eye by her side, to their rooms.

"Good night, dear Eye."

Eye took her hand and squeezed it hard, "Good night, Heart. Have lovely dreams."

"You too." She stepped into her room. *"Off!"* she commanded when the lights came on. The lights blinked off. Heart stood in the darkness, looking up at her star window. She had told Keeper G a small lie when she said she'd not recorded the star shower the previous week. Because, of course, she had programmed the window a year ago to record that stunning star shower. Anyone who knew her at all would know she could never forget such a significant cosmic event.

Keeper G knew her at least that well, and she knew he knew that she never lied. She could not have communicated more clearly without saying it directly, that he could no longer count on what she said.

He could just take that back to Keeper A, she thought, and you're welcome. It wasn't enough to pick on Eye. Hopefully, Keeper A would begin to wonder if Keeper G was reliable. That would be the best possible outcome, wouldn't it?

Heart knew revenge was a waste of energy, even if she seethed with frustration and anger. But could she really go on like this for three years? Could she?

She tried to tell herself that over time it would get easier. She would figure out which were her attention-grabbing habits and do away with them. She would develop new habits. She would change for Keeper A, while trying not to change for Eye.

Thinking how to do this made her head want to pop off.

She stretched out on her bed and turned on the breathtaking 3-D star shower. The meteorites fell around her in profusion. Their pastel colors left trails of light throughout the room.

Was there ever anything so beautiful?

Well, yes, she answered herself. Just as she'd said to Loruza at lunch today, the Mechanical Aurora Borealis in the sky above The Museum of Scientific Improbabilities and Unpredictable Oddities yesterday had been this kind of breathtaking beauty, while belonging, specifically, to her own planet, to her own home.

But, more to the point, the Mechanical Aurora Borealis had unmistakably responded to her. She knew this to be true. She'd tried to ignore it, but now, lying in bed with stars falling around her, feeling as big as the sky, a sense of destiny flowed over her. Her destiny. She could not evade it. She could try to be small and quiet and uninteresting and unimportant. She could devote her life to attempting to protect Eye from every awful thing that might ever happen to him.

Or she could devise a plan to step out from this pettiness, and move as her inner compass, her gut, her intelligence, and her emotions insisted that she do.

She weighed Keeper A's cloaked and vile threats against her devotion to Eye. She finally came to a conclusion that was so obvious, she wondered why it took her all day to figure it out.

With this insight, she could now begin to make a viable plan. All she needed was courage like she'd never had before in her life. The courage she'd had to muster last night to go to Eye in the deprivation chamber was a gnat's eye in comparison to the courage she now had to discover within herself.

For Eye's sake, she would find her courage, or make it, or fake it. Whatever it took.

The insight that had broken upon her mind while all the lights of the stars fell about her was that Keeper A would never touch a hair on Eye's head if Heart disappeared.

He would be the most privileged, he would be the most adored, he would be the most cared for. Who cared if Keeper G and even Loruza were Keeper A spies? It did not matter.

She, Heart, herself, could think her way around Keeper A.

She saw now how clear her path had been all along. She saw how her destiny had played out in everything that happened, right down to the detail of not going to The Museum of Scientific Improbabilities and Unpredictable Oddities until yesterday.

And she saw that now she must move forward, alone. Although she would miss Eye profoundly, every day, every minute, she would make a future for them where they were truly meant to be. Not this shadow life, living like ridiculous and pampered bee larvae.

It would be hard on Eye when she disappeared. She'd tell him a bit about her plan, but she dared not give him the details that were rapidly falling into place in her mind. For his own safety.

She turned off the star shower to lie in the dark, looking up at the tiny, remote stars, where worlds upon worlds spun in endless cycles. She wondered if, far away, somewhere out there, some other creature, different from herself and yet, perhaps, not so very different, puzzled over a dilemma in its life. If that being's light was just reaching her now, it would be a story eons old.

But she wished that creature well, all the same. She hoped that the far away or long ago being had found a solution to its problems. She rolled over onto her side, looking at the wall, thinking. In the end, it only mattered that one does the best one could, to the best of one's understanding and ability.

The one thing—the only thing—that had been her private fantasy, and now would be her driving force, she had never told anyone, not even Eye. Only moving toward her goal with unwavering focus, like a single thread in a plaid, weaving the bits of pattern together as she went, was her dream of seeing that one day Eye had eyes. Real, seeing, beautiful eyes.

From this point forward, every action she took and everything she encountered either contributed to, or was in the way of, that result.

*　*

Heart stayed awake most of the night devising her plan, finally falling asleep in the wee hours of the morning. Eye knocked on her door as the lilting voice called the Darling Undesirables to breakfast. Heart had not even bothered to change into night clothes, so, other than wearing the same thing she'd worn the previous day, which didn't bother her one way or another, and splashing some water on her face and a toothbrush across her teeth, she was ready to go.

She leapt up from the bed and opened the door.

"Hey," Eye said.

"Hey."

"You're wearing the same thing you had on yesterday."

"Yes. But don't tell anyone."

"I won't. Good thing almost no one has my heightened sense of smell."

"Is it bad?"

"No, dear Heart. You smell wonderful. More is just better. Of course, what is particular about what you were wearing yesterday, is all the stress you went through. Spicy."

"All right, all right. Let's go to breakfast, then I'll come back and change."

"Doesn't matter," Eye insisted while Heart pulled on her shoes. They stepped into the hall and, under the cover of all the bright chatter of Keepers and Darling

Undesirables, Eye came close to Heart and whispered, "I'm going crazy wondering what happened yesterday in Keeper A's office."

Heart glanced around, smiling, "Yes. You're right, a great privilege. Not everyone has had the opportunity to see the beautiful scrollwork, the lovely pale green billowing drapes. The carpet is so plush, you practically lose your feet in it. I'm so fortunate to have been invited to Keeper A's office to talk about our visit to The Museum of Scientific Improbabilities and Unpredictable Oddities. That she chose me from all the Darling Undesirables who went is quite an honor."

Keeper K came from behind and as he passed her, he smiled broadly and patted her shoulder.

"Yes, dearest Heart, it is indeed an honor to have an audience with Keeper A. But who would be more appropriate than you? You know what they say about you?"

"They? Say? They who, and say what?"

"Silly girl." Keeper K flapped his hands like a giddy girl, clearly delighted to be the one to tell Heart the buzz phrase going around. "'They' is everyone, of course. And the saying is,

"Just because Heart doesn't have a heart
"Doesn't mean she's not smart, because she's smart,
"She has the power to make the skies part!"

"Oh," Eye groaned, putting his forehead into his hands and almost tripping over the end of the people mover in the dining hall so that both Heart and Keeper K had to grab him.

"I second that groan," Heart said once they were at the end of the people mover. "Please don't repeat it. I want to live a quiet life."

"Don't repeat it?" Keeper K giggled. "I made it up! I fed it to a newshound lurking around the front fence this morning, and it shot around the globe."

Heart feigned dismay for Keeper K's benefit while experiencing an authentic deep anxiety. She'd stayed awake all night devising a plan to be so low-key that she fell off Keeper A's radar. This turn of events ruined that possibility.

"But why, Keeper K, would you even start such a saying?"

"I guess you've not seen the morning news."

"No, I've not," Heart said, anxiety mounting.

They entered the dining hall. Keeper K nodded at the space above the dining tables. "Well, you will now. Enjoy your breakfast!"

Heart stopped in the middle of the entryway, with her eyes raised to a gigantic image of herself looking up at the fabulous Mechanical Aurora Borealis above The Museum of Scientific Improbabilities and Unpredictable Oddities.

The accompanying commentary from the newshound made sweeping and ridiculously grandiose statements about Heart. She longed with every cell of her heartless body to melt into the floor and disappear.

All the Keepers and all the Darling Undesirables who understood what was happening—looked at the 3-D and then at her, and, over the commentary that "this was the first time in history an individual clearly influenced the Mechanical Aurora Borealis," everyone began clapping and cheering.

Mystified, Heart thought how she'd done nothing. *Nothing!* But stand there, feeling the light of the Mechanical Aurora Borealis pulling on her, like it might come down and make a path for her to walk right up into the sky. But she'd not done anything to merit the Mechanical Aurora Borealis's unique behavior. If, indeed it was true.

Someone began to chant:
"Heart, Heart, Heart
Makes the skies part!"

Soon the room reverberated with the chant. Heart stood frozen, a frown etched on her features. Finally, Eye took her hand and led her to her chair. A first! She sat, staring hard at the tablecloth, then glanced at Loruza, who grinned from ear to ear, clapping and chanting along with everyone else.

This would not sit well with Keeper A.

Gradually the room returned to something resembling normal, bizarre enough on the most mundane of days.

Loruza reached over and filled Heart's water glass. "I can't imagine what that was like—standing under the Mechanical Aurora Borealis and having it respond to you!"

"It was—it was just as you and everyone in the world have seen. I stopped to look at the Mechanical Aurora Borealis. It was so beautiful and … so … powerful. Then it changed. It made that arch. People in the museum said they'd never seen it do that before, and asked me how I did it. But I didn't do anything."

Loruza nodded. "I would have been awestruck too. Incredible, the way the lights moved into shapes and became an archway. Mysterious and compelling. Did you feel anything?"

Heart shrugged. "It felt sort of like tiny fingers of electricity. I was awestruck, yes. People passed by me on both sides, but I was a stone in a stream."

Loruza reached over and patted Heart's hand. "Lovely, Heart. Truly lovely. I don't know what it means, but it couldn't have happened to a nicer or sweeter person."

"Miss Heart," the gentle voice of the audio system hummed, "Keeper A requests your presence, directly."

"Just as I expected," Heart muttered, dismayed, but covering with a false calm. "Excuse me, Loruza."

Loruza nodded. "I'll see you at lunch and we'll continue our chat."

The call to Keeper A's office started a chain reaction of Darling Undesirables, the dining attendants, and the Keepers, chanting again, rising in volume as Heart stood.

She clasped her hand to Eye's shoulder for a moment. He reached up and patted her hand. "It'll be all right," he whispered. "You're famous now, makes us safer, doesn't it?"

"Don't know," Heart said. She hurried outside and along the little paths, anxiety growing with every step.

The double doors of Keeper A's inner office swung inward as Heart climbed the stairs. Through the doorway, Heart saw Keepers B and C on one side of the huge desk, and Keepers D and E on the other.

Why was Keeper D still here? Heart had never seen a Keeper on the premises after dismissal, most especially not after the profound offense of returning to a Darling Undesirables Facility without one of their charges.

Heart approached Keeper A's desk. Without uttering a word, Keeper A waved her hand over her console. The drapes turned to shutters, slammed over the windows. The room became black in an instant. The 3-D Heart had seen in the lunchroom sprang up. Keeper A reached into the airspace of the 3-D, pulling it above them, into the center of the room, then spread her hands, enlarging it.

"*What—Is—This?*" She intoned in her soft, angry voice that Heart longed never to hear.

What did Keeper A expect her to say? What it was could not be more clear, in brilliant 3-D, right before them, larger than the actual event.

"I asked you, what is this?"

"It's a 3-D of me outside the front door of The Museum of Scientific Improbabilities and Unpredictable Oddities when we arrived."

"Don't be impertinent," Keeper A warned.

"Don't be impertinent," Keeper D repeated.

"How did you make the Mechanical Aurora Borealis do that?" Keeper A demanded.

"I didn't. I don't know why it did that. I'd never seen the Mechanical Aurora Borealis, as you know. When I saw it, I didn't know that was unusual. Not until afterward when everyone talked about it."

As Keeper A watched the 3-D in a continuous loop, Heart saw a strange series of emotions cross her perfect features in the reflection of the moving image of the 3-D across her face. What Heart saw, that the other Keepers could not see standing beside her was anger, sadness, pathos, loneliness, mystification, then back to anger.

If only, Heart wished, if only she could shrink and sink into the depths of the carpet, becoming pale green fluffy threads and then, be utterly forgotten.

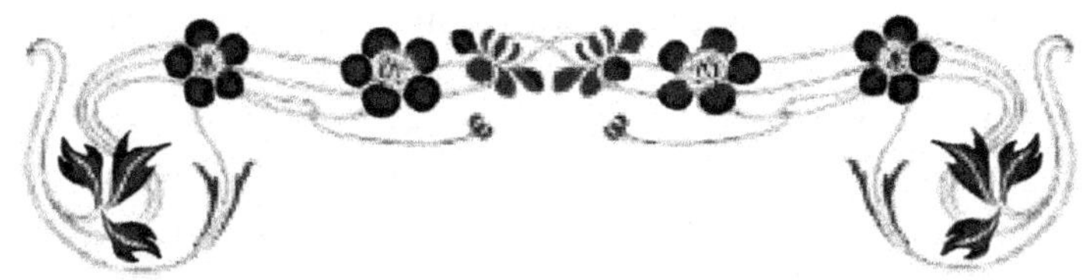

Chapter 8

Keeper A suddenly dismissed Heart without further comment.

Heart took in the strange look of fascination and frustration in Keeper A's expression as she turned to leave—while all the Keepers added their dark, disapproving scrutiny. Not one of them showed any spark of caring or compassion for her. What had she done to deserve their inexcusable and inexplicable disfavor, she wondered, while immensely relieved to be sent away without further threats or interrogation.

She went directly to Eye in his room, where he'd returned after breakfast.

"What a lot of fuss," he said as she entered his room. "One would think you walked on water without dark energy assistance."

"One would think." She got his yard work jacket from the closet. "Let's do some weeding on our flower bed along the side fence, it's looking rather neglected."

"Right now?"

"Sure."

Eye caught the tone of her voice. "Let's go. We can't have our flowers looking sad," he said. "We've spent a lot of time on them. I'm glad you noticed."

On their way to the fence, they stopped at the little gingerbread tool cottage behind their residence to pick up a few small gardening tools. The hand tools would allow Heart and Eye to kneel side by side and chat in privacy, Heart hoped. At least for a few minutes.

When they got to the flower bed, Heart put a small song maker beside them and programmed a run of light-hearted music she and Eye knew well, so the happy tunes would not only cover their conversation, but the two of them could burst out singing if a Keeper came to check on them.

Heart and Eye kneeled over the flowers, pulling out nearly non-existent weeds, gently tilling the soil around their base and sprinkling a bit of water on them.

"Listen carefully, Eye. I wish I could talk to you for an hour, but we'll be lucky if we get ten minutes. I must leave."

Eye gasped. "Leave?" he cried.

"*Shhh!*" Heart leaned her head close to his. "Darling Eye, we both must be strong. I have to know you'll be all right."

"If you're not here? I won't be all right. You know that. What would life be for me if you were not here?"

"It'll be difficult for both of us. I may be your eyes, but you are my heart."

"You have tons of heart. And you know perfectly well that you're much more to me than just my eyes."

"I know. We're each other's family. But sometimes family must be apart physically. You know we'll never be apart emotionally."

"But why? Why must you leave?"

"Many reasons. But I leave to make a future for us, for you and me. I can't tell you more because for one thing, I haven't worked out the details, and for another, there must be no place in your mind where you know what I'm doing.

"Even telling you that I must leave is dangerous, but I couldn't leave without saying something to you. You must appear as shocked as everyone else when I turn up missing. I hope to make it look like I've been kidnapped. The only thing I ask of you ...."

"I don't think these flowers need attention just now," Keeper E said behind them.

Frustrated that he'd snuck up on them, Heart acted as though she hadn't heard him. "No, you're wrong Eye, that's the fifth verse of 'La, La, La, Love,' and we're on the third verse." Then she turned and smiled up at Keeper E. "I didn't hear you over our songs. Have you come to see how we've helped our poor little flowers? They've become quite pathetic." Heart moved aside and waved her garden tool at the work she and Eye had accomplished.

The flowers did, indeed look considerably perked up in comparison to the flowers further along the fence. Their cheerful faces lifted to the sun, dead flowers removed, soil turned and watered.

"Well, yes, they look quite lovely," Keeper E agreed. "I hadn't noticed they'd become a bit wilted. But don't you garden in the afternoon?"

"In the afternoons we've been working on the rock garden. I wanted to spend a little time with these flowers since Eye and I have worked so hard on them all spring. Many of these flowers we grew from seeds."

"Yes. Seeds," Eye piped up. "It was amazing for me to feel them under the soil, popping out of their seeds, and then I could feel them breaking the surface of the earth."

Heart grinned at Eye, and then up at Keeper E. "Isn't Eye incredible? I could never feel the seeds germinating under the surface of the earth. Do you think you could, Keeper E?"

"I'm sure I could not. All right, then, carry on, but finish in the next few minutes so you'll have time to get washed for lunch."

Heart nodded. "Will do!" She watched as Keeper E moved to the residence building, out of the sun. Keeper E hated being in sunlight.

"Good!" She whispered. "No one else will bother us now that we've gotten Keeper E's directive to continue." She moved further down the row of flowers, and Eye came next to her.

"The only thing you ask of me …." Eye picked up where they'd been interrupted.

"The only thing I ask is that you register shock and dismay when you hear I'm missing, just as if we've never had this conversation. Your reaction is vitally important to both of our lives."

"I will do it, Heart, it won't be hard. I'll be in real pain if you do as you threaten."

"It's not a threat, Eye, it's a necessary plan of action. As I say, the only way I know I can succeed is because I must do it for you—for us.

"You know how we can communicate now, with our minds. Even though I'll be far away, you must listen for me. And … pay attention to anything that seems unusual. It might be me. It might be code. Keep your wits about you."

"Oh, Heart, you ask a lot."

"Life asks a lot, Eye. But we can handle it." She put down her trowel and gave Eye's hand a squeeze. "The last piece of information I'm going to give you for the time being is, do not believe wild stories about me. Don't believe I've died, or anything like that."

"You think they'd spread such a rumor?"

"Anything is possible. Let's get ready for lunch."

*   *

After lunch they worked in the rock garden with several other Darling Undesirables, tending the rose moss, thyme and ajuga, washing the rocks, arranging the furniture and the fairy and gnome figurines under the direction of Butterfly, whose bony protrusions from her shoulder blades resembled stunted wings. She insisted that all her clothing be constructed to permit the exposure of what she referred to as her "broken wings."

A delicate girl, with fairy features, she knew how to crack the whip and get the most out of her Darling Undesirable crew. Everyone loved Butterfly and vied for the privilege to tend the rock garden.

"When I came here yesterday," Butterfly said to Heart and Eye as they knelt in the garden, "the table and chair had moved!"

"Oh, dear," Heart said sympathetically, feeling guilty.

"Yes. And see here? The table has a couple of scratches on it, just as if the chair had been put on it."

"Oh! I see these little scratches. I'll go get the paint and touch it up. It'll be good as before."

"But don't you see?" Butterfly fairly fluttered up to Heart, looking up into her eyes.

Heart's smile froze on her face. What was Butterfly about to say? There was a small possibility that she had been awake and saw what Heart did with the chair and table. But she would have expected Butterfly to say something right away, or even come out in the night to confront her.

Blythe Ayne – 81

"I don't know. What ought I to see?"

"That the fairies love this furniture that I got for them. Oh! I would so, so have adored to see them at play. I do see them, every now and then, you know."

"I remember you telling me you've seen them."

"But only for a few seconds. It's like—it's like you see them when you're thinking about something else, and so there they are, just as plain as day. I mean, really just a real as me seeing you right now. Then you think, 'Oh! Goodness! It's a fairy!' and that thought makes some other part of your brain shut them out. It's quite frustrating. Especially for me as I'm sure I'm part fairy."

Heart had no reason not to believe there were fairies. She'd never seen any, but they would stay clear of humans if they had a choice, wouldn't they? Even if this time the 'fairy' that rearranged Butterfly's fairy furniture was herself. Given that it would be cruel to Butterfly and dangerous to herself, to tell the truth, Heart kept silent and permitted the untruth to germinate.

She knew she needed to develop her ability to let untruths remain untouched, as she embarked on the great adventure taking shape.

*　　*

Perhaps the most significant piece of Heart's plan required the assistance of Swen. She had to trust that her intuition about him was accurate and that he was not in Keeper A's pocket. She felt he had a soft spot for her, and that he would appreciate her unexpected behavior.

After all, that was the nature of events that made news—anomalous human behavior.

It was a risk to trust him, yes. But she had to trust someone, or some … creature. She couldn't leave, on her own, when she'd never lived outside the delicate and protected garden where she and her peer Darling Undesirables lived, in the lap of luxury, being taught nothing of life skills. Their lives decreed by law to be nothing other than pleasurable and smooth sailing. As if that could assuage the feelings of guilt of a society that permitted experimentation with combinations of dark matter, mechanical materials, and complexes of human cells.

As she and Eye walked toward their residence after dinner she said loud enough for those beside them to hear without drawing undue attention, "let's take a walk along the back fence line and check out the flowers there, too."

"Sure," Eye agreed.

They ambled by the rock garden. Heart felt watched. She slowed her pace, pointing out every bit of minutiae to Eye that she could. "The sun looks pretty, glinting off the laundry building's western windows."

Eye responded with careful attention. "I thought that the windows of the laundry room were lower than the top of the fence line."

"They are, you clever boy, but just at this moment, the sun is caught in the panes, and even as we talk, the light fades from the windows. And here's something interesting I never noticed before. The grass on the right side of the path is a different shade of green from the grass on the left side of the path."

"Strange," Eye said.

"Yes. Strange. I wonder why it is."

"It's probably a different kind of grass," Eye suggested.

Heart plucked a few blades of grass from each side of the path and held them close for inspection. "I can't see a difference, except for the color. The one on the right is a deep green, and the grass on the left is a sort of blue-green."

"Let me see." Eye held out his hands and Heart put the grass that she had in her right hand in his right hand, and the grass from her left hand in his left. He inhaled each of the grasses in turn, then pulled them across his cheek. "Well, the dark green grass is more tart and slightly more sawtoothed, and the blue-green is a bit sweeter and softer. So, I'd say, different species of grass."

"That's a fun school project, to ask the gardener what the different grasses are and why there are different grasses planted here."

"Good idea," Eye agreed.

They ambled on until they came to the back fence. Heart felt her anxiety rise, but she kept her surface calm. "Butterfly looked so adorable today in a pink and green iridescent body suit."

"Now, that is something I really would like to see. Is she very cute?"

"Butterfly? Why, yes, she is very cute. She's tiny and really does look like fairies in children's storybooks. She walks on her tiptoes most of the time. It's not an affectation. I see her sometimes thinking about putting her feet down flat, usually in the dining hall, when she's trying to be like everyone else …." Heart paused and she and Eye burst out in laughter.

"Like everyone else? What does that even mean here?" Eye said.

"Oh! Too funny! Anyway, darling Butterfly is exactly as she seems. If some experimenters dreamed of making a fairy, they came quite close. If some bio developer discovered a way to capture a fairy, if there are such things, for experimental purposes, I'd find that easier to believe than that she's a human bio error."

"Let's believe she's truly part fairy," Eye suggested.

"Yes, let's."

They took the last few steps to the back fence. "The flowers don't look too bad here. It's pretty shaded. It's nice, isn't it?"

"Lovely," Eye agreed.

"The lenten rose, hosta and coral bells all look great. The astilbe isn't as happy. I wonder if it wants more sun."

"Maybe we need to ask to transplant them along the other wall."

"That's a good idea. It'd look great over there." Heart bent over, "Oh, is this a snail?" She knelt down, and Eye knelt beside her. "Swen," she whispered, "Swen, are you by any chance there?"

"I am, indeed, by every chance, here. I've been watching you meandering toward the back fence for fifteen minutes."

"Trying not to draw attention. You know I can't stay here for more than a few seconds, but I'm asking you, can I trust you with my life?"

"Heart!" Swen and Eye quietly exclaimed together.

Silence hung, as if it had been nailed to the fence between them for several seconds.

"You can trust me with any secret, or anything you want to trust me with," Swen finally whispered back.

"He's a newshound," Eye protested.

"How do you know?" Swen asked, incensed.

"I can smell it. And, before you get more insulted, it's not dog, it's something that's connected with how information travels on dark energy."

"Oh! Swen," Heart exclaimed, alarmed, "is what I'm saying traveling who-knows-where?"

"*No!* It's only being heard by me. I'm a senior newshound, I can turn off communications for confidential interviews. You should know that from your social studies."

"I don't know anything anymore. Who can be trusted, who's a spy, who cares about Darling Undesirables and who doesn't—it's all up for grabs. That's what I know, that's what I've learned over the last two days."

"Well, all I can say is, you can trust me. I will keep your secrets. I'm nervous, though, about you asking me to protect your life. That might be beyond my abilities. I will if I can."

"That's good enough for me. Please stick around."

"I'm always here, on permanent Darling Undesirables duty."

Heart felt an anxious, creepy sensation up her spine. "Gotta go!" She stood. Eye was already standing. She took Eye's hand, and they meandered back to the rock garden.

"Did you feel that too?" Heart asked.

"A creepy up the back thing?"

"What was that?"

"I don't know, but I hope it didn't come from your new friend."

As they passed the rock garden, Heart suddenly felt very calm. "Wait a minute. Now that I'm calmed down a bit, that feeling was a lot like the feeling I had when I was looking at the Mechanical Aurora Borealis. It wasn't a bad feeling, was it?"

"I'm not sure. It surprised me so. We're already nervous. Maybe I felt it through you."

"Maybe. Anyway, Eye, you must remember everything we just did, and keep it locked away in your memory."

"Yes, Heart. Locked and safe."

*　　*

Later, alone in her room, Heart pulled out the paisley baby bunting she'd been wearing when discovered on Keeper A's doorstep, almost fifteen years ago. If she held the fabric long enough, it began to pulse.

Now, as she held the soft fabric, the individual paisleys gradually began to swim about, occasionally softly bumping into one another. It even appeared as though they communicated with one another. She could feel the fabric hum and throb as she held it. Could it help her find her way, help her make wise decisions, help her discover the route she needed to take?

Heart lost herself in the vibration as the fabric hummed. Pictures formed in her mind. First, a star shower. But not just any star shower, the star shower that she'd let pour over her the night before. She felt the hum of the star shower and relaxed as the paisley forms moved, with a gentle insistence, against her hands. The images of the star shower faded, and as they did, the beloved little moon, Pink sailed across the image's sky. Then there was void.

Exhaustion swept over Heart—the previous days had been overwhelming. She tucked the paisley fabric under her pillow and fell into a deep, deep asleep.

*   *

But she awoke in the middle of the night with a start.

She had to leave. Now. Right now. No hesitation, no second thoughts, no more planning. She had a sudden, unshakable realization that leaving now was the only way she could be sure Eye would register true shock at her disappearance. She knew he'd never imagine she might leave right away. She would not have believed it of herself. But for certain Swen was at the fence right now. What if she waited days and he left? It could happen.

What if it got out that she'd stayed behind at The Museum of Scientific Improbabilities and Unpredictable Oddities, despite Keeper A's determination to keep it secret? She'd be at the top of the news again, continuing at the forefront of Keeper A's angry attention. She had hoped to wait until everything calmed down, but what if things didn't calm down? The situation would escalate, getting worse and worse.

Now or never.

What must she take? She pined over what she must leave. Her plaids and paisleys must come, and the shooting star pendant.

She had to take something of all the little gifts Eye had given her. The bracelet of stone was perfect. He'd worked on polishing each stone until it was shiny, and he'd set every one by himself, with Keeper Q's supervision.

She'd take what money she had. Not much, for sure. She'd take a small communication device, but ask Swen if he thought it had tracking capabilities and dump it if it did.

She reached into the small drawer by her bedside and pulled the shooting star pendant over her head, then put the stone bracelet on her wrist. She crept out of bed, moving slowly. Slow movements, and crossing the room to enter the bathroom did not usually make the recording devices come on. She crossed to the bathroom and gathered a small comb, a washcloth and a toothbrush.

Moving stealthily into her closet next to the bathroom, in total darkness, she dug out a little backpack she never used, then gathered her plaids and paisleys, knowing each of them by the texture of their patterns. She pulled on her black jacket and stuffed gloves in the pockets. Then she stuck the paisley blanket into the backpack.

Was this all she needed? How strange! With all her possessions and all the luxury she lived in, she could walk out with a small pile, and not need anything else.

She probably ought to take something to eat, although her need for food was unusually minimal. At least, that's What Keeper Doctor had told her.

She kept her little bits of money in a drawer by the door, along with a few packets of things to eat—the ones Eye liked.

Stepping back into her room from the bathroom, Heart threw a few things helter-skelter, then tore the bed up, moving in slow motion, leaning over to make herself smaller and less noticeable. Then she slowly crossed the room, took the money and food packets out of the drawer, stuck them in the backpack, left the drawer open, turning items over on the desk.

She hoped it looked as though she'd been kidnapped, at least enough to make the Keepers think so. It would instigate a different sort of search than if it was believed she'd left on her own.

Certainly strange enough! No Darling Undesirable under eighteen had ever left a Darling Undesirable residence of their own accord. Why ever would such pampered darlings of society leave? In any case, most of them didn't have the mental capacity to even consider running away.

Glancing one more time around her room, she said a silent good-bye. Sad. She would truly miss her celestial geodesic window, but she must forge on, and rapidly.

Shapeshifting into the door as she opened it, she passed through, then shut it behind her. Setting her mind on her focus—she stole past Eye's door. So difficult!

She longed to leave him a note, but she could not.

She wanted to peek into his room, and dared not.

Creeping slowly down the hall, she shapeshifted from door to wall to door, so taxing to shapeshift while moving, and never sure if it worked. She looked the same to herself. She didn't understand how the shapeshifting worked, she just knew that when she activated a certain spot in her mind, she appeared to others like whatever she happened to be standing by.

She'd learned very young that invisibility was invincibility, and when she put her mind to the one, the other was her reward.

Finally, she came to the back stairs. In this dark stairwell, she more easily became invisible. She scurried down the stairs and out the back door. Only fifty feet to the back fence, and then her exhausting shapeshifting would be done—for the moment, at least.

She smiled, thinking of her conversation with Eye, about the ways in which the grass was different on the two sides of the path. Thinking about those differences made it easy to shapeshift into the grass and trees around her, their living scent and organic makeup let her flow into them with ease. She glided on the gentle breeze to the back fence.

But when she reached it she curled herself into a ball on the ground. Exhausted, tapped, depressed, scared. Pulling off her backpack, she wrapped her arms around it and held it to her stomach.

I could go back, she thought, I could creep back to my room and no one would know anything. I could go on as before, living a sheltered, safe life, with every now and then an unpleasant moment with a Keeper, but most of the time being adored, receiving presents, and, most importantly, being with Eye.

I don't have to leave, she argued with herself. Does it even make sense? Will I succeed? Stay here, conform. Just wait. That's what you'd already agreed with yourself to do.

She continued to badger herself with unanswerable questions, feeling her resolve rapidly ebbing.

I'm being ridiculous about Keeper A, Heart continued her interior monologue. She has to keep everything going as smoothly as possible in this relentless madhouse, with Darling Undesirables who give her an endless sea of troubles. Like me! Disrupting her routine, consuming her attention with my drama. So what if she said a few nasty things? She doesn't mean them. How else can she keep me in line?

Keeper D? I don't like her, I never will. She's unskilled at her job. But does she really deserve to lose her position, just because I broke every rule? Just because I outsmarted her, at the end of a day that must have been incredibly exhausting for her.

What am I thinking? I'm a Darling Undesirable. I may have disordered thinking, like most of my peers. I probably have disordered thinking. Just because I'm smarter than they are doesn't mean I don't have a mental disorder.

"What are you doing?" Swen whispered from the other side of the fence.

Startled, Heart jumped. "Having second thoughts. A whole plethora of second, and third and fourth thoughts. I think maybe I'm crazy and my logic is disordered."

"I don't think you're crazy. I don't know why you're intent on leaving your little life of luxury, but I guess it has to be pretty serious for you to have come this far—something to do with Eye, no doubt, and his safety."

"Well, yes. That's one of the two reasons. The things Keeper A said in her office … terrible. Terrible! But maybe not real. Maybe just to make me behave."

"Don't believe it."

"Don't believe which?"

"Believe your gut."

"Believe my gut." The second reason Heart knew she must leave The Darling Undesirables Facility at Long Prairie came to her as if it stood before her, here and now, in the garden. The Gear Horse. Until she got to him, she could not make one jot of a plan beyond that.

She inhaled and exhaled, deeply, slowly. "I must do this. It's my destiny. I leave to protect Eye, I leave to learn my future, I leave to make a future for Eye and myself." She kept the Gear Horse to herself. "Can you dig a tunnel?"

"It's right in front of you at the base of the fence. Shove your backpack through."

Heart crawled through the tunnel Swen had dug, then sat unmoving on the other side. "I'm free," she uttered softly. "I've left, I can do as I please."

"Wouldn't it be lovely if that were so?" Swen said, sitting on his haunches beside her. "But now you are wanted by society, and I'm your accomplice."

Heart nodded, disgruntled. "That's another way of looking at it. Look, I don't know you at all—you helped me the other night, and you appear to be helping me now. But if you're going to be dark and gloomy, I will not enjoy the company."

"I'm not usually 'dark and gloomy,' but I am all for a decent reality check now and then, else you find yourself in deep waters wondering how you fell in the ocean."

"More metaphors," Heart said. "Droll."

"I'm a writer."

Yes. Well, I guess we'll sort things out as we go, but please, I need the positive take on things, not the negative."

"Right. Positive. But, dearest Heart, you are not free. You are a particularly adored ward of society. You will be missed. Your absence will raise worldwide alarms. You will be looked for. If you think I'm being negative to express that truth, you're right, we're going to have hard times ahead. I want to help if I can, but don't make it extra hard on me." Swen looked at her imploringly with his huge, down-turned puppy-dog, deeply intelligent, irresistible eyes.

Heart paused, trying to resist his imploring look, and failing. "You're right," she said. "One-hundred percent right. One-thousand percent right. You're as right as right can be. I'll try not to make things harder on you—

on us!—than they already are. I suppose I will, though, because I'm so naive, and I apologize ahead of time. Also, I thank you ahead of time for your help. Is there anything I can do right now to make it easier?"

"Do you have any money?"

"Well, that doesn't seem like a very nice place to start."

"We'll need money. You can't run around without a form of exchange."

"Again, you're right." She pulled her money from the backpack and showed it to Swen.

"That's not money!"

"What is it?"

"It's just as they say right on them, 'Darling Undesirables Exchange Coupons.'"

"Isn't that money?"

"No. What do you think, the whole world uses pictures of Darling Undesirables on their money?"

"Well …yes."

"There's ego for you."

"But, Swen, I don't know anything else. Maybe I really had better not go. Maybe I'm more stupid than I thought. I've lived in this sheltered environment my whole life, with most of my peers mentally defective, including, it seems, many of the Keepers. Maybe I have a dangerously wrong idea about my abilities.

"If I seem to be showing an unattractive display of ego when I'm simply naive, I will get on your nerves. You'll abandon me somewhere like trash, or turn me over for the reward that's sure to be offered."

"Hmmm," Swen said, raising a paw to his mouth and tapping it thoughtfully. "Some good ideas there. Silly little DU, I'm not going to do either of those things. Furthermore, I will get used to your boggling naïveté."

Heart nodded, relieved. "While, at the same time, I'll be becoming less bogglingly naïve … I hope."

"We do hope. All right then, young princess, what is your heart's desire—metaphorically speaking, of course."

"I must go to The Museum of Scientific Improbabilities and Unpredictable Oddities."

Chapter 9

"The Museum of Scientific Improbabilities and Unpredictable Oddities?—oh, that's nice, that's good. The Museum of Scientific Improbabilities and Unpredictable Oddities. Could we get any more public? Wasn't your day there precisely what has brought you to this side of the fence, outside of your safe, cocooned life?" Swen nudged her backpack. "Here, put this thing on."

"Well, yes." Heart slipped into her backpack. "What's your point?"

"Why would you want to return to the very place that brought about the stress you've gone through the last few days?"

The question stopped Heart in her tracks. Wasn't it perfectly obvious to anyone who had seen the video that she would want to see the Mechanical Aurora Borealis again? Never mind the Gear Horse, which, for the moment, she intended to keep secret.

Swen spoke her mind out loud. "If you think you're going to walk up to The Museum of Scientific Improbabilities and Unpredictable Oddities and have the Mechanical Aurora Borealis just, I don't know, do something else, or more than what it did before, you are indeed kind of nuts."

"How so?"

"I don't know why the Mechanical Aurora Borealis responded to you the way it did, but it's a light show. There might be something about you that tripped some trigger in its mechanism, that made a pretty show it hasn't previously done. But it can't be anything more than that. Or maybe there is someone who runs the lights, and when they saw you, the most darling of the Darling Undesirables, they made a show to capture the world's attention. For obvious reasons."

Swen shook his long, doggie head, ears flopping about his chin. "Going to The Museum of Scientific Improbabilities and Unpredictable Oddities is about the most unwise thing you can do if you're trying to keep from getting caught and sent back."

Heart thought about the possibility that someone, somewhere, ran the light show, taking advantage of her presence to get the world's attention. But would she have felt that tug at her body, if that was all it was?

No. She would not. "Let's get out of here." She moved ahead forcefully, with no idea where she headed. "I think sitting here chatting by the wall is just about the most unwise thing I can do at this moment," she added over her shoulder.

"You're right," Swen agreed, trotting up to her. "But I want to make sure you have at least a clue what you're doing, and if you really don't, then your thought about going back to your bedie-by might be a wise move."

"I do have a clue what I'm doing," Heart said, her indignation rising. "I need to go to The Museum of Scientific Improbabilities and Unpredictable Oddities. I need you to help me get there. I'm counting on you completely, because I cannot do it on my own."

Swen shrugged, a peculiarly human gesture. "Yeah. All right. Let's move out." He crept close to the edge of the fence. Single file, they moved away from Keeper A's residence, away from Eye's room, away from her room, away from everything Heart had ever known.

She shadowed Swen, hunkering down to his height. There was no one to see them this side of the fence and she felt safe not shapeshifting, still a bit tapped from the previous stint.

"Why do you even care?" she asked. "If I get caught, I get caught. It's no skin off your long, fur-covered snout."

"Charming. So kind. I care because I could get in a big pile of dog-do if I'm found to be your accomplice. Oh! How many things are wrong with that picture? I didn't report the news of, for instance, this precise moment, which would, if I did, quite frankly, set me up for life. And, you know, I'm going to live a *verrry* long time. I would be in trouble, and I'm not even sure what the limits of punishment are, to make off with a Darling Undesirable, even if she recruited me. Do you know what they would do to me?"

"No," Heart answered, alarmed.

"They'd "disassemble" me for usable parts. You know …" He paused to turn to her and drew a paw across his throat. "*Agh*, gurgle, gurgle," he added melodramatically. "Yeah, I care."

"Oh dear," Heart sat down on the ground and put her hands over her face. "Oh, *dear!*"

Swen came back to her and nuzzled her hands. "Wow! You *are* delicate. Hey, don't take it so hard. I was exaggerating. Come on, let's go."

"No. You weren't exaggerating. You're absolutely right. I can't go on. I'm terrible and selfish. I didn't think of you for one fleeting second. Not one second. I just thought about me. Well, me and Eye. But still, very selfish. I can't understand why you're doing this. The worst that can happen to me is being sent back to a luxurious life at The Darling Undesirables Residence. The worst that can happen to you is—the worst! Why are you doing this?"

"Grand adventure, my dear. A grand adventure is worth a gamble, even with life. This is the news story of news stories. So what if I don't get to tell the story for years? I got to live it. What we're doing right now is all a newshound lives for. It's in our genetic make-up and hard-wired in our mechanical components.

"So I think we can agree that we've agreed. Come on, we've got to get away from here before the sun comes up. And I need to come up with a route that's not too public, yet not too convoluted. Plus now I have to figure out how to get some money. I haven't needed any, living off the Darling Undesirables waste. It's the lap of luxury, what they throw out where you live. Lived."

"I can believe it." Heart gestured for Swen to move on. "Guilt is generous."

"Cool," Swen chuckled. "I see you have wisdom bits of your own. Or was that a fluke?"

"I don't know. You'll have to stick with me to find out."

"'*The Travels of Swen and Heart.*'"

Heart cleared her throat. "I think that's '*The Travels of Heart and Swen.*'"

Swen chuckled again, a funny little deep-throated doggie sound, Heart thought, if bio-dogs chuckled.

"I stand corrected. Of course, you come first, in every regard. As the protagonist, and as a lady."

"*A lady! Hah!* I'm not even certain what I am, I mean, as an organism. But I'm pretty sure 'lady' is off the mark."

"You're as much a lady as I am a dog."

Heart nodded. "I'll leave it at that. We're two grand adventurers, thrown together by fate. I'm the remora on your back, dependent upon your direction. How long will it take us to get to The Museum of Scientific Improbabilities and Unpredictable Oddities on foot?"

"I don't know. Let's get through today and see where we are, then I can make a reasonable estimation."

"Where will we hide when the sun comes up?"

"Again, at this moment, clueless. But I have to figure out something pretty soon, we don't have long. We've been puttering around and jabbering."

"I'll shut up." Heart moved ahead of Swen. He adapted to her quickened pace and pulled ahead. Heart followed him silently, in a direction, she trusted, that would bring her, sooner rather than later, to the Gear Horse.

Was it possible the Gear Horse knew she moved toward him? She repeatedly saw his image in her mind's eye, so real, so palpable, she felt he must know she was coming.

It wasn't long before the little songbirds that brought up the sun started to sing in raucous profusion all around them. She and Swen had come to a large city park. Giant, ancient trees surrounded them, and a bubbling stream ran among the trees. Dawn crept in a lacy pink-peach light, low among the trees while a radiant orange light shot up into the sky.

Swen suddenly turned at a right angle and flew off the path, splashing across the stream. Heart splashed after him without hesitation. As she left the path, she saw, some distance ahead, a woman with a tiny creature, probably a dog, on a leash, walking in the early morning.

"Hey," Swen said when they'd put some distance between themselves and the woman with the small creature, "that was pretty good, the way you just followed me."

"I'm trusting you. When I trust someone, I trust him. I didn't see that woman when you did, but I saw her when you zipped off the path and realized that the last thing we need is to come face to face with a bio dog. Right?"

"Absolutely correct. A bio dog cannot resist sending up a howl when they come muzzle to muzzle with a newshound. Poor things. We make them crazy and confuse the poo right out of them. Sometimes literally. If you ever want to find me or one of my peers, just get your hands on a bio dog. Big or little, doesn't make matter."

"Making a mental note. If wanting to find Swen, use bio dog. Watch out for poo."

"Right." He looked around. "Hey, this is a nice spot. Let's rest here."

Heart took in her surroundings. Giant conifers rose up around them to a small patch of sky, high above. Fragrant grasses and trillium carpeted the ground, and a tiny stream gurgled over rocks a few feet away—picture-perfect beautiful. "Wow! I could live here."

"So could I," Swen agreed. "If you could help me disengage my newshound ganglia, I could just be your dog—with the benefit of being able to talk. It would be a sweet life. Do you wanna?"

"Are you serious."

"Seventy-five percent. Yes. Twenty-five percent, still curious about the story that's unfolding. I could be convinced to stay."

Heart took off her backpack, threw the paisley blanket over her knees, put the backpack under her head and studied the towering trees. Although she'd seen trees this huge in 3-Ds, she'd never been anywhere near a real one in her life. The 3-Ds were not the same.

"It's a temptation." She felt sleep creeping over her. She was tired! "Temp-ta-tion. But first ... muse-m and gear hhhh ...."

"Gear hhh," Swen whispered softly, pulling the paisley blanket up around Heart's chin. *"Hmmm ...."* Then he snuggled his muzzle under her chin as well, wide awake, watching, but unmoving as an iron doorstep, for several hours.

*   *

"Eye!" Heart cried when she awoke with a start, sitting bolt upright.

"Shhhh!" Swen warned.

She looked around, remembering where she was. "Oh!" She lay back down on the ground. "Oh! Poor Eye. He came into my dreamscape. He's so distressed."

"You told him you were going to leave."

"But even I didn't know I was going to leave last night. I took myself by surprise. I wanted Eye to have an authentic strong reaction from being truly shocked. But, oh! I can't stand his pain."

"He'll be all right."

"Yes." Heart didn't believe it. She'd never felt Eye so strongly distressed, not even in the sensory deprivation chamber. "I wonder if there's a way I can communicate with him ...."

"Don't think it, Heart. Too dangerous."

"You're right." But the thought made her recall the communication device she'd brought along, and that she'd forgotten to ask Swen if it had a tracking component. "Oh dear."

"Now what?"

She dug around in her backpack. "I just remembered I brought this communication device. I meant to ask you if it could be used to track me. But with all our talking, I forgot." She held it out to Swen.

"Holy doggie dungeons!" He took it in his paws and studied it. "Yes, they could use it to find out where you are right now, but only with its particular receiver. Who knows you have this thing?"

"Just Eye. We picked the two of them out of a big pile of presents so we could talk to one another anywhere."

"Like walkie-talkies."

"Like what?"

"A really old, old, old device. Let's see. I get it—here, do what I say." He handed the device back to her. "I have an opposable thumb in my tool kit, but you have one attached right to your hand, so follow my directions."

Swen proceeded to tell Heart how to disable the tracking component of the device. "There now, we're safe," he said when they were done. "You can send outgoing but there's no incoming and no tracking."

"So that's the end of my getting to know how Eye is, other than in my dreams."

"Or on the news. I just happen to have this 3-D news screen." Swen pushed a button on his chest, and a newscast hovered in the air in front of them.

"… Intrigue in the world of the Darling Undesirables today, when the world's darlingest Darling turned up missing, with her room in shambles."

"Shambles! Not quite," Heart interjected.

"It's news, dear. Hush."

"As everyone knows, Heart's heart is Eye, who is distraught at what appears to be a clear-cut case of kidnapping."

"Well, that's good, at least," Heart commented. "That they think I've been kidnapped."

"Yeah. Good." Swen clicked the newscast off.

"You sound cautious."

"I am. A newshound is always looking for the red herring."

"You're looking for a fish at this moment?"

"No. There really is a lot you don't know, isn't there?"

"As I said."

"A red herring is misdirection. Do they actually think you've been kidnapped? Or are they spreading that tale for a variety of reasons? Examples: they want to lull you into a sense of having gotten away with it. They don't want to have looked like a Darling Undesirable can just walk out at any time on a whim. They're gathering forces to find you ...."

"Or all of the above," Heart added.

"Or all of the above."

"For the moment, though we'll stay here and wait for dark, yes?"

"Seems best."

They lapsed into silence.

"I can shapeshift."

"I saw that. That's helpful."

"It's helpful to a certain extent. Only as far as whatever is looking for me is dependent on sight. But if there's something that tracks using other senses, shapeshifting is probably not worth much."

"Good point," Swen said. "Like scent."

–"Into? ...."

"Into one of the mechanical inventions. But when Keeper A came, she pulled me right away from the gears. There is this cute little man with ...."

"Keys all over him."

"Exactly!" Heart gestured back and forth across her body. "Keys all over him. He was like a percussion instrument when he walked. Ching-ching-chang-alang."

Swen laughed, and repeated, "Ching-ching-chang-alang?"

"Umm-hum. You know about him?"

"I know about him and I know him."

"What's to know about him?"

"I'll tell you later. But first, finish telling me what happened to you."

"Well, the Key Man was shocked when Keeper A put her hands on me. But she was able to find me with her enhanced olfactory receptors, which she energizes by pressing between her eyebrows." Heart demonstrated.

Swen nodded. "Third eye activation. Sure."

"Then she dragged me back to the Darling Undesirables Facility at Long Prairie."

"So they might use dark matter scent entities."

"Oh, that sounds scary."

"Yes." Swen agreed, deep in thought.

"What are you thinking?"

"Just considering contingency plans."

"While we're thinking about it, what about dark matter audio entities, that search me out by my sound. Or dark matter touch entities, that find me by where I moved?"

"All possibilities," Swen agreed quietly.

"I didn't think about any of this."

Swen nuzzled her hand. "You didn't know about them. How could you think about them?"

"True. But if you're right about the red herring thing ...."

"Precisely. Which is why I'm contemplating changing my approach. But I have to think it through a bit."

"Shall I be quiet?"

"Not necessary. My computer is considering various possibilities, and the wisest responses we can make. It'll come up with a plan in a few minutes. Please continue chattering on."

"Chattering on?" Peeved, Heart lay silently back on the grass, putting her arms under her head and looking up into the sky.

"I didn't mean that like it sounded. I find you chatter most pleasant."

"You're not making it better."

"Please, continue your conversation. Is there anything I might have in my database you'd like to know about? My database has practically everything in it."

"Yes," Heart said softly. There is a subject I'm extremely curious about."

"And what is that, dear Heart?"

"I would like to know … I can't understand why … why is Father Inventor spoken of in hushed tones, with great reverence and respect, and at the same time, he is hunted, with statements on walls and in the corner of the 3-D and, just all over the place that he is a wanted criminal, to be considered very dangerous. I've asked Keepers, and even the nice ones get upset when I do.

"I've tried to pose the question in different ways, but I just can't seem to say it so that it doesn't raise temper. Anything about him is blocked on all my research devices. It's the single most burning question I have, next to the other burning question I have, which I believe will be answered when we get to The Museum of Scientific Improbabilities and Unpredictable Oddities. I've wondered about Father Inventor most of my life."

Swen was quiet for a long time. Heart finally propped herself up on her elbow to turn around and look at him, afraid she would see, somehow on his hound face, the anger and disapproval she'd come to know with Keepers whenever she asked this question.

But she didn't see anger. She saw unmistakable pity furrowed in his expression. "What? What is it? I've caused you to feel a huge emotion, that's obvious."

"Yes. You have. Your Keepers' anger is not directed at you. They're quite poor with their emotions, aren't they, for a group who supposedly has been highly trained to care for Darling Undesirables. But then, you're not the usual Darling, are you?"

"I'm not."

"Your intelligence has been a challenge for them. Most Keepers are kind souls and love the Darling Undesirables. But they are not prepared to be challenged intellectually."

"Talk about chattering! Will you please answer my question?"

"I will. Father Inventor changed the world. Before his genius discovered how to harness dark energy, our little world was going down. Humanity had choked the life out of it, and the clock was ticking the countdown. Megalopolises winked out. Overnight, huge cities shut down. People were trapped in thousands in thousands upon thousands in elevators, at the tops of buildings, behind gates, in trains—wherever power was required.

"Communication died in an instant—no one could get help or talk to anyone. People left the cities with not much more on them then your little backpack here. It was—beyond terrible, but I won't trouble your young mind with more details.

"That's all blocked from you, because of the laws protecting Darling Undesirables from any unpleasant information that might make them sad.

"Father Inventor had been working on perpetual motion machines, hence all the beautiful clockwork inventions. He made pretty things of his inventions, but at the same time, he was trying to puzzle out dark energy, trying to employ it. That was the perpetual motion component of his machines.

"As the world spun more and more out of control, he worked frenetically. Desperate, he turned from mechanical applications to bio applications in his experiments."

"Bio applications?"

"Yes. In other words, the mechanical components were not capable of reaching into the potential of dark energy that he needed to tap, even though it came close.

At some point, he had his lightning insight, the lynchpin of genius, that bio matter would be able to go the distance that mechanical applications could not."

"His initial bio-dark energy inventions used plant matter, and suddenly the world was alive again. Power was ignited by a small amount of plant genetics in combination with dark energy.

"He was revered, and rightly so. Then he was glorified and made essentially into a god.

"Meanwhile, one of his assistants got it in his head to turn upon his great teacher and benefactor. He sold some of Father Inventor's greatest secrets to a band of renegade scientists.

"And then the unethical went on a rampage. No one could stop it. No authorities, no protest groups—no one. All of a sudden, the human family had a new, huge problem to deal with."

"The Darling Undesirables," Heart said quietly, looking down into the grass, understanding, now, all the times she'd seen the Keepers' anger when she asked about Father Inventor.

"Yes," Swen said. "The Darling Undesirables."

"But … you don't think he was responsible?"

"Not directly. Indirectly, of course. But not directly."

"Then–why don't the Keepers feel as you do?"

"Survival. At least in part. Untold funds are poured into the 'find Father Inventor' coffers. These funds go to the Darling Undesirables residences, which are, as you know, the Keepers' livelihood."

"So … they aren't really looking for Father Inventor? All the news and signs and posters and notices, they don't actually do what they're saying, looking for him?"

"No. They don't. The result of the posters is the same as an extremely effective advertising campaign to get money to support the Darling Undesirables, their residences, their Keepers and the rest of the staff. It's big business."

"Humanity never learns, does it?"

"It does not appear … wait!"

"What?"

"*Shhh!* Something comes—throw your things together."

Heart didn't need to be told twice. She flung everything into her backpack, and as she moved to pull it on, she was jerked off the ground. Her backpack flew from her hand.

"*Ohhhhh*, Swen!" She cried, instantly above the tree line. She watched her backpack tumble to the ground. She couldn't see Swen at all. The entire park disappeared from view as she flew faster than she imagined possible, freezing in the cold air. Something held onto both of her arms, but whatever it was, she could not see it against the bright sky.

"I … I can't breathe," she gasped. "Can't breathe." Might the invisible tentacles drop her? What would it be like to fall and fall and fall? "Eye," she whispered. If she was being taken back to The Darling Undesirables Facility at Long Prairie, if she survived, she would at least be back with Eye.

She began to lose consciousness. Then it seemed as if the tentacles made a sharp turn. They slowed down, then lowered in the sky. Heart felt warmer. She saw the park loom in front of her, the giant trees came closer. The tentacles lowered her down among the trees. Then she could see them—sky blue tentacles, wrapped around both of her arms with balloon-like projections, deflating even while she looked at them.

Although they seemed bio, they appeared to have no intelligence of their own. Below she saw Swen, jabbing away at a device as she floated down to him.

He glanced at her. "All right then!"

She wanted to run to him and give him a hug, but the tentacles remained wrapped around her arms. Swen appeared to be entirely preoccupied.

"Hey, Heart here. On the heels of a terrible adventure."

"I know. How do you think you came back?"

"Don't know."

"Gyroscoptic Dark Energy Entangler."

"Gyroscoptic …."

"Dark energy boomerang. Made those whatever-they-are bring you back."

"Can we get them off me?"

"Want to look at them first. I'm afraid if I get them off they might zing off like rubber bands back where they came from. It's a good idea to understand them, don't you agree?"

"I do. But, *ick!*"

"You can handle 'ick' as long as you're not in pain."

"I'm not in pain. I was. I couldn't breathe. I was losing consciousness. Then they turned around. Because of your Gyroscoptic Dark Energy thingy-thing-thing."

"Right." Swen came close to one of the tentacles with a small device that clicked when he held it to the part wrapped around Heart's arm, and went silent at the balloon end. "Whatever programming or intelligence it has, it's in the tentacles. I'd really like to dissect one, but we don't have time. We've got to let them go and get out of here as fast as we can."

"I'm ready."

"I'm going to turn on the Gyroscoptic Dark Energy Entangler again. I don't know if it'll be uncomfortable for you or not being this close to it, and you being … anyway, brace yourself, just in case. The important thing is they'll be too confused to track and grab you again. I believe they'll make their way back to where they came from."

"Me being what?"

"You being … you. Hang on."

"Hang onto what?"

"Don't know."

Heart watched Swen watch her intently as he turned the dial on the Gyroscoptic Dark Energy Entangler. She felt a peculiar sensation as if about to levitate and plunge off a mountain in the same instant. *"Auuggghhh!"* She crumpled to her knees and felt her eyes roll back into her head. At the same time, the tentacles dropped off her arms, landing limp on the ground.

"Holy dog doo," Swen exclaimed, "I hope I didn't kill them. That won't be good if they're classified as protected exotic pets. Let's get outta here."

Heart barely heard him. She'd managed to jump to her feet, grab her backpack, and had already sprinted away. She looked back to see Swen putting his instruments into his chest pack, then start loping after her. As he did so, she saw behind him the tentacles rising from the ground, they spun in awkward, dizzy circles, then gradually rose up into the sky, where, soon, they became invisible.

She trusted Swen, that the tentacles would be confused and unable to track her, but she was also savvy enough to imagine that their programming to bring her back might prevail. She broke into a flat-out run.

Chapter 10

It was wonderful! Heart had never come close to a full-out, save-her-life run. Not once in her life. The ambulatory Darling Undesirables ran without enthusiasm around the inside perimeter of the fence once per week, with the Keepers cheering them on halfheartedly, much more engaged in chatting among themselves than paying attention to the exercise of their charges.

Swen loped up to her side. He had a grin on his shaggy, doggy face. He caught her eye and angled to the left, and she followed him.

"Shapeshift if you can," he called to her.

Heart tried to become the grass, the benches, the trees as they sped by, but the effort slowed her down. Observing her, Swen slowed to match her pace. "See that monolithic rock ahead? Let's stop behind it for a minute. I want to explain my plan."

Heart nodded and sprinted toward the rock, leaving shapeshifting aside. They encountered no one. She felt safe when she dashed around to the back side of the building-sized rock, standing up against another rock half its size. Heart hoped the rock would block signals she might be giving off to any wayward weird devices.

Swen came around the edge of the rock and sat on his haunches. Heart sat, cross-legged, on the ground in front of him.

"That was fun!" Swen said. "Too bad we're running to save ourselves instead of just having a good run."

"I'm not even breathing heavily," Heart said. "Whenever I've seen people run on a 3-D, they always breathe heavily."

"I noticed this about you." Swen continued on without segue, "I'm taking us into The Periphery."

"The Periphery? No! I need to get to The Museum of Scientific Improbabilities and Unpredictable Oddities."

"I know. And the only way I can assure that you'll get there is by going through The Periphery. All of the Keepers gadgets and the tracking devices of whoever else they're working with can't cross the Dark Energy Wall. I'm almost one-hundred percent certain that I can get you to The Museum of Scientific Improbabilities and Unpredictable Oddities going through The Periphery. But out here, this way, trying to outrun weird devices that can't be outrun and things we don't even know about, while you try to shapeshift to hide from devices that use other means of sensing you—I can't even place odds on it. But they're not good."

"What are you saying? We can't get inside The Periphery any more than tracking devices. Even if we could, that's crazy. I won't be safe there, in the land of criminals. They'll capture me for ransom for sure."

"Ah!" Swen said, actually winking at her, melting something in her, even if not a heart she didn't have, just like the museum doorman and the docent had. "You're so many kinds of wrong, my dear. First of all, I can get into The Periphery at will. Secondly, you'll be *soooo* very safe there, I can't even begin to tell you. Thirdly, It's not all criminals. And last, but not least, they have no interest or use for anything they would ransom from this side."

Heart wrinkled up her brow at Swen's self-assurance. "What if you're wrong?'"

"I'm not wrong. By the way, how did you like that bit of flying?"

Heart shuddered. "That was, I think, the worst experience of my life. If Keeper A wanted me to be punished, she succeeded. Horrible!"

"All right. That won't happen on The Other Side."

"The Periphery?"

"The Periphery."

"If only criminals can go to The Periphery, and they are only admitted by the PeaceKeepers, and only Peace-Keepers have the ability to open a hole in the Dark Energy Wall, how do you get in?"

"You'll laugh when you see how we get in."

"I could use a good laugh."

"We'll wait here until dark. I think you're probably nearly impossible to find behind this massive rock.

"Or we could run for it right now," Swen continued. "It's good you can run so fast and appear to be able to go without stopping. But at some point, we may attract attention. If we go slow so you can shapeshift, another sensory device may lock onto you."

"There's no clear choice," Heart observed.

"Right. Here's the fun part. I'm letting you choose which option you prefer."

"Hmmm. Well, you have your Gyroscoptic Dark Energy Thingy-thing-thing. That helps."

"True."

"I might be wrong, but I do feel relatively safe here."

"Good."

"And, although I seem to be able to run without getting tired, shapeshifting wears me down if I do it while in motion. I'd rather not. I'd rather preserve my energy."

"Also good thinking."

"Running like we were, how long will it take us to get to The Periphery?"

"I think it'll take us about two hours. Do you think you can run for two hours?"

"I have no idea. Maybe I'll hit a wall before we get to The Wall," Heart added in a droll tone.

Swen nodded thoughtfully, scratching a floppy ear. "Another unknown. We'll just have to deal with it if it happens. Sounds like you want to stay here until later."

Heart nodded. "Until dusk at least."

"Good. I'll set the Gyroscoptic Dark Energy Entangler on low pulse. It'll hopefully confuse tracking devices but not draw attention to itself. At full power, it would cause nearby 3-D devices to go berserk, and makes an ultrasonic sound that some dogs need to sing to. Dog song is music to my ears, but humans do not appreciate it."

Heart nodded. "I'll sit here and think about my insanity to agree to go to The Periphery, while you take a doggie nap, happily dreaming about … I don't have any idea what you might think of as a happy dream…."

"I'll just replay that run. I loved it. Never ran with a human who could keep up with me."

"Pleasant dreams, then."

*   *

Swen really did fall into a deep sleep. Heart chuckled softly when his legs began to run in his sleep. Who knew what their near future held? These few minutes in his private happy dream might be his last for a while.

When the giant rock's shadow on the smaller rock reached the ground beyond, Heart became agitated. It was time to leave.

"Swen," She said softly, patting him on the top of his head between his long ears. He'd slept the whole time.

Swen sat up abruptly. "Holy dog-doo, I really slept. Is it time to go?"

"I think so. It's still light, but the shadows are long. And … it just feels like it's time to go."

"Let's do it." He put the Gyroscoptic Dark Energy Entangler in his chest pack. "I'm completely charged up. Did you sleep?"

"Not for one second. But I'm already all charged up. I'm going into The Periphery. Just thinking about it kept me wide awake."

"Nothing to be scared of."

"So you say. That's why they send awful criminals there, a place that's not even frightening to naive Darling Undesirables."

"Well, I'm glad you see it that way."

"Sarcasm, Swen."

"I know. Let's go."

They stepped to the edge of the giant rock, and, even though they'd only been there a few hours, Heart felt reluctant to leave. When would she be this comfortable again, when would she feel this safe again? She'd soon be in the place where criminals and sad children lived, without light, without heat.

"Just a minute, Swen."

He paused with one paw in mid air. "Yes?"

"Once in The Periphery, how long will it take to get to The Museum of Scientific Improbabilities and Unpredictable Oddities?"

"I don't know, Heart. In distance, it is the long way around. But we might get some rides. Or we might have to walk. One thing for sure though."

"What's that?"

"We won't have to run unless we want to."

"I hope that's true. I forgot to ask—have you been there yourself, or are you so sure you know how to get in because some other newshound has told you how to?"

"I beg your pardon!" Swen said, clearly insulted. "I'm the one who discovered how to get through The Wall. I'll show you the news bit where I'm interviewed for *The Hound*. Really! Have I been there myself. Like I would risk your life if I hadn't been there. Holy dog doo!"

"Sorry. Sorry, Swen, I didn't think that was an insulting question. I thought it was a logical question."

"Well," Swen paused. "It was." He lay low to the ground and slunk out from behind the rock, then looked about. He wagged his snout for Heart to join him.

The sun was brighter than she'd anticipated, and she feared she'd made a bad decision. But Swen had already loped some distance ahead. She sprang after him in the nearly deserted park. A few runners ignored her and her dog, or said an offhanded "hi" without a second glance.

It was perfect.

*   *

Heart and Swen ran and ran. They ran while the lengthening shadows turned to dusk and dusk transformed into a dark, silken twilight. They soon left the park and ran among big, old, elegant homes, half-timbered, brick, stone. Homes that in their foundations remembered a time when they were not pulsing with power and life from harnessed dark energy. Homes that shone brightly, from which music and laughter poured.

Through the windows, Heart glimpsed at small bits of ordinary life, for ordinary people. People with families and jobs and pets and regular school. Homes with parents and children, and grandparents, aunts, uncles, cousins. Homes where people decided for themselves what they would eat, and chose for themselves the clothes they'd wear.

All these new thoughts tumbled through her mind, jumbled up, while she kept running, running, running. What would it be like, to have a life of one's own, she wondered as she ran and ran.

It seemed downright peculiar that no one gave her a second glance. As people walked by her, or brought their hovercrafts into their garages, no one glanced at this girl and her dog. Even as they walked into their homes and looked at their 3-D Recap of Day's Events and saw her, larger than life, hovering in the center of their living rooms.

Humanity, she surmised, was exceedingly odd.

Gradually the huge, elegant old homes gave way to smaller vintage homes. Heart much preferred these homes with their cozy front porches, their tidy yards lined with the same flowers she and Eye planted, sending up delightful aromas in the evening air. Companionable ancient trees hovered around the charming homes like gigantic guardian angels.

Then she and Swen came to the end of the small, tidy, older homes, and, abruptly, the houses they ran by were ramshackle, yards poorly kept, skinny cats and dogs chasing one another down the road.

Heart had never seen anything like it. The few people who were out looked at her, hard, like they wondered why a girl would be running. But still, no one appeared to recognize her.

"Swen," she called.

He fell back to her side.

"How much longer? I—I don't like it here. It feels sad. I don't like it."

"We've only got a short distance to go. See the shadow of those gigantic trees in the distance? That's where we're going. It's a park, and The Wall goes through the park."

"Good." She added speed to her feet. "If it's like this *here*, it must be so much worse on the other side of The Wall."

"Save you judgment until you get there. Right now, concentrate on running."

"Right."

The mean, sad houses came to an abrupt halt at the Great Hover Way. Heart forgot that they would come to it before getting to The Wall. She recalled looking down on the dark energy flow, just a few nights before in the Darling Undesirables airbus.

"Swen!"

He fell back again.

"How will we cross the Great Hover Way?"

"Oh, that's nothing. In fact, here we are."

They came to a downward grade, and Heart soon found herself in a tunnel. "The Great Hover Way walk tunnel! I forgot about it."

Lights came on in the tunnel as they ran.

"We're likely to encounter people," Swen said. "You might want to shapeshift, since we'll be so close to them and they might recognize you."

"Not too difficult, these stone walls are all the same." Heart slowed while going into the shape of the stones that flew by. Just in time, as they passed a runner with his own dog. The dog stopped short, sensing both the newshound and the anomaly of shapeshifting Heart, and started howling. The runner turned, looking at Swen. Heart and Swen ran around a curve. To their relief, the runner decided to continue as they heard him call to his dog and his footsteps receded.

The only other event in the tunnel was an elderly woman walking a very small dog.

"Hello, doggie, are you all alone?" The woman called sweetly to Swen, when he flew by.

As they ran deeper into the tunnel, Heart felt increasingly strange. Her steps slowed and the effort to remain shapeshifted seemed nearly impossible.

"Swen," she called, as he pulled further and further away from her, unaware of her difficulty.

He looked back, then ran to her side.

"What's happening?"

"I don't know. It feels like something is weighing me down."

"Are you getting tired?"

"It doesn't feel like it. I—just—feel—heavy."

They kept running, although Heart continued to slow.

"We're about in the center of the tunnel. Perhaps it's the power of the Dark Energy."

Just as Swen said this, they began to incline slightly.

"Oh!" Heart exclaimed, beginning to feel lighter. "I think you must be right. I'm feeling lighter and lighter—and lighter!" She picked up her speed. Before long they ran out into the crisp night air. The Great Hover Way glowed above and behind them as they ran into the park.

"Let's stop," Swen said. He pulled up to a trio of small ornamental trees with orange spiky leaves glowing in the soft Great Hover Way light.

Heart glanced down at her plaid sleeve, where the red threads pulsed with their own light, making them appear to stand out from the rest of the fabric. "I am clearly on the right path," she said, pointing to her sleeve.

"I've heard about your predilection for plaid," Swen said, "but I never knew why."

"Because it's a map. When I'm hurt or confused or abused, I pick a color in the plaid, like, for example, green is for when I'm confused, yellow when I want to learn something new, and red for adventure, and follow it in the fabric with my mind and it calms me, or let's me have an insight, or whatever.

"My red threads are glowing on their own. It must be so huge, what I'm doing now, for the red threads to glow."

"Of course it's huge, you funny girl! Oh, look! I can see the red thread glowing!"

Nodding, Heart tore her gaze from the plaid and looked around. "Why have we stopped?"

"I need to think for a minute, about your reaction to Dark Energy, if that's what happened."

"Oh!" Heart exclaimed with sudden insight. "The Wall is Dark Energy, so if I have a negative reaction to just a little bit of it, when we come to The Wall ...."

"Precisely. You may not be able to cross."

"But--why not continue running on this side of The Wall? It has worked well. No one paid any attention to us, and we've come a long way."

Swen shook his head. "I picked the path we ran on carefully. People coming home in the evening just want to get home. They don't pay attention to a girl out in the evening, running with her dog. Also, and maybe you didn't realize you were doing this, you cast a bit of shadow over you. Probably a low amount of shapeshifting, just enough so you didn't look strange, but you features were indiscernible.

"All well and good in the evening in a residential area. But quite different in the city, which is what we're faced with if we don't cross into The Periphery." Swen pointed his muzzle behind Heart.

She turned and saw the glow of the city light rising above the tree line.

"Girls don't run in the city," Swen continued. "Dogs are not allowed off-leash in the city. Newshounds are regularly stopped and asked to show credentials. The Museum of Scientific Improbabilities and Unpredictable Oddities is at the farthest end of the city from where we are. We would never make it. However, on the other side of The Wall, we can move as we please. And, most important, we will be accepted as we are, wherever we go."

"Why are you so sure of that?"

"You'll see."

"I'll see—if I can cross."

"Yes. If you can cross."

"Let's find out." Heart stood. "I think the plaid cannot be wrong. So far, I'm going in the right direction."

Swen led the way, ambling along at a slow run. Heart realized he was keeping a close watch on her. She felt fine, nothing like she had in the Great Hover Way walk tunnel. The confusing commingled glow of the Hover Way and the city dimmed. She could see the stars above. The loamy earth and the evergreen trees vied with one another to produce the most compelling aroma, and little night creatures chirped their various songs making the evening utterly delightful.

If only Eye were with her, that would be perfection!

Reveling in these pleasant thoughts and feelings as she ran, Heart suddenly found herself flung to her knees.

"Swen," she cried.

He rushed to her.

"Can't—move. Can't—s-s-speak."

"Oh no, oh no." Swen sat on his haunches and actually wrung his paws together. "Oh dear. We're still some distance from The Wall. That came on very suddenly."

Heart nodded.

"Not gradual at all!"

Heart could not now even nod.

Swen noticed the plaid of her shirt. "The red has dimmed on your plaid! In fact, now the purple is starting to glow."

"Danger," Heart faintly whispered.

"Danger. What can I do?"

"Drag—me—back."

"Of course. That's obvious. I'm so worried I'm not thinking clearly." Swen grabbed the strap of Heart's backpack in his teeth, and gently tugged her back a few feet.

She sprang to her feet. "Awful! Awful-terrible-horrible feeling. *Aughh!*" She danced yet further back from the invisible line as if shaking insects from her body, then sank to the ground.

Swen came up and sat in front of her, hanging his head and looking very hang-doggie. "I'm sorry."

"You don't have anything to apologize for, Swen. You're just trying to help me. You couldn't know."

"No, I didn't know. Since prisoners …." he stopped.

"Since prisoners … what?"

"Well, I've never known a prisoner to have this reaction."

"Once again, proving my freakishness. Poor little Darling Undesirable. Freak, freak, freak!" She stood up, filled with anger, yet not knowing what to be angry about, or who to be angry with.

Looking down at her sleeve, the red again glowed, while the purple had entirely receded. "The red thread is happy again. I'm out of danger, now I'm on the right track."

Swen shrugged. "We'll have to let your shirt dictate our motion."

Heart turned ninety degrees to her right and took a few steps. The red threads faded to nothing, and she felt a slight tug of the horrible, knee-melting sensation. She turned one-hundred and eighty degrees, and took a few steps. As she crossed the spot where they'd stopped first, the red threads glowed, then faded to nothing as she passed the spot. Then the purple began to glow.

She returned to the spot Swen had dragged her, and watched as the red threads glowed.

"Apparently I'm not to move from this spot—or retreat."

"There must be something you can do or remember that will open up the way, or shift your energy so that we can get to The Wall from here."

"Something I can remember? …." Heart sat back down on the ground and put her chin in her palms. "I feel a memory, but I can't pull it forward … It's not worth much to have a memory if you can't remember it!"

"I don't think that your red threads would glow so energetically," Swen said logically, "and be so precise about where they glow and don't glow, if there wasn't a solution, right here in this spot."

"Oh!" Heart tore off her backpack and spilled out its contents. Wrapping her left arm in the paisley blanket, while watching the plaid sleeve on her right arm, she stood and walked forward to the spot where she had crumpled to her knees. She reached her paisley-covered arm into the Dark Energy space. The red threads continued to glow and she didn't feel the horrible dark tug. She pulled her arm back.

"I believe if I'm wrapped entirely in my paisley blanket, I can be in the Dark Energy. But I really must be entirely cocooned in it."

"I'll have to drag you on … something," Swen said.

"Well, yes."

"Let's get at it. Gather all the twigs you can find and a bunch of tall grass. We'll make a travois."

"You're so smart!"

The two of them scurried about, gathering sizable twigs, small branches, and tall grass into a pile of twigs and a pile of grass. Heart began to weave the grass among the twigs, while Swen devised an attachment to the travois to his harness. Before long, a makeshift, but strong travois lay between them. Heart crammed everything but her paisley blanket back into her backpack, then pulled it on. She lay down carefully on the travois, rolling herself up in the small paisley blanket.

"Ready," she called from inside.

She felt Swen poking along her sides, making sure the paisley covered her completely, then he moved out. Ready to yell, and braced to not even be able to yell, she watched in fascination as the paisleys in the blanket swam about, bumping into and interacting with one another, the usually muted blues and greens and browns of the fabric becoming brilliantly lighted.

"Whoa!" Swen yelped, apparently having looked back at the glow that surrounded her. "What a light show! Can you see it?"

"See it? I'm inside it!"

"Come in, Barky," Swen said.

"What?"

"I'm calling my cousin. With this travois hooked onto me, I'll need help getting through The Wall. I sent him our coordinates so he'll know where we are when we come to The Wall."

"Your cousin? You're machine-bio."

"Yes. And my bio is from his mother's sister. You know, his aunt is my mom."

"Are we talking dogs here?"

"Dogs. Yes."

"Can your cousin be trusted?"

"Everyone in The Periphery can be trusted."

"They're criminals."

"On this side, they're criminals. On The Other Side, they are not. They've made new lives."

Heart suddenly heard barking nearby, but clearly on the other side of a wall. She stirred about.

"Don't move, Heart. We are at The Dark Energy Wall. With your reaction to Dark Energy, it might … destroy you."

"Right. Not moving." Heart held onto the edges of the paisley blanket while she felt Swen shift in the travois and heard him digging furiously. At the same time there was an echo of digging a few feet away.

Then the barking came right in her ear. And strange wonder of wonders, Swen began barking as well. She felt the travois being let gently to the ground, then picked up again. She was pulled sharply downwards and soon, sharply upwards, then rapidly some distance on flat ground.

When the travois came to a stop, she heard many footsteps approach. Cheering broke out all around. Swen patted her arm under her blanket. "You're safe now. Come on out and say hello."

Cautiously, Heart removed her paisley blanket, tremendously relieved to feel no horrible bodily disturbance. A circle of people with fiery torches bent over her whispering, "Heart! It's Heart! Hello, Heart!"

She jumped to her feet. A dog, who looked like a Swen clone, came up and licked her hand.

"Hello," she said, feeling anxious, trapped. Swen had faded away from her side. "Swen! What's happening?"

"You're being welcomed by the People of The Periphery."

"Not to worry, dear," An elderly woman pushed her way through the crowd. "Back off you all. Give the girl a tich to breathe in!"

Everyone backed away several feet, revealing Swen, sitting on his haunches, clearly smiling and quite proud of himself.

"You think you're something, don't you?" Heart asked.

"Rather much, yes."

Everyone broke into laughter like it was the best joke in a decade.

"Swen *is* rather much," a young man agreed. "Look! Here's you, Heart, in our midst."

"But—I'm just passing through."

Again everyone broke into laughter as if she'd said something incredibly amusing. Heart wondered if these people were perhaps a bit like many Darling Undesirables, missing a number of brain synapses.

"No dear, we're not slow," the old woman said, reading Heart's mind. There's a lot you do not know, that we *do* know. So you'll have to forgive us for our seeming oddness as your story unfolds. It's a story we've known for ages. We can't help but chuckle as you quote from *Ourbook*. But never mind that."

The woman turned to the crowd. "I need two torches, the rest of you, scat. It's enough privilege that you are here at the moment of Heart's arrival, is it not?"

There were utterances of agreement as everyone dispersed except the young man who had spoken, and a young woman who looked very much like him. They moved to either side of the line that had formed around Heart. The old woman on one side, Swen on the other, Barky beside him, then the torch bearers on the ends.

They walked into the woods, which Heart barely made out in the flickering light of the torches.

The small group soon reached a rustic, adorable cottage among flowering magnolia trees. The elderly woman opened the low door, and they all moved into the small cottage. Inside, Heart looked about at the cozy surroundings in the dancing light of the fireplace. The young woman hung a kettle of water over the fire to boil.

"Here, Heart, sit here," the old woman gestured to a rough-hewn wooden chair. "Swen, good dog that he is, will sit by your side, I'll sit over here, across from you. Amdrona will make us something to eat and drink. You must relax. Running for hours. My, my, quite remarkable."

"Yes," Heart agreed while watching Amdrona move with stunning grace in the small space around the homely stove. She'd never seen a woman so sure or so natural in her body. Certainly not the way Heart imagined a prisoner would move.

"Amdrona is third generation," the old woman commented as she continued to read Heart's thought. "Not a prisoner. She could leave any moment, if she chose."

"But she doesn't." Heart decided to accept the old woman's ability to read her mind as if it was completely ordinary. She turned to Amdrona. "You don't chose to leave?"

"I do not."

Heart wanted to know more, but at the same time, she had a feeling that to ask would be rude. Swen put his muzzle in her lap. As she patted his forehead, she calmed immensely.

"What are you called?" Heart asked the elderly woman.

"Usually, 'Mother.'"

"That would be strange for me," Heart protested.

"Call me what you will. Anything but 'old woman' that's in your head. Try to be more creative."

"I will try." Heart felt embarrassed.

"You have questions. Let us contemplate some of your questions before you continue on your journey to The Museum of Scientific Improbabilities and Unpredictable Oddities."

Heart looked down at Swen, disapproving.

"I told her nothing, Heart."

"He told me nothing. Not only am I a thought-reader, as you are already aware, but I know you future, Heart, as if it's history. That is to say, your possible futures. You will be faced with many decisions, and you'll be making many choices. We are all most intrigued with your decisions. That you've made it to this side of The Wall is written in *Ourbook* as, "The Dark Wall Crossing."

"I don't want to know this," Heart protested. "I want to get to The Museum of Scientific Improbabilities and Unpredictable Oddities. And I want to have Eye living with me—somewhere."

"I understand."

Heart saw that, indeed, this wise woman did understand. "May I call you 'The Mystic'?" she asked.

She smiled. "You may."

"All right then, I have questions, dear Mystic."

The young man, who had stepped outside, returned and sat beside The Mystic when Amdrona brought a tray of cups and something brewing in a pot that did not smell like tea or any beverage Heart had ever been acquainted with, to the table. On a clay plate were slices of a flat toasty, dark bread, and another plate held beautifully arranged fruit and cheese. Amdrona sat on the other side of The Mystic.

Heart, who rarely had an interest in eating anything, found herself longing to devour everything before her.

"Thank everyone and everything who contributed to the plenty on our the table," Amdrona intoned like a small prayer. She piled fruit and cheese on a slice of bread, and gestured Heart to do the same.

Heart dug in, then the young man reached out and pulled the tray to himself, piled a slice of bread high. Heart expected him to shove it in his mouth, but he handed it to The Mystic.

"May I give some to Swen?" Heart asked.

"Of course," Amdrona said, smiling down at him and popping some cheese into his mouth.

"I want to know," Heart said, "well, so many things. But, first, what is it like to live here?"

"It's good to live here," The Mystic answered.

"How can it be good, when you don't have Dark Energy lights and appliances and heat? When you live by, as I see, fire?"

"We have all the transformers and clockwork machines," the young man said. "They were all sent over here from the Dark Energy side when they switched to total Dark Energy."

"But we like our cozy firelight," Amdrona added. "We like living simply. We like being close to nature, in small homes, where stepping out the door means touching earth."

"I see." Heart took in the idea. It was not bad. She screwed up her courage to ask the most burning question of all her burning questions as she and Swen had been interrupted when she'd asked the question before.

"Tell me about Father Inventor. If he's been banished, but he's not in The Periphery, where is he?"

Her question made everyone laugh.

"You mean, Mr. Thompson?" the young man asked.

"Mr. Thompson? No, I mean Father Inventor."

"'Father Inventor,'" The Mystic said, "has a name, and his name is Mr. Thompson. Mr. Thompson lives in a location of exile of his own choosing. That is to say, he lives off-planet in a place he created."

"So," Heart said, putting many things together, "The Mechanical Aurora Borealis at The Museum of Scientific Improbabilities and Unpredictable Oddities is not just a light show. It comes from a place Father Inventor, who is also known as 'Mr. Thompson,' created. It is off-world, and that's where he lives."

"That about sums it up," The Mystic said, smiling at Heart with a pleased expression.

PART
TWO

Chapter 11

The Mystic and Heart talked long into the night. The Mystic had an unflagging energy that matched Heart's urgent need to learn. During the night, Heart felt a gentle weight on each of her feet. Looking under the little table she saw Swen's muzzle resting on one foot and Barky's on the other. She grinned from ear to ear and completely lost the thread of the conversation.

She looked up at The Mystic, who had stopped talking when Heart peeked under the table. "The hounds … " she said simply.

The Mystic nodded. "You are loved. And trusted. And protected."

"Yes," Heart agreed. "And protected. Strange." A myriad thoughts ran through her mind as she considered the protection at her feet. She'd never before wondered if she was protected. The life she led was a sheltered life at

The Darling Undesirables Facility at Long Prairie. Until just the last few days, when her life changed completely, she'd never felt unsafe.

"Do I need to be protected while in The Periphery? So far, it doesn't seem like I do."

"Your choices will answer your question," The Mystic said, cryptically. She reached over and patted Amdrona on the shoulder. Heart saw that the beautiful young woman looked exhausted. Amdrona moved to a small cot in the shadows of the cottage that Heart had not previously noticed, and lay down. The Young Man to Heart's left had already put his head on his forearms and fallen fast asleep.

"Poor thing," the Mystic whispered, maternally stroking the Young Man's cheek. "It has been a very exciting evening."

He raised his head and they exchanged a glance. He got up from the table and stepped outside.

"It's exciting to be present when prophecy is fulfilled," the Mystic said. "They are young things, their energy burns up like a large fire. Mine burns steady, like a candle."

"And mine? Why aren't I falling asleep like the two of them? I've had the biggest day of my life, and I'm wide awake." Heart heard some stirring along the wall of the cottage, and she pictured the young man making himself a bed next to the wall.

The Mystic nodded in response to her mental image. "Well, you Heart, you …." She trailed off.

"I?"

"You are Heart. You can know no more and no less than that at this time."

Heart felt a spike of irritation at yet another cryptic bundle of words.

The Mystic smiled a crooked little smile. "I do understand your frustration, dear Heart. But I can only give you answers to questions that help you make your choices, not that make the choices for you. You can be at peace with that. You may also choose not to be at peace with that. But remember, every choice you make takes you down a path. And if you discover you're heading down a path you don't prefer, it's more difficult to back out than to go down the path you intended in the first place."

"More cryptic words." Heart was taken aback by the anger she felt rising. Why this anger? The Mystic was gentle and kind. Truly, authentically, kind. Why feel anger toward a kind woman, who had taken her into her home, who had fed her and surrounded her with people—and creatures—who cared about her?

In growing agitation, she stood, disrupting both sleeping dogs. She moved about the little cottage, edgy. Wanting to say something, ask something. But the words, the question wouldn't form. Anyway, the Mystic would just give her a cryptic non-answer, wouldn't she?

Swen came out from under the table and stood by her chair, watching her pace the few steps across the cottage, while Barky put his head back on his paws and returned to sleep. But Swen said nothing as he watched her, and Heart felt he and The Mystic knew something about her that she did not know. Knew something about this moment that she had yet to discover.

Oddly, she noticed, as she paced about the room, it seemed to grow. She looked over at Swen and—surely he was now fifteen feet distant instead of five. She turned the opposite direction to see if the other end of the room had receded, which it had. She felt drawn to the fireplace. A small fire, mostly embers, glowed there, but Heart's attention was taken by a shiny, golden surface above the low mantle. She stepped over to it and looked at the glowing image held within the confines of the golden reflective surface. As she came near the surface, the image came close, as she turned to look at The Mystic and Swen, the image turned.

"What am I looking at? Who is that? Who am I seeing?"

"That's you, Heart," the Mystic answered.

The room snapped back to its cozy size.

"Me?" She returned her gaze to the golden-lit surface. "I've seen myself in holos. I don't look anything like … this …" She moved her hand across her face. The reflection moved her hand across her face.

The girl looking back at her was not scruffy, gaunt and raggedy-looking as she always appeared in holos. This girl was a young woman, with a deep intelligence in her now-golden eyes, a radiating light poured off her glowing skin, her hair, a rich amber hue, gleamed in the pale firelight.

"That is the real you, Heart," Swen said. That is the you I see." He ambled over and stood by her. "Perhaps slightly less golden, as the mirror is not usual, but the glow, the intelligence, the power of you—there, that's how I see you. That's how everyone here sees you. All Darling Undesirables are cloaked in holos by law, as a protection."

"So, when we were running today, we didn't have to be careful."

"Well, yes, we have to be careful. Because there are people who can see through the holo cloaking. And there were all the people who saw you live at The Museum of Scientific Improbabilities and Unpredictable Oddities."

Heart was drawn back to her image. "That's me," she whispered, and the golden image mouthed the words with her. "Not as much of a lost little thing as I thought!"

"Indeed not," The Mystic agreed.

Heart pulled herself away from her golden image and returned to sit across from The Mystic. "So, what was that about? Why did the room get gigantic and then snap back to this cozy little space?"

"Ah! That was your mind making a shift into a more real understanding of where you are now. Just a piece of brain chemistry, helping you become aware that who you are and where you are are bigger than at first it seems. You were coming into the energetic space beyond the three dimensions of here and the one dimension of now."

Heart nodded, but without complete understanding. "All of this is in your *Ourbook*?"

"Cryptically expressed, yes."

"I'd like to look at that someday, but right at this moment, I think it's time for me to get on my way to The Museum of Scientific Improbabilities and Unpredictable Oddities."

The Mystic nodded. "I think you're right. Poor Zack barely got stretched out. Go stir him up, Swen, if you don't mind, dear."

"Don't mind a bit."

Heart watched, puzzled, as Swen muzzled his way through the door. "Who's Swen stirring up, and why?"

"Zack." The Mystic gestured to the now empty chair to her right. "He's going with you."

"Why? Why is he going with us?" Heart didn't want anyone but Swen with her. They moved fast and efficiently.

"Because he has transportation."

"Transport. All right then, we'll get there yet this morning. That's good. But how does a transport work if you have no dark energy?"

"I didn't say 'a transport' I said 'transportation.' You will not get there this morning. You will not get there today."

"We won't get there today! When will we get there?"

"When you arrive." The Mystic got up and stirred about the cottage, gathering food and some other items that Heart could not make out. She put it all in a lovely woven bag of gold and russet threads and handed it to Heart. "For your journey."

At that, Zack stepped through the door. "Ready?"

Heart nodded. "More than ready." She passed through the charming little door. In the faint glow of the pre-dawn light, she saw a small cart hooked up to a pair of donkeys. "Oh! I didn't know there were still donkeys alive!"

"We have quite a few here on The Other Side," Zack said, clearly proud of his little grey team.

"But … but … well, they certainly are not run by Dark Energy."

Zack and The Mystic burst our laughing while Amdrona came to the door of the cottage, and Swen and Barky came bounding up to the little cart, barking their good-byes to one another.

"I see now why it will take me days to get to The Museum of Scientific Improbabilities and Unpredictable Oddities. But is it really all right to make them pull all the weight of the cart and me and Zack …."

"I'll mostly trot alongside," Swen said.

"Of course!" Zack said. "They were very excited to get harnessed up. It's been a long time since we took a road trip. I'm excited too! I've got some old friends and cousins I haven't seen in a long, long time, who live near the Museum. Grand adventure. Hop in!"

Zack gave her a hand up into the little cart, where she found a beautiful and luxurious red blanket spread out. There was also a small bundle of hay, a bucket of grain, and a closed container that Heart thought must be water for the animals. Heart put the bag The Mystic had given her and her backpack under the driver's seat, and Zack put a similar bag under the seat as well, then he climbed into the driver's seat.

"We're off!" He shook the reins. The cart jerked into motion. Barky and Swen exchanged a few parting barks, while The Mystic and Amdrona waved.

"Travel safely," Amdrona called. "Travel safely, dear Heart!"

* *

As the donkey cart pulled away from The Mystic's cottage, Heart, sitting sideways in the back of the cart, silently watched the little cottage become tinier and tinier as the gigantic conifers of the forest closed in around it, like the life-spark at the center of an egg, protected round about by the flow of life from the plants, then more protection from the little deciduous trees, and even more protection from the gigantic, ancient trees, all surrounded by the atmosphere of pure, clean air and the forest energies themselves.

When she could no longer see the little cottage, nor even the illusion of its image, she turned her attention forward. Much to her surprise, in the near distance, the giant forest trees gave way to a gorgeous and far-reaching stand of oak trees, wildly green with the long rays of the morning sun pouring through their branches. Joy and exuberance welled up in Heart and burst from the center of her chest out through her fingers and toes.

It was so lovely here!

Not that The Darling Undesirables Facility at Long Prairie was not lovely. It was. But it was a prison. Heart had read this word in her studies and didn't truly understand what it meant until this exact moment. This moment when she knew herself to be free. Her decisions were her own. Her choices were her own. The results of her choices and decisions were hers, too. There was no feeling like it in the world, in all of life, she knew, like this feeling. Delightful. Exhilarating. Promising. Frightening.

Did she have the wisdom to make wise choices? she wondered.

Blythe Ayne – 139

Probably not. But she would learn. Wasn't that what life was about, making decisions, making wrong choices, learning not to do that again, discovering the right choices, and moving forward?

Leaving The Darling Undesirables Facility at Long Prairie was the best decision of her young life. She wanted to tell everyone, everywhere—if they felt trapped, if life was not what they meant it to be, they must break out, and head into the forest of their dreams.

You could only do this alone, she thought. Then she noticed Swen, trotting alongside the cart at her back, with a really, silly, goofy grin on his long snout, clearly every bit as happy as she, and perhaps for the same reasons. The beauty. The freedom. The adventure. And then she realized that, trotting along beside the cart, at her back, he was protecting her. He may be wearing a goofy grin, but Heart became profoundly aware that she was neither alone nor unprotected. Then she had the thought that it was good to take a journey with a friend. Someone who had your back. Someone who cared about you.

Her attention was drawn to Zack, also in his own reverie, saying a quiet word or two now and then to his darling donkeys. Heart leaned over to watch their cute little, sure-footed feet as they made rapid delicate drum sounds on the dirt path.

She could ride and ride like this forever!

However, an image of the Gear Horse rose in her mind, insistent, compelling. No, she could not ride and ride like this forever. She urgently needed to get to The Museum of Scientific Improbabilities and Unpredictable Oddities. First things first. And Eye, of course. It was all about Eye. But somehow, the Gear Horse was a part of that, was a part of her life, a part of her fulfilling her destiny, and a part of caring for Eye. Whatever it took. Whatever it meant.

Only one thought nagged at Heart now. The knowledge that she could move faster on foot than she was moving, sitting here like royalty, the only passenger in a private carriage. True, a modest carriage. But a slow-moving carriage. Her anxiety mounted as this thought overtook her mind. Just as she was about to say something—yet not exactly sure what—Zack said, "We'll pull over her. Water the donkeys, and Swen, you probably wouldn't mind a bit of water, right?"

Swen nodded, his floppy ears flapping about his grin. "Wouldn't mind, no. Great. Great idea."

A little three-sided lean-to on the side of the road came into view. Zack pulled to a stop in front of it, and got down from the cart. The donkeys watched him with rapt attention while he opened a small door in the back of the shed. He then pulled out a huge, and obviously heavy, barrel and a smaller tub. The barrel had a tap on it, which Zack opened, filling the tub with water, then led the donkeys to it. They stood side by side, drinking up the water with great gusto.

Zack pulled out a small bucket from the cupboard and filled it with water for Swen.

"Thank you, Zack," Swen said politely, then began lapping at the water.

Heart chuckled at the incongruity of his impeccable manners with his dog-ness.

He looked up at her. "Not nice!"

Heart put her hand to her mouth in fake-apology. "No. Not nice. You are so lovable, you—you whatever you are, bio-machine dog-friend."

"That's better." Swen went back to his water drinking.

Heart hopped down from the cart and walked around to the back of the shed and out among the oak trees. She went up to one and rubbed her hand on its bark, absorbing the sensation of the ridges and roughness.

Zack joined her. "Beautiful, aren't they?"

"Yes." Heart pulled her hand from the trunk of the tree, then intertwined her fingers behind her back, with an edge of discomfort when Zack walked up to her. She glanced sideways to see if Swen was still drinking his water, hoping he might join them. But he was still fully engrossed.

Why, she wondered, did she feel uneasy?

"Sorry if I startled you," Zack took a small step back.

"No, not startled." She tried to think it through before speaking, feeling curious about her own reaction. "I … Oh! I understand—I'm not used to … to being around people I don't know, one-on-one. I've never been alone with anyone I don't know."

"Have you been uncomfortable this whole morning, riding with me?"

"No. That was different, Swen was right there, and we weren't face-to-face. It's interesting …." Heart trailed off, wondering if Zack found it interesting too.

Zack nodded. "I understand, Heart. It's good that you have this caution about strangers. But soon, we won't be strangers. Soon, you will not need to be afraid of me …."

"I'm not afraid!" Heart exclaimed, shocked at the word. Afraid? No.

"We all have fears, Heart." Zack sat down at the base of the oak tree between them. "Fears inform us of our path. We must learn whether to face something that induces fear, and forge through it, or to move away from it as the wisest choice."

There! He said aloud the conversation she'd just been having with herself.

"I know!" she sounded defensive, and wondered at her tone. Zack was not a Keeper. He was kind and good and generous and had given up whatever he would otherwise be doing, to take her to The Museum of Scientific Improbabilities and Unpredictable Oddities.

Zack looked up at her, raising an eyebrow.

"That didn't sound like I meant it to … I mean," she said, softening her tone, and contemplating her feelings, "I mean, that's precisely what I was thinking back there on the road, about my choice and my decisions and about the freedom I now have, that I've never had, and how—if something is frightening, I have to keep on, and work my way through it."

Zack nodded.

"That was right before I had the thought that I could move faster on my own two feet, which I was about to say, when you pulled over here to water the—the creatures." Swen was not exactly an animal. "And I really do thank you for your help, but I believe Swen and I must take off on our own so that I can get to The Museum of Scientific Improbabilities and Unpredictable Oddities sometime tomorrow."

Zack burst out in a loud guffaw.

"What,"Heart's irritation at his response reaching a new high, "is so hilarious?"

"Get to The Museum of Scientific Improbabilities and Unpredictable Oddities by tomorrow on foot? You're trying to be funny."

"I most certainly am not 'trying to be funny.' I am, as you know, trying to get there as quickly as possible."

"My dear Heart, there's quick and there's sure. Furthermore, there's possible and impossible. Do you have any idea at all how far you must travel?"

"It takes an hour and a half to two hours by Dark Energy craft to travel from The Darling Undesirables Facility at Long Prairie to The Museum of Scientific Improbabilities and Unpredictable Oddities. Swen and I ran for several hours yesterday …."

"Yes, and good job, too. You covered about eighty miles, fifty more or less towards The Museum of Scientific Improbabilities and Unpredictable Oddities, and thirty to cross into The Periphery. The Darling Undesirables Facility at Long Prairie is about seven hundred miles from The Museum of Scientific Improbabilities and Unpredictable Oddities. A low atmosphere Dark Energy vehicle airways cruising speed is about 500 miles per hour. We've gone almost fifty miles so far today. That's about six hundred miles yet to go. Six or seven days, if nothing goes wrong. You cannot go six or seven days without supplies."

"Six or seven days?" Surprised and disappointed Heart turned away from Zack, seeing again!—how much she didn't know. How much she didn't think things through. How was it possible that she did not do on her own the reasoning Zack just voiced? It really didn't seem like herself.

"I think I know what you're thinking." Zack stood and moved around to face her. "Don't be hard on yourself. You had to act fast, and you've been in motion since you made the huge, important decision to leave The Darling Undesirables Facility. You made the right choice.

"What do you think would have happened if you'd thought all of this through, adding up miles to The Museum of Scientific Improbabilities and Unpredictable Oddities, the time on foot, and the need for supplies, and all of the numerous details?"

Heart shook her head ever so slightly. "I … I would not have left."

"That's right. You wouldn't. You're on the road now, you're in motion. People, and—" he gestured toward Swen, who had finished drinking his water, and stood patiently by the donkeys, "creatures, are helping you along the way. The smartest choice you can make, if you will allow me to advise you, is to let us help you with the details, and you continue with what you know you must do."

"But—six or seven days! Many things can go wrong. It feels too long. Is there another mode of transportation that can go faster?"

"There isn't. We used to have some vehicles, but they've long ago fallen out of commission when everyone here learned that we were not in a hurry to get anywhere."

"Very nice," Heart said with a twinge of sarcasm. "That is, until someone actually has to get somewhere …."

"We'll get there, Heart. One of our mantras is 'everything that happens is supposed to happen.'"

Heart frowned. "That says no one should ever bother to do anything."

"Perhaps. If a person needs it to say that, then it works that way for them. But what it says—to me—is, everything that happens is a result of previous things you've done, and everything is a result of what you've put into motion. So, if you don't like where you are right now, then right now you have to put into motion what you believe needs to be in the future."

"Hmmm …" Heart mulled the idea over. "So, if I …."

Swen came loping up to them. "Gotta move. They've taken down a section of wall …."

Zack leapt toward the donkeys, "Let's go!" he called to Heart.

"What? What's happening? What's going on?" She watched as Swen turned and ran away from her. "Wait! What's happening?"

"*Come on,*" Swen hollered back at her.

Heart ran to the front of the shed. Zack was rapidly putting things away. Swen had climbed in the back of the cart, fussing with one of his numerous communication devices on his chest pack, where it had been thrown.

"How can you know that?" Zack asked, hurrying up to the cart, he did not climb onto his little seat, but instead, took the reins and brought them in front of the cart and began to lead the donkeys off the road and into the Oak forest.

"When they opened the wall," Heart heard Swen say, "communication flowed through. I'm getting news as if I'm on The First Side."

Heart stood in the roadway, watching them.

"Come on, Heart."

"What's happening?" she called after Zack and Swen as the cart pulled away from her downhill.

"They're looking for you, Heart," Swen shouted. "They tracked you to The Wall and took down a section, where we came through ...."

Then, instantly, Heart heard nothing, saw nothing. The cart, Swen, Zack, and the donkeys could neither be seen nor heard.

She dashed into the forest.

*   *

She ran straight downhill in the direction the cart had headed, stumbling over tree roots and ferns, but soon ran smack into the cart, which, she'd not noticed before, was painted with leaves in a forest camouflage.

"*Opf! Ouch!* I couldn't see you!" Heart jumped into the cart.

" That would be the objective," Swen said, hunkered over his device.

"What's ...."

"Don't mean to be rude, Heart, but be quiet."

Heart shut up. She looked for Zack, who she finally saw squatting down in front of the donkeys, holding their reins, and patting the muzzle of one of them who looked like a coiled spring ready to go off, just waiting for instruction about which direction to go.

Heart returned her attention to Swen. Holographic words appeared around him, but she couldn't make any sense of what they were saying. She waited impatiently.

"Okay," he finally said.

Zack stood and came around to the back of the cart.

"They've shut off a section of the wall where Heart and I came through last night. Apparently only about four feet wide, so, for sure they've just let through a few bots. Maybe a bunch of those things we dealt with yesterday."

Heart shuddered at the thought of more of those awful balloon tentacles carrying her off.

"I think we'd better keep in motion. They were able to hone in on her yesterday, but the hole in the wall is small, so the Dark Energy is weak. We have to trust that the camo will adequately block her. It'll be slow going, because we're off the road, and I have to stay in the cart to monitor and fuss with my instruments."

Zack nodded and even as Swen was finishing his sentence, Zack pulled out the bag from under the seat and unwrapped a lightweight bit of camouflage fabric with the same pattern on it, Heart observed, as was painted on the cart. "Lie down, Heart."

"Wait—wait!"

"What?" Zack held the camo up, ready to fling it over her. "We have to keep in motion, Heart."

"I don't want to lie down. I have to be ready to jump if those—those whatever-they-ares come after me."

"They won't know you're here if you're under the camo," Swen said.

"This flimsy thing?"

"This flimsy thing is bio-blocking, mechanical-blocking, and even to a certain extent, dark energy-blocking. Now lie down, please," Zack said.

"All right." Heart stretched out on her back and Zack flung the camo over her. "Bio-blocking, mechanical-blocking, dark-energy-blocking," she repeated. "I hope so."

She heard Zack walk around to the front of the cart and pick up the reins. Apparently, he was going to walk, leading the donkey team and the little cart through the forest.

"*WAIT!*" Heart sat bolt upright. "What about the Mystic and Amdrona and, and … everyone else. If the bots came through there, they're in danger."

The cart moved on as if she hadn't spoken.

"The bots are looking for you. They may not even perceive other life forms at all. Let Zack and me do what we know we must do, and what we know how to do. While you keep your mind on what you must do. Which is? …."

"First, get to The Museum of Scientific Improbabilities and Unpredictable Oddities …."

"Right. Now please get back under the camo. Relax a bit. You need to rest."

As wound up as she was, Heart fell deep asleep, waking up sometime later to a buzzing, trilling sound, unlike anything she'd ever heard. When she opened her eyes, she was frustrated by not being able to see through the camo. As she began to pull it off, the conversation between Swen and Zack arrested her movements.

"Here they come," Swen said quietly.

"Yeah. I thought I heard them."

"I trust she'll sleep through it."

"Hmmm," Zack said. That doesn't seem likely. I didn't know she could sleep this much."

"She's gone through an endless bout of weird events, she needs to get recharged—hopefully, this sleep has done it."

"Have you been in touch with Mr. Thompson?" Zack asked.

"No. He doesn't need me to tell him what's happening. He knows."

"Probably," Zack agreed. "We just want to make sure that she's …."

Swen interrupted, "Here they come."

Mr. Thompson!? Why were they talking about Father Inventor so casually? And they needed to make sure that she was—what? And, last but not least, she couldn't see because, she finally realized, it was night—she'd slept for many hours!

The trilling sound broke her thoughts—these were not the same bots that had hauled her off before. These were much more frightening, by their sound alone.

She stirred.

"You awake?" Swen asked softly.

"Yes. The sound—that noise."

"Right. Don't move. It's the bots."

"So I figured."

"Don't move."

"Yes. I figur …"

"*Shh!* Don't be audible."

Right. Shut up. Be still.

The nearly unbearable trilling seemed to come right down to the cart, while Zack continued to lead the donkeys through the dark forest.

The trilling hovered over Zack. Heart longed to see— and desperately hoped not to see! what made this sound that banged in her chest like a sledgehammer.

Weirdly—very weirdly—Swen stirred about, prob- ably hiding his equipment, she thought, and barked, very dog-like, as if excited and upset by the bot. He jounced around in the cart, and next thing she knew, her paisley blanket, paisleys stirring about faintly in their own light, was "trompled" under the camo into her hand.

Somehow he knew what the sound was doing to her. He continued to pretend dog-distress, making the cart rock about so no one could see her subtle movements as she put her blanket over her head.

Much better!

The trilling became faint and stopped hurting. Further, she could now hear that the object was talking with Zack! Horror upon horror.

"Why," the object's trilling-grinding voice asked, "are you leading your cart through the forest in the night?"

"Because," Zack answered as calm as if talking with Swen, "I need to be at my destination by morning."

"What is your activity at your destination?"

"I'm meeting with my relatives for breakfast."

"What is your business?"

"I am to frighten a little mouse under a chair."

WHAT? Heart almost squawked aloud. Are you trying to get us all hauled off?

Swen barked loudly to cover his guffaw.

This was funny? Heart didn't understand.

"Very well," the bot said. "Carry on. Make sure the mouse is fully under the chair before undertaking another project."

"Of course," Zack answered. He'd not stopped for one moment but had steadily walked on, the little donkeys and cart coming along behind.

Heart heard a zipping sound and imagined it was the bot, moving away at fantastic speed.

"Can I come out?" she whispered.

Swen pulled back the camo with his paw and Heart removed her paisley blanket from her head. "What? I mean just—*what?*"

Swen finally let erupt his contained guffaw to such an extent that he could not even speak. Zack, reins in hand, came back beside Heart. "We're good now, for a while at least. I'm going back up to the road. Hang on, steep climb."

Swen jumped out of the cart and trotted alongside. "They're mechanical bots, Heart. What they're looking for when they stop someone—besides you, because that's their mission—is suspicious behavior, emotional upheaval like fear, anger or guilt, and a lack of mission. Well, we're suspicious because we're traveling at night. But Zack was cool as the night air. No emotion for the bot to grab onto. Good job, by the way, Zack."

"Thanks."

And then a mission. Doesn't matter what it is, it just has to follow a form 'I am doing fill in the blank with blank.' Zack's mission at his destination is to frighten a little mouse under a chair." Swen chuckled again. "Kept me cool, and probably helped Zack a bit too."

"Keep your cool," Zack exclaimed, "Sheesh, it's a good thing you didn't register with them as anything other than 'simple canine,' which showed up on his monitor, to my relief. I thought I had a hyena in the cart."

"Simple canine! I beg someone's pardon!"

"Be glad!" Heart said.

"Well, yes, of course—didn't attract any attention." Swen nodded slightly. "But umbrage must be taken."

"Umbrage noted," Zack said. "Now that we're, back on the road we'll make better time. Although Molly needs a rest, I want to keep going until I'm closer to any of my cousins, so if the bots turn up again, it looks like I'm where I said I'd be." Zack paused the cart while he situated the reins over the backs of the donkeys and climbed onto the driver's seat.

"Who's Molly?" Heart asked. There was someone else with them?

"Molly, your faithful four-footed cart-mover on the right from where you're sitting. Molly and Lolly."

"Oh, Molly and Lolly—I've not been properly introduced. It's lovely to meet you!"

The donkeys ignored her, continuing to put their eight little sure-footed feet, one in front of the other, on the dusty road ....

But why did only Molly need rest, Heart wondered, as a picture of the Gear Horse came brilliantly into mind, setting aside all thoughts other than getting to The Museum of Scientific Improbabilities and Unpredictable Oddities as soon as possible.

Chapter 12

"Too easy," Swen said when they were in motion again.

"Yes," Zack nodded.

"What do you mean?" Heart asked, dismayed. "They left. They wouldn't have left if … if they didn't accept what you told them."

"You're probably right."

"What are you not saying?"

Zack remained silent and still as stone on the driver's seat except for the movement of the cart. She glanced over at Swen. Trotting alongside, looking at the trees and all but whistling, so preoccupied with not answering her.

"Here's what I don't understand. I don't understand what's the big deal about me. I mean, okay, Heart. A Darling Undesirable without a heart. Lots of publicity and money and … and stuff for The Darling

Undesirables Residence of Long Prairie. But, beyond that, who cares?

"Let's get logical," she continued. "I'm a financial benefit for one residence, and maybe residual funds for the larger, whatever—organization. But, I'm not a dummy, these bots are very expensive. Taking down a chunk of The Periphery Wall for bots to get in, that's not free. Zipping about looking for me. Again, not free.

At some point, looking for me has got to be more resource consuming than having me. Yes?"

Swen looked up at Zack. "Well, she's right. She's not a dummy."

Heart scowled. "Is that sarcastic?"

"Not in the least," Swen answered. "No. Not sarcastic. Just—don't know what to say to your impeccable logic, except ...."

"With care, Swen," Zack interrupted.

"Right." Swen shook his muzzle, pruning up his wide mouth. A bizarrely human expression. Heart hated the bad, un-trusting feeling that welled up in her thin chest. What were they not telling her?

What?

She became quiet, thinking through every moment of her last few days. How Swen had been steadfastly on the other side of the fence at The Darling Undesirables Residence of Long Prairie. How he had brought her here. How she'd come trippingly along, without even flinching. And at the same time, so suspicious of the Keepers and the only home she'd known all her life.

What would the people in The Periphery have to gain by her presence here? There might be something she had not even a tiny notion about.

Oh, you are *soooo* ridiculous, she said to herself. There are an infinite number if things you don't know about. Pick one.

She didn't know if she was being used by the people on this side of The Wall ....

She didn't know if the bots were trying to take her home to safety ….

She didn't know if humans were not sent to get her, because they could not be safe here ….

She didn't know … she didn't know … she didn't know ….

She didn't know if she ought to jump from the little cart and run flat out, as fast as she could, back the way they came. She didn't know if she could, would she make it?

No. She knew. Swen would have her in his jowls in under a minute.

She must bide her time. She must listen carefully. She would keep her eyes wide open, and her mouth tight shut.

She hoped against hope that perhaps they actually were moving in a direction more toward The Museum of Scientific Improbabilities and Unpredictable Oddities than away.

She'd known loneliness many times in her life. But she'd never felt loneliness like this. To be with others who claimed to be friends, but who—the thought gathered into a dark place in her heartless chest—may have an agenda for her that bore no resemblance to embracing her best interests.

"You're awful quiet," Swen finally said.

"And you."

"True."

Zack looked over his shoulder at Heart. She could feel him trying to peel off the protection into which she'd just cloaked her thoughts. It certainly felt as though he read her mind.

She took her mind to her run with Swen, across the park, under the tall trees. She decided to play this loop in her mind when either of them gave her a silent study.

But what she really wanted to do was think about Eye. How was he? Had she left him alone for no good reason? Had she abandoned him when all she'd needed to do, as she wisely told herself a mere three days ago, was to wait until she was eighteen?

That was all she had to do. Again, she found herself haunted by the fear that she was not nearly as smart as she thought she was. Surrounded by a population of mentally deficient peers and mental midget Keepers—with the exception of Keeper A, Eye, and Loruza—she'd never been intellectually challenged.

Faulty thinking brought her here. Faulty thinking made her abandon Eye.

Faulty thinking and she was out in an unknown wilderness, alone with strangers, who could talk pretty, but gave her fake no-answers to her questions.

"I am not betraying you," Swen's doggy-voice came clearly into her mind. Damn! She'd stopped thinking about the run.

She turned to look over her shoulder at him, and was startled when he jumped up into the cart behind her. He looked her in the eye, into her soul, with his big, mopey, down-turned eyes, his brown fur adding to his overall appearance of sadness. He shook his head slowly, holding her gaze, and whispered quietly, "I … Would … never. At heart, dear Heart, I'm a dog. I bond. It's my nature. I'm bonded to you. Don't shut me out. I won't be able to focus, it'll interfere with my ability to protect you."

Zack began whistling a bright tune. Heart glanced at him, frowning. Whistling happily? Odd.

"I know, you'll hate these words right now," Swen whispered. "But they are the truest words I have. Trust me! You must trust me. You've no other option."

Silently, she thought through his words. He was right. They were the only words she could hang onto in this moment.

Trust him. And so she would. With strong reservation.

*　*

They traveled on in silence for the better part of two days and two nights. Swen occasionally put his muzzle on her knee. She did not remove it. He'd fall asleep, and then, Heart noticed she was patting him on the head, without even realizing it.

Okay. They were bonded. He to her. She to him. Through thick and thin, right and wrong, good and bad. That was that. But it didn't answer the question of where Zack came in.

On the morning of the third day, after having kept in motion much of the night, Heart stirred about and Swen woke up. "I'm going to walk for a while, I need to stretch." She moved to the end of the cart. Swen got up to jump off with her, but she stayed him with a hand on his neck. "You stay here. Just let me be alone for a bit."

She stepped off the cart to the ground, then turned and looked at the cart, bemused.

"Strange!"

"What's that?" Swen asked as the cart pulled away from her.

She took a few strides to catch up to it. "Did the cart shrink? When I got on it, I had to use both hands to hoist myself up and now—I just stepped off."

Swen nodded like it was the most natural thing. "Maybe you've grown."

"Two inches in a handful of days—when I haven't grown at all in almost three years?"

Swen shrugged.

It must be another event like when the room at The Mystic's cabin expanded and then snapped back into shape, she thought. But it still did seem as if everything was a bit shorter than it had been.

Heart loped past the cart, feeling her limbs work the kinks out after all the time in the back of the little cart. She matched, then exceeded the stride of the little donkeys. What she really wanted to do was run, but she thought Swen and Zack would get the wrong idea and chase her.

For the moment, she was with them. Waiting. Watching. Willing to see how things went. What she wanted right now was to quietly be able to think through some thoughts without her brain getting poked at. She didn't know how far Zack and Swen's ability to mind-read reached, but putting some distance between herself and them would help her regain a sense of privacy, and clear out the cogs.

She trotted along, breathing in the lush green of the forest, awash with a lovely wallow of happiness and liberation, knowing she was on the right path, taking the right actions.

But … what about Zack? He was human. Humans may well have something up their collective sleeves that Swen knew nothing about. Maybe Swen had been duped all along, ever since becoming a high-ranking newshound, with significant connections and hands-on—or paws-on—sophisticated technology.

Maybe there was a plot to break out of The Periphery. The local population could quite readily be thinking of using her as a trading chip.

Heart turned to look at the cart, only to realize she'd left it some distance behind. It finally came around the bend. That was when she noticed Molly, all but dragging her delicate little hooves.

"Zack," she called, "Molly is suffering!"

"I know. There's another shed a bit further. We'll stop there."

Heart turned and sprinted away. "I'll get her water and grain out."

Heart came to the shed, a couple hundred yards further along the road. She pulled out the buckets for the donkeys' and Swen's water, filling them from the large tank, just as she'd seen Zack do several times on the trip. She filled a bucket with grain, then stood watching the road.

But the little cart did not appear. Where were they? Her anxiety mounted. She began to run back the direction she'd come, when the cart, with only Lolly in harness, came toward her on the road.

"Where ..." Then she saw Swen, Molly's reins in his mouth, slowly coming along behind, Molly looking pathetically bedraggled.

"Oh!" Heart rushed toward her and patted her neck as the three of them drew up to the food and water. Molly drank deeply, but only nibbled at the grain. "She's absolutely too exhausted to go on," Heart said looking up at Zack from where she sat on the ground next to Molly, who had sat down after her long drink.

"She's spent, it's true." Zack let Lolly out of the cart harness and led her to the water. "I guess we'll have to take a break here until she's recouped. But she's been amazing. We've made unanticipated progress." Zack dug out a small device from his coat pocket that Heart had not noticed before. "We're almost one-hundred-and-fifty miles farther than my calculations had predicted we'd be by this time!"

He leaned down and patted Molly's soft, gray nose. "Good girl, Molly!"

Lolly, who'd moved from the water bucket, where she'd practically inhaled the water to the bottom of the bucket, to the grain bucket, and was now doing the same with its contents, gave Zack a glance as he patted Molly, and stroked her neck.

"You are incredible, too!" Heart said, smiling and nodding at Lolly, who did not seem to give her the least bit of attention.

"Oh, right," Zack turned to Lolly. "Good work, girl. More grain?" He moved to pour more grain into the bucket.

Heart wondered at the strange disconnect between Lolly and Zack, while there was a noticeable bond between Molly and Zack. And herself, too! she thought, as Molly put her nose in Heart's hand and snuffled. A clear request for food.

"Okay, Molly." Heart stood, got another bucket and filled it from the grain barrel.

"Is she hungry now?"

"I think so." Heart stopped in front of Zack as she was about to pass him. No, now, this was too, too strange. She had—no argument—previously barely come to his armpit, and now his throat was at her eye level. "I … Have … Grown …."

"We've all grown. This is no experience for the weak-kneed."

"I mean, I've grown two inches taller in two days."

Zack shrugged, looking equally as hang-dogged as Swen had about the same subject.

"Shrug? Just—shrug?" She looked at Swen, sitting by Molly, then back to Zack. "You two know something, so start talking …."

At that very moment, a sharp bleat sounded, coming from somewhere on Zack's person. "Just a minute." He moved off a few feet and became engaged in an animated conversation. His face broke out in smiles—or so it appeared from his profile in Heart's shadowed view.

She wondered if she would be equally delighted by whatever he learned, or if, perhaps, she might do well to become alarmed. She took the bucket of grain to Molly, who stood and began munching it down.

"Great news," he said, returning. "That was my cousin, Jackson. He's come up with a short cut across The Periphery to The Museum of Scientific Improbabilities and Unpredictable Oddities that'll save almost a day's travel. He and his family have been tracking us psychically, so he knows where we are. He advised that we rest, let Molly recoup, and he'll be here in a few hours."

"Tracking us psychically?"

"That doesn't surprise you, I hope."

"Yes, it does. And no, it doesn't. Eye and I communicate that way all the time. Or did, before I ran away."

"With us, it helps if there's a genetic strand. We learned how to 'jump onto' that strand and share thoughts. It's kind of like a highway. Jackson and I are what we call 'cousin-brothers'—we were born on the same day, and, because of that, we're even more psychically hooked up."

Heart nodded. "A thought highway among relatives. So when I feel like you're reading my mind, you're not, really. Because we don't share the genetic highway."

"Hmmm," Zack did the tiresome turning away movement that he and Swen were employing far too much. "I'm not sure your statement is entirely correct."

"Or," Heart appended, "my statement is entirely incorrect."

"Not precisely accurate in a couple aspects," Swen entered the discussion.

"Rewriting the copy, newshound?" Heart asked, giving him a frustrated, approaching angry look, wondering in what way her comment might not be "precisely accurate." Either Zack could read her mind, with or without the genetic highway. Or … "Are we related, somehow, Zack?"

The question would remain unanswered.

The horrifying trilling of bots—dozens, hundreds of bots, could be heard in the near distance.

"Here it comes," Zack whispered.

"Yes," Swen agreed, "Here it comes."

"It? Hardly 'it.' 'They' you mean." Heart shuddered.

"By it –" Swen started ….

"*Hush!* Swen." Zack had jumped to his feet and moved rapidly around the cart.

"What, Swen?" Heart demanded.

"We mean, 'The First Turning Point Battle.' She deserves to know something, Zack."

"That's nothing," Heart protested as the trilling grew.

Zack threw Heart's paisley blanket to her. "Cover up. And be ready to do as I say. I don't care what you think of me, just … please, for everyone's sake, do as I say. If we survive, we can jabber away about it until we're older than the hills."

He got out the device he used to communicate with Jackson. "Jackson, it's begun. How long?" He listened, nodded, stepped to the side of the road and surveyed the plain that fell away from the road, beyond the trees, and secreted the device in his coat. "Half an hour." He gestured to the plain. "Look."

Heart could hardly take her mind off Molly, and how to protect her if some battle was about to ensue, but she stood and joined Zack. Shocked, she backed away from the edge of the road. "What? What am I seeing?"

The plain was teeming with movement, but the figures were too far away to distinguish their form.

"That's us, Heart. The people and the life forms of The Periphery. Gathered to protect you. To assure that you get to your destination."

"But—WHY?"

"Again, this is not the time for ques …."

The horrible trilling broke through as if dashing a barrier, and, almost instantly, the air became filled with a red mist rapidly growing into a fog.

Bots poured through the red fog in droves, diving to the plains below and all around Heart. Zack turned the cart over, pulling from its underside a mysterious device that looked like a musical wind instrument. Heart stood unmoving, without a clue what she ought to do, but as she watched, Zack made great swaths across the trilling bots, blowing into his sound weapon—or whatever it was. It completely cancelled out the nearly unbearable trilling. The red fog disappeared in Zack's motion and sound. Bots fell to the ground but were not put out of commission, as they writhed and appeared to re-gather their strength.

Heart strained to see through the ebb and flow of the red fog, trying to get a clear picture of what the individual bots looked like. But that proved nearly impossible, as their thick droves amassed into a red haze more dense than the fog. Finally, she could make out that they resembled the tentacled bots that had hauled her into the sky, except with many more tentacles, maybe six or eight each, impossible to tell, as they whirled in a frenzy that appeared to generate a wind, knocking down everything in their path.

Heart watched the battle raging on the plain below. Both sides were not faring well. Flighted bots and grounded beings fell left and right. None of the people—or whatever they were—below, appeared to have a weapon that gave them the advantage that Zack's strange device gave their little band on the road.

Zack continued to wield his sound weapon, bringing down dozens of bots. Then he ran over to Heart and grabbed her around the waist, carrying her into the shed. "Will … you … *PLEASE* … not … make … Things … more … difficult … for … me. *PLEASE!*" He plopped her unceremoniously by Molly.

Heart looked around for Swen—where was he in all this melee? She finally spotted him by Lolly, just outside the shed on the opposite side, fussing energetically with something in his chest pack. She rushed over to him. "What are you trying to do?"

"Trying to get my opposable thumb out of my chest pack. I think the bots dark energy has it jammed."

"Or maybe you're just freaking out and aren't being very effective …." She moved his paw aside and opened the pac and began to reach inside.

"That's good," Swen said, moving her hand aside and pulling out a small packet. "I'm good now. Get back in the shed."

"What's so fantastic about the shed, Swen. Just a makeshift pile of boards."

"Not exactly." Swen put the little packet in his mouth and shoved Heart back into the shed. "The shed is shielded—invisible to the bots."

"Oh!!"

She watched the action of the bots and noticed that they flew into the wall of the shed, not as if attacking it in the same dive-bombing way they were trying to get at Zack, but as if, indeed, they did not see it. When they collided with the shed, they fell to the ground, writhing. "Well, then, you and Lolly get in here right now!"

Don't worry about them," Zack said. "They both know what they're doing."

"Both?" What did Lolly have to do with the battle, other than hunker down next to Molly? Heart crawled over to Molly and threw the camo blanket over her, but for all her calmness with the battle and weirdness swirling around, Molly reacted dramatically to the camo blanket, bucking it off and running from the shed.

"Molly," Heart cried as the little donkey bolted into the thick of red fog and trilling, diving bots. "MOLLY!" She screamed.

Zack looked in the direction Molly ran, as she approached the edge of the road, a dozen bots flew toward her with a furious trilling. Zack waved his sound weapon, and most of them dropped, but before he could even wave the other direction, bots flung themselves at Molly.

Zack turned back to look at Lolly. Heart couldn't understand why or how he could take his attention off Molly for a fleeting second. "Swen, move!"

Swen jumped into the shed and leapt to Heart's side. "Get your paisley blanket on!" He ordered.

But she stood, transfixed, unable to make a move.

"Convert!" Zack shouted.

Before Heart's eyes, darling Lolly appeared to blow apart. Heart ducked, expecting to be hit by bits of flesh that had been Lolly. But instead, a fantastical creature materialized from the inside-out donkey, blood-red, merging with the fog. Giant fangs and claws appeared from among the indistinct pile of bio and mechanical materials. A massive head like nothing Heart had ever seen, nor could ever imagine seeing, pulled out from what had been the interior of Lolly's neck and head.

Completely open on its underside, the creature appeared similar to—but again, nothing like—a gigantic, animate, blood red, bear rug. In two giant leaps, the appalling thing was upon Molly, swallowing her in one movement.

"*NO, NO, NO!*" Heart screamed, leaping forward, yet held back by a hand from nowhere.

She writhed, struggling to get loose. The thought that something might be about to devour her didn't even cross her mind.

She had to get to Molly—even though, as she looked, it was clear, through the red fog, that there was no Molly to get to. The blood red monster screamed and tore bots from the air, flinging them like balloons into the red fog.

Continuing to defend their small stand, Zack ran back to the shed. "Jackson's here, Swen. Across the road. Get her over there."

Heart looked toward where Zack gestured to the other side of the road, which could barely be seen through the haze of red and the gathering shadows of evening. She saw nothing.

Meanwhile, the strange, invisible hand from behind forced her out of the shed, and across the road. She fell in the underbrush, immediately picked up by a tall, muscular man, blond with dark eyes, but who otherwise looked so much like Zack she gasped.

"Jackson, here," he said, putting her down and taking her hand. "We must hurry."

"But … Swen …."

"Here, Heart."

She looked in the direction of his voice and saw, now the strange invisible hand—a dog paw with an attached thumb. It had been Swen all along holding her, but she'd gone into shock when she saw Lolly explode.

She turned to look at the carnage. "We can't leave Zack! I won't. Are you both crazy? And the people—or whatever they are—below, we can't leave them." She tried to extricate her hand from Jackson's grip to no avail. "You *ARE NOT* going to leave Zack!"

"Look, Heart, his only chance of survival is if we get you away from here. We must do so quickly while Zack and Lolly have their strength." Jackson began to drag her through the underbrush. "Do not make it harder on me, *PLEASE!*"

"Is that all you two can think to say? I'm trying to do the right thing."

"Then come with me. The bots are looking for you. They will soon discover you're not there, and they'll come searching. Good thing you brought the camo blanket, Swen."

"Yeah," Swen said, throwing it over Heart. "Trying to make it easier for all of us."

They stumbled a few yards into the underbrush. "Just … just one moment …." Heart begged. She turned and peered through the red fog, the gathering darkness, the ferns, and underbrush. She saw one last sweep of Zack's arm with his sound weapon. She would keep this vision deep within herself, insisting that he survived. This valiant man, who she'd had awful thoughts about—who perhaps had even been able to know her every mean thought— had not hesitated to put his life on the line for her. His life and his dear little donkeys' lives. Or whatever they were.

It was a thought she could not wrap her mind or feelings around. Bigger than huge. She wanted to burst into tears, which she'd never done in her life. She wasn't even sure she could cry.

Why would he sacrifice himself for her? How could she possibly be worth it? And—if he survived—how could she ever, ever, ever repay him?

Chapter 13

"Stop gawking," Jackson ordered, pulling her along. Heart yanked her arm from his grip. "Excuse me!" She took a step away from him and nearly lost her balance, stumbling over a downed branch. "I'm not gawking, I'm trying to see if your cousin is still alive."

"He's alive. Let's keep it that way. Get on the move, now! Follow me." Jackson turned and forged through the ferns and foliage as smoothly as if on open road.

Despite how much she disliked his manner, she couldn't help but admire his skill and grace navigating the nearly impenetrable forest. But, problematically, she could not keep up, and, worse, the rapidly gathering dark made it more and more difficult by the moment. Thankfully, Swen stayed by her side, as best he could.

That was when she noticed he kept up with her, while limping on only three legs.

"Did you get wounded? Why are you limping?"

Swen held up his right front paw that still had his opposable thumb attached to it. "Haven't had time to take this off, and really dare not run on it, or I'll damage it. Can't afford that, I'm certain-sure to need it endlessly, hanging out with you."

"Well, let's take a moment for you to take care of that." Heart stopped.

But Jackson did not. He continued his large, easy stride through the forest, and was out of sight in moments. Swen struggled with his device, looking where Jackson had disappeared, clearly becoming flustered.

"He's out of sight. Not good, Heart."

"No. Not good. What's the matter with him?"

"Don't know. Damn this thing."

"Can I help?"

"Probably." Swen held up the pads of his paw. "See this thing-a-ma-thingy has to slide through that whatsie-whatsit." He tried to point, but it was so dark, Heart couldn't see where he pointed.

"Why didn't you have me help you with this before?"

"Well, I don't know, Heart. Maybe because other things were going on."

"Right. Other things."

"What is with you two?" Jackson materialized between them as if from nowhere.

"*Yikes!*" Heart squeaked when both she and Swen returned to the ground from practically jumping out of their skins. "What the …."

"Indeed! Is it necessary to scare the dog food right out of me?" Swen complained.

Heart giggled nervously. "Yeah. And me too, do you have to scare the dog food right out of me?"

"Is there something funny about what we're doing?" Jackson asked, turning on a small light and shining it on Swen's paw. The light cast shadows up on his face, augmenting the frustration that furrowed his brow.

"Nothing funny," Heart retorted. "Sheesh, you are an unpleasant sort, aren't you?"

"Am I supposed to be pleasant?" Jackson asked, disentangling and removing Swen's appliance in a trice, sticking it in Swen's chestpac, then turning off the light and moving out again.

"No. Not supposed to be nice. Not supposed to be polite. Not supposed to give us a remote clue where you're headed, or anything. Just stand around and give orders, then move through the forest in the dark like you're on a highway in the daytime, and be nasty to everyone who doesn't have your skills," Heart rattled, following him as best she could.

Swen trotted alongside Heart, gaining his stride, now that he had the use of all his feet.

"Thank you, Jackson, sir. Thank you for unsticking my prosthesis," Swen called after him. "Much appreciated."

There was not a sound from Jackson.

"A nasty bit of work," Heart whispered. "Looks like Zack, nothing like Zack."

"True, true," Swen agreed. "Different coloring, but same everything else, in looks. Not in character. True."

Again, Jackson appeared at their side as if by magic. "Will you two *SHUT UP!* I'm making a path, tracking, watching both of you stumble and bumble about, trying to get in contact with Zack, trying to keep in contact with the helpers on the other side, and I'm hooked into you two for any sounds you make, with this nonstop noise from you!"

Heart and Swen hung their heads.

"I don't have to be nice," Jackson continued. "I have to get you to your destination, Heart. You and your," he gave Swen a hard look … "whatever he is—companion. If you insist on keeping him."

"Insist on keeping him? I wouldn't be here at all, if not for him."

"So I've heard. Still, he's entirely dispensable."

"He is not!"

"I am not," Swen confirmed.

Jackson shook his head, turned and moved out. "Come!" he ordered, then muttered just loud enough that they could hear him. "He's a canine, and not even real canine."

This was apparently the final insult. Swen broke away from Heart and moved forward to Jackson. "I'll have you know, my bio-canine is all canine, of the highest caliber and breeding. You know, you can insult me, but don't you dare …."

Jackson actually chuckled. "I know, I know. 'Don't dare insult my mother.'"

"Well, that's right." Mollified, Swen fell back to Heart. "I'm going to shut up now. But here's my final word, Heart. He is a nasty bit of work."

*   *

They moved through the forest with the shadows becoming a solid wall of night, but Jackson produced a faint glow on the plants he passed, and in this manner, the three of them made non-stop progress through the forest for several hours, without uttering a word.

Heart had no idea how far they had to go, nor how long it would take. She tried to pull her mind from the sights and sounds of the battle they'd left raging that played, again and again, unbidden, in her mind.

Then Jackson stopped and Heart, now steadily two strides behind him, collided with him.

"Whoa, What? ...."

Jackson held up one hand and put the other on his clavicles. He appeared to be listening intently. Then he nodded. "Right," he said.

He turned to Heart. "It's Zack. He survived. The battle is over."

"He's been fighting all this time?"

"So it would seem."

"Oh!" Heart pictured Zack fighting the hoards of relentless machines, pouring through the air in their red fog. "And Molly?"

"Don't know."

"Don't know," Heart repeated in a whisper.

"But, Heart," Swen put his muzzle in her hand at her side, "Zack is all right."

"Yes. Zack is all right. He's been fighting all this time. Awful. What is worth so much terror?"

Jackson stopped and turned to her. Even in the darkness, she could see a light shining from his eyes. "You ... don't know what all this is worth?"

"Not yet, Jackson," Swen interjected. "Freewill must prevail."

"Oh." Jackson's tone was so subdued he didn't sound like himself. "Well, I don't know *Ourbook* like I ought."

"What?" Heart blurted.

"So. Yeah. I see," Jackson thought aloud. "You, talking dog. Protector."

"Yes. Apparently. Yes."

"Well then, apologies, Mr. Swen."

"Please, just—Swen."

"Right. Well, that explains ... I couldn't understand why she ... does ... why ... she ... doesn't ....."

"Yeah," Swen reassured. "That's why."

"Oh!" Heart said, frustrated with anger. "I am so sick of cryptic talk. Either say it or shut up. And I mean, you, the both of you, just shut up ...."

She pushed past Jackson and stormed ahead on the non-existent path.

Jackson came up to her side. "Do you know where you're going?"

"Does it matter?"

"Very much so." Jackson took the lead again.

*　　*

The peculiar threesome moved on through the night. They didn't stop. They didn't talk. For a while Heart counted ferns she could make out in the light of the natural moon along with little Pink's delicate light. Yellow was not, at present, in the sky overhead. Heart, as always, felt warmed and comforted by Pink up there, seeming to caress her with a cozy, friendly light.

But she soon gave up counting ferns and, instead, began to wonder how long she had to thrash through underbrush and stumble over downed tree branches.

Then she wondered how she would cross The Wall. And then wondered why she hadn't already been working out this problem.

She broke their silence and their almost rhythmic swishing among the plants. "We'll have to make something for me to lie on, in order to cross under the wall."

"Cousins have constructed a travois this night." Jackson did not pause.

"Really!?"

"Thank the Dog Gods," Swen muttered.

"Good," Heart said. "Thanks for telling me, so I didn't have to contemplate that chore that last umpteen miles."

Predictably, Jackson said nothing.

"How much farther?"

"Not much."

"Jackson, please be so kind as to honor my question with a more specific answer."

"We stop here." He stopped short, stepping aside to stoop over and rustle about in the ferns.

Heart stumbled forward and immediately felt the horrible pull of the Dark Energy of The Wall. She fell to the ground, unable to pick herself up. "I can't …."

"I said, 'we stop here.'"

"You did." Heart felt her strength pour into the ground as she tried to move away from the force that sapped her strength.

Swen rushed up to her, put his muzzle down to her face. "Can you wrap your arms around my neck?"

As she tried to do so, Jackson came over to her, picked her up and set her down where he'd said, "We stop here." "How you've survived, one can only wonder."

"I lived in a pampered compound. I've been 'out' for a week. I've been running, I've been in places I never imagined existed, met people the likes of which I never imagined existed, done things I never knew I could—and you wonder how I've survived. Well, quite well, thank you!"

"Are you angry?"

Swen chuckled.

"*I … just … cannot … believe … you!*" Heart shut her mouth with a silent oath to never again say another word to Jackson.

He returned to what he'd been doing, uncovering an exquisitely constructed travois of woven branches, ferns, and vines hidden under the ferns.

"*Beautiful!*" Heart breathed, ignoring her oath of silence.

"Nice work," Jackson noted. "Right, so here's the Harness for Swen."

Heart pulled her paisley blanket off her backpack. The little paisleys began to light up and move around on the fabric in her hands.

Jackson stood over her, watching the fabric become animated. "Fascinating."

Heart stood to hoist her backpack back on, but stopped in shock. "Unbelievable, unbelievable!"

"What?" Jackson and Swen said together.

"Well, look, Jackson. I'm looking straight across at your chin. When we started trekking through the forest, I barely came to your shoulder. I thought at the time that you and Zack must be the exact same height."

"Well, I don't know what to say to that."

"Neither do I, except either I've grown another two inches while scrambling through the forest, or you are shrinking."

Jackson, completely unruffled by her statement, looked down at Swen. "Not shrinking. Mr. Swen comes right to my knee, same as when we started. But I do see that you're taller, no mistake."

"Let's get going," Swen interrupted.

"Good idea," Jackson agreed.

"Wait a minute, dog. You know something."

"Well, dear Heart, I know a lot of things. And so too will you, quite soon. But at this moment, we must keep moving." He looked up into the sky. Heart saw he directed his attention to Pink. "There is much to do this night." He moved beyond where Heart had been brought to the ground. "Where am I to dig the tunnel?"

"It, too, has been attended to by the cousins. I will show you. Wait here," Jackson ordered Heart, while he and Swen disappeared in the night.

"Not going anywhere," she said to herself. She pulled the paisley blanket closer, worrying that her unprecedented and weird growth would prevent the blanket from covering her. But it appeared the blanket had grown as well.

And then—a flash of light! Golden-pinky light that played through her brain—she could feel it, this stunning, beautiful light. In its glow stood the Gear Horse, poised, tense, looking at her, looking into her.

He was near—very near. And she would soon be by his side.

Where she belonged.

*   *

Swen and Jackson stealthily came back to her.

"It's good, Heart. Short distance, smooth path, a wide, beautiful tunnel. Are you ready?"

"I'm so ready. Let's go!"

"Jackson is going to pull, too. The cousins put a rope on the travois for him."

"Are you coming with us?" Heart asked, surprised.

"Sure," Jackson said. "All right, let's get you wrapped up. You'd better put the camo blanket in your backpack." He helped Heart slip off her backpack. She put the camo blanket in her backpack, while Jackson held the paisley blanket. Heart was curious to see that the paisleys, while paler and slower, still had light and movement in his hands. Was this true of everyone in The Periphery, she wondered?

She held her backpack to her chest while Jackson securely wrapped the paisley blanket around her. Then a very strange thing happened. Jackson pulled the paisley blanket from her face, took her face in his two hands, and kissed her gently on the forehead.

She would not have been more surprised if he had slapped her. Indeed, that would have seemed more like him. She looked at him, in the darkness, in the strange light that seemed to emit from his eyes.

Blythe Ayne – 175

"Let's go," he said quietly.

She lay down on the travois, mystified by what his puzzling behavior meant, while he and Swen made sure the paisley blanket was completely wrapped around her. Soon she moved as smoothly as if in a troika crossing an ice-covered lake.

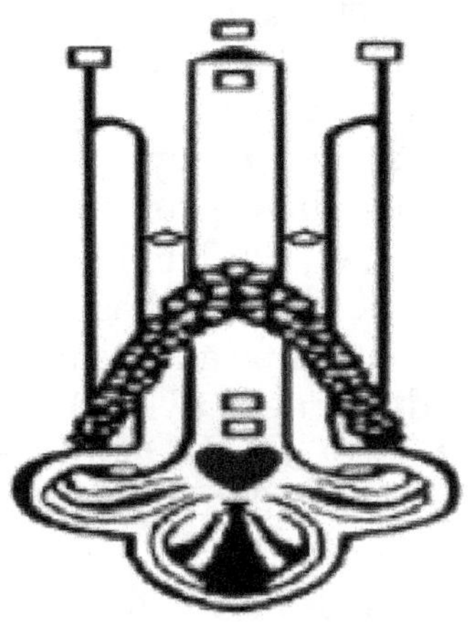

Chapter 14

She began to wonder, for the first time—and it surprised her that she hadn't thought about it before—where they would come out on the other side. How far might she have to run and to hide before they came to The Museum of Scientific Improbabilities and Unpredictable Oddities?

And, what, she asked herself, was she going to do when she got there? All these kind people in The Periphery had helped her, had been wonderful, sweet, lovely. But what was she going to do when she got to The Museum of Scientific Improbabilities and Unpredictable Oddities?

She reminded herself of her priorities.

Number one: For reasons she didn't understand, she had to get near the Gear Horse.

Number two: Her motivation for leaving The Darling Undesirables Residence of Long Prairie was to find and to make a home for herself and Eye. She longed to completely disappear from this crazy public that treated them like caged, fascinating creatures, or curios in a cabinet. Not human beings.

The travois paused. Heart knew this meant they were at the mouth of the tunnel. She heard shuffling and pictured in her mind's eye Jackson getting on his hands and knees, then Swen following, dragging her through the tunnel. She kept her silence but felt nothing but gratitude that she had experienced none of the totally debilitating weakness of The Wall. There was a small bit of dialogue between Jackson and Swen, but she could not make out the words. She felt herself being pulled down, then flat for a few feet, then back upwards again.

Suddenly there was light and cheering and hands helping her stand. She'd not expected a welcome of any sort, least of all a cheering contingent of several voices. Crossing out of The Periphery was reminiscent of crossing *into* The Periphery.

Confused, bemused, she looked around her.

Shock! Here she stood—inside The Museum of Scientific Improbabilities and Unpredictable Oddities! And even more astonishing, she found herself surrounded by the sweet round-faced docent, the winking doorman, and the little clanking Key Man.

Swen sat on his haunches to the side, grinning as if he had planned a totally successful surprise birthday party.

"I'm here!" Heart said simply, at a loss for any more observation than that.

"Yes," The cheerful docent said, "you are here, here you are!" Also seeming at a loss for more words, equally delighted.

The Key Man and the Doorman simply nodded, grinning.

Heart looked down at the tunnel she'd just come through. "But ... where's Jackson?"

"Jackson?" The doorman came over to the tunnel and peered into the darkness. "*The* Jackson? He was with you?"

"I don't know about 'the' Jackson, but Jackson, Zack's cousin, brought us here. And he said he was coming through the tunnel with us. Didn't he, Swen?"

"He did, it's true. But …."

"Where is he?" Heart interrupted.

"That's what I'm trying to tell you. At the tunnel, he said he would push while I pulled. But he didn't. I mean, I could tell he wasn't pushing. So, I guess he didn't come through."

"Why would he say he was, and then not?"

"That's Jackson," the docent said. "He hates to say good-bye. It is likely his greatest weakness."

"His only weakness," the Doorman added.

"So who is he that you're so impressed?" Heart began to lovingly fold her paisley blanket. It had saved her life yet again.

"He saved the lives of everyone in The Periphery," the Doorman said.

"And he raised interest in The Museum of Scientific Improbabilities and Unpredictable Oddities when they were going to close it, so much that people demanded it stay open and operating, on threat of civil insurrection," the Key Man added.

"And he assisted in another wonderful event that you will learn about in due time," the docent said. "But first off, let me introduce myself and my cohorts properly."

Heart nodded. "That probably would be better than calling you 'The Docent,' 'The Doorman,' and 'The Key Man.'"

The three of them giggled. "Well," The docent said, "the Key Man is Key Man, but the doorman is Peter, and I'm Martha."

"And we are all," Peter said, giving her his endearing wink, "at your service."

"Thank you," Heart said simply. "But I don't need anyone to 'serve' me. I just want to go somewhere and live quietly."

"We all do, my dear," Martha said. "Passionately. But at this moment, we must get the tunnel closed up, and get you situated."

"I don't need to be situated. I've only come here to do one thing, and then I have other things I must do."

"True, true, true! Many things you must do." Martha nodded and grinned, grinned and nodded. "The first item of business on your agenda is to talk with the Gear Horse. Of course! We know that. But even before that, we have to get you cloaked. No more of this shielding fabric or that shielding fabric, although we are most appreciative and grateful to the fabrics, and hope they will continue to do their work." Martha reached out and stroked Heart's rolled up paisley blanket, and it flashed a bright, white lightning.

"Oh! The paisley likes you."

"It should."

"Why?"

"I wove it," Martha said.

"You wove it?...."

"And energized it with bios from someone profoundly beloved to me." Martha's relentless cheerful round smile took on a deep sadness.

"How is it that it was wrapped around me as an infant if you wove it?" Heart tried to understand what Martha was saying, but it didn't make sense.

"You will learn more of that some other day, my dearest Heart. But, as I say, right now, we must get you situated."

"Situated ..." Heart repeated, her mind full to over-flowing with how it could be that Martha made her paisley blanket, why she was only a docent in the museum, and, most compelling question of all, when would she get to be with the Gear Horse?

Martha reached up and put the paisley blanket in Heart's backpack, then took her by the hand. Heart could hardly believe how short the little woman had become. "Will you tell me one thing, at least?"

"What's that?"

"How can I have possibly grown two—or more!—inches in the last few hours?"

Martha giggled and giggled.

"Is that funny?"

"Yes and no."

"Do you know why—or even how—it can happen?"

"Yes. I know why. I know how. But all in due time, dear Heart. All in due time."

*   *

Martha took Heart down the long hall she'd gone down the first night Heart had been there, when she left for the day. Darkness filled every corner, although little lights along the bottom of the wall lit up as they approached.

Heart, filled with questions, decided that the smartest thing she might do at the moment was to be silent and observe. That was one thing she'd learned in life. Sometimes questions got better answers by silent observation than by asking questions.

Martha, too, seemed content to remain quiet for the time being, which surely must be out of character, Heart thought. She occupied the back of her mind with counting the steps she took—just in case she might need that bit of information, and in the front of her mind, she listed her questions, starting with:

Why and how had she grown two inches in the last few hours and two inches the two days before?

Why did Jackson say he was coming and then didn't?

*   *

"Here we are." Martha inserted a gear-shaped key in an opening on a door with a brass plate on it that read: Recent & New Acquisitions to the Antiquities Clockwork Collection. A soft whirring came from the door, which then swung open. Heart saw that the door, itself, was a clockwork invention.

The room hummed gently with Dark Energy. A bright, warm, peach-toned light turned on as they stepped inside.

All around, in great and unceremonious heaps, Heart saw piled gorgeous, exotic, terrible, destroyed, broken, intact, rusted metal, shiny brass, stainless steel and even wooden clockwork inventions that exceeded anything she could have imagined. Beyond anything anyone without a key to this room could imagine.

"*Oh! … My!*" Heart whispered.

"Amazing, yes?" Martha watched Heart take in the room.

"More than amazing! All this invention, all this art, all this craftsmanship, piled up, so … so …."

"I know. It seems disrespectful. But every day restoration of these remarkable inventions is in progress. The important thing is, this apparent disarray will contribute to your safety."

"How so?"

"Today we cataloged this beautiful little carousel, a new acquisition. So, here's our plan. During the day when the public is in the museum, you'll stay in here. If anyone comes in that you don't know, you'll shapeshift into the carousel. Do you think you can do that?"

Heart studied the little carousel, perfect for a young child's room. A colorful little lion, tiger, unicorn, and dragon with saddles on their backs chased one another in a circle. "Strange combination of creatures," she observed.

Martha chuckled. "I guess it is a rather odd mix. The important question now is, can you shapeshift into the carousel, or one of the animals—however it works for you?"

"I think I probably can. It's easier for me to shapeshift into things that are monochromatic, and the carousel is so colorful. But I can try. "

"Try now."

"Right now?"

"Yes. If you can't do it, we will have to come up with a new plan."

"New plan. I see. But—I only want to ...."

"Be with the Gear Horse. I know. And you will! But your safety comes first."

"My safety? From who, from what? Why is it that amazing people like Zack and Jackson and The Mystic—and now, perhaps even you—appear willing to put yourselves in harm's way for me?"

Martha nodded but remained cryptic. "Soon you will know the answers to your questions. Soon, you'll learn many extraordinary things. But right now, it's of utmost importance that I see if you can successfully shapeshift into this little carousel."

Heart released all of her questions and all of the tension she had gathered during the impossibly eventful day. She relaxed into the child's merry-go-round. She felt into it for the most comfortable spot to settle. She smiled as a beckoning warmth rose up around the dragon. Soon the scales, gaudy colors, a long neck, a short, small head, and a fake and childish evil grin came upon her. She wanted to laugh, the shifting event was playful and surprisingly easy.

"Wonderful, wonderful," Martha fairly sang. "I even watched you transition, and I can't see you. Now let me show you your room."

Heart, quite enjoying the little metal dragon and the whole happy energy of the carousel, would not have minded relaxing in this shape longer, but the hope—the need!—to be with the Gear Horse brought her quickly back into her own form.

She pulled herself from the carousel. "My room? Here?"

"Yes. Right here."

"But ... why would I stay here?"

"Because everything you need to learn is here, in The Museum of Scientific Improbabilities and Unpredictable Oddities."

"Everything I need to learn? What must I learn?"

"You'll see. We need to learn things from you, as well."

"You need to learn things from me? I don't know anything to teach you. My goodness, you know more things, I think, than anyone I know, besides, maybe The Mystic. I'm afraid you're going to be sadly disappointed if you think I have something to teach you."

"No, I won't Heart. But never mind, it's not important to discuss that at this moment. Everything will unfold, just as it's supposed to."

Martha led Heart to the back wall of the Recent & New Acquisitions to the Antiquities Clockwork Collection. She had in hand another key, similar to the first one, yet considerably smaller, made of a mysterious-looking white metal. She stuck the key in the blank wall, where only a tiny hole was visible. After some disconcerting whirring, a small door opened in the wall upon a darling pink and yellow room, practically bursting with lace and frills.

Mystified, Heart followed Martha into the room, so incongruous to the room on the opposite side of the wall. "What is this place?"

"This is your room, Heart."

"My room? But …."

"I know, dear Heart. Its 'character,' shall we say, is not anything like you. But I trust that you'll be able to find yourself at home here, even so."

"No. It's not like me, that's true …" Heart agreed, while another myriad pile of questions welled up. Overwhelmed, she said nothing.

"Key Man put every single thing in here—for you."

"Key Man did this?" She moved to a small fake window, reaching out to lightly touch its frilly pink curtain. She leaned over to study a lamp on the bedside table. A girl in a hooped, floorlength skirt of several shades of yellow, layered and pleated, billowing to her feet, held the lamp in the shape of an umbrella, over her head. The yellow light from the fixture bathed the bedside table in a warm glow.

"Yes. He did this for you."

"It's so sweet! Does he see me as a sweet and frilly girl?"

"I'm not sure, Heart. I'd say it's more probable that he thinks all girls are like this. His experience with girls is extremely limited. Well, nonexistent, actually. He doesn't interact with the public at all, as he's in here most of the time, tending to the clockworks."

Heart tried to picture herself spending time in this overly-pastel, delicate, even fragile-feeling room with its knickknacks and spindly furniture, and frills. Although it felt incongruous, she fell, fast and completely, in love with the room. It called to her, she responded. The loving energy the peculiar-yet-endearing little Key Man had put into it wrapped around her. She felt safe, needed, loved.

"See? He lined the dresser drawers with this beautiful pastel paper of paisleys." Martha pulled open a drawer, and Heart looked in.

"Pink and yellow, like the room. Paisleys. I like that. But why so much pink and yellow?"

"When he learned you were coming, he listened to every quote you ever made that he could get. He was looking for what you said about colors, you see. It was interesting. We both knew you've talked about plaids, we've heard you. But when he went to your quotes, all references to plaids have been removed ...."

"Really? Why?"

"Because you talk about their energy and power. The media has been instructed to eradicate all mystical references by anyone who is a 'media pet.' As I'm sure you know, you are the number one 'media pet.' But he did turn up a statement from you about paisleys. You said they are symbolic of life, like a seed."

Heart nodded. "Paisleys are even more sacred than plaids. I don't like to talk about it to the media though, because I can tell they don't understand. This paisley paper is wonderful. But do you know why he's filled the room with so much pink and yellow?"

"Because there are so many of your quotes where you talk about how much you love the moons, Pink and Yellow. You almost never talk about the two neglected little Blues."

"It's true. I do love Yellow, but I especially adore Pink. Something—something about her draws me to her … I'm sure everyone feels the same way. She's so charming up there, glowing and smiling down on us."

"Unhappily, everyone does not feel the same. I guess you've not heard about the movement to bring down the artificial moons."

"*Oh! No!* No, I did not know there was anyone who felt that way. Terrible. Frightening. Why? Why do they want them down?"

"Because, they say, the moons are not 'natural.' These people call themselves The Purists. They cause a lot of problems for the likes of us."

"Us? Who is 'us'?"

"Me, Key Man, Peter, the people in The Periphery, Father Inventor, and you, our own very dearest Heart."

"Oh!" Heart whispered, sinking into the little yellow rocking chair, trying to fold up her suddenly long legs, then sticking them out awkwardly. "Because I don't have a heart I'm not 'natural.'" She paused, taking in this new and different picture of herself. She knew herself to be— or seeming to be—everyone's Darling. But now, she had an insight about the "Undesirable" part.

"But why you?" she asked Martha. "You're not a Darling Undesirable."

"True. But I'm one of those who care for and care about the Darlings."

"You are? How so?"

"You'll see more when we get deeper into your training."

"And why would these 'Purists' care about the people in The Periphery? What I saw is that they are very sweet, minding their own business, making a life."

Martha nodded. "You're right. But The Purists are convinced that the people of The Periphery are bio-mechanical. They want them gone. The most vehement Purists even want the clockwork inventions here in the museum destroyed."

"Oh!" Heart leapt up, knocking over the little rocking chair. *"That's too much!* The Gear Horse, and, and the others—they have intelligence. You can't allow people to go around destroying intelligent beings."

"That's what we believe, too." Martha righted the rocking chair. "That's why we need you to help us protect them."

"What can I possibly do?" Agitated, Heart paced the room. "I would be happy to help. But what can I possibly do?"

"So much, Heart. And I'm sure that you will. You, and the Gear Horse."

"Speaking of which …."

"I know. Soon. As I said, first we must get you situated."

Heart looked around her little room. "I'm situated. This room is totally sweet. I'm so moved that Key Man did this for me. I love it. I love it. Even without plaids …."

"Plaids. I've been waiting for you to mention plaids. Look here…" Martha slid open the closet door. Hanging neatly within were three outfits, each of a different bold plaid, clashing with the gentle room, but sheer beauty to Heart's eyes.

"Oh!" she sighed, moving to the closet as if drawn magnetically. "Gorgeous!" She ran her hands over the soft, rich, flannel plaids.

"You might want to put one of them on," Martha suggested, "as you've very nearly outgrown the outfit you're wearing."

Heart looked down at herself, thinking about her clothing for the first time since before the battle in The Periphery. Her sleeves were halfway up her forearms, and her pant legs hiked up her calves. She suddenly became conscious of the discomfort through her shoulders and waist.

"Well, I guess so!" She giggled. She gazed at the beautiful plaids hanging in the closet with longing. "Is it truly all right? I can try on any of these I choose?"

"My darling Heart, these are your clothes. You may do with them as you please. Mix and match. Whatever. They are yours."

Heart gathered the flannel clothing up in her arms and carried every bit of it to the bed, then spread them out lovingly, stroking their colors, studying their weavings. Although primary colors dominated in their threads, she noticed a beautiful lavender thread running through all of the plaids. "I love this thread," she said, pointing it out. At her touch, it lit up, glowing.

"Me too," Martha agreed. "That color will give you strength."

Heart didn't even ask what she meant, she just wanted to be wearing any plaid with that lovely lavender.

She slowly pulled off her formerly favorite plaid shirt that she had now outgrown in so many ways, and pulled on the new blue, green, yellow and lavender plaid shirt. She ran her hands over the softest, most delicious feeling flannel she'd ever worn in her life. Then she changed into the matching plaid pants, heavenly and warm, although the outfit was slightly too big, she'd never felt this "at home" in her clothes in her life. She moved to the floor length mirror in the corner of the room and gasped at her reflection.

Once again she encountered that golden glowing girl she'd seen at The Mystic's cabin.

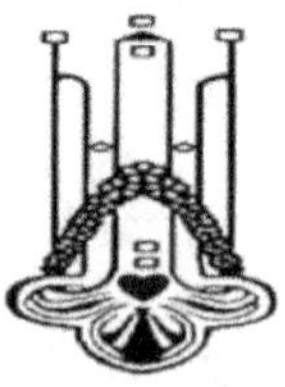

Chapter 15

Martha handed Heart the strange little mechanical key to her invisible door in the back wall of the Recent & New Acquisitions to the Antiquities Clockwork Collection, after Heart hung her plaids back up in the closet. As they stepped out of the hidden pastel room, Heart gave it a last study, feeling awe and gratitude, that someone cared for her this much.

They walked down the long, dark hall in companionable silence, Heart feeling as close to Martha, whom she had known for, at most, a few hours, as she ever felt with anyone. Other than, of course, Eye.

Oh! How she wanted to ask Martha about Eye, while at the same time, she discovered she was unable to scare up the courage. If she didn't ask, she could imagine the best. If she did ask, she would perhaps learn something she didn't want to know. But it was hard to imagine the best, and her mind was beset with anxieties and worries about him.

Mind reading, as it seemed, Martha said, "I think you might like to know that Eye is all right. I know about Keeper A's threats—don't ask me how as it's yet again another of those things you'll learn with time. But you can trust that I have inside information, and he's fine."

"Thank … thank you!" Heart whispered, feeling a gigantic emotional balloon in her diaphragm well up. 'I … I … well … just … thank you."

"I know, Heart. You don't need to say anything. He was truly and profoundly upset the first day you were gone from The Darling Undesirables Residence of Long Prairie. But we have our ways of contact and I dared to break one of our rules—no direct contact with Darling Undesirables who are in a residence. But his agony was more than I could endure. So, well, anyway, he learned that you were fine, and he became calm."

" I…" Heart didn't know what she was about to say. "I miss him so much!" In that moment she realized that she missed him with a deep, untouchable ache that she'd ignored since she stepped foot from her room.

She'd put those feelings aside. And since she'd been on the run from that moment until this, they sat quietly in her mind, waiting for her to slow down, waiting to pour out.

Martha put her arm around Heart's waist and gave her a hug. "I know, sweetie, I know. But you did the right thing by leaving and you're doing the right thing now. Just keep following the drive in you, it will not lead you astray."

Heart nodded. "The one thing that is, has, and I'm pretty sure will continue to drive me, is being with the Gear Horse."

"We know. Although I'm sure we must seem particularly obtuse or deaf."

They approached the light of the front entryway where stood Key Man, Peter, Swen, and two other gigantic men, who looked, at the distance, to be made of clockworks. And, indeed as she came up to the little group, it was perfectly clear that the two additions to the group were twin, nearly seven foot tall, clockwork men.

"Heart, I'd like you to meet Wonderman One and Wonderman Two, our helpers."

Heart took each of their extended clockwork hands in turn. She felt a slight quivering as their energy passed through them into her. Their identical faces, an intricate field of meshing cogs and wheels, churned into various facial expressions.

"I'm very pleased to meet you," she said to them.

"Pleased to meet you, too," they replied in unison, their somewhat mechanical voices soft and penetrating.

"They are rather early prototypes of mechanical men," Key Man said. "So they may seem stiff and, well, *mechanical*, even perhaps a bit frightening. But I assure you, they are as gentle as kittens. And devoted to you, Heart."

The two giant men began to make the most compelling mechanical purring sound, grinning mischievous grins.

Heart burst out in giggles.

"All right, enough grandstanding from you two. By the way, Heart, you look lovely in your new plaid," Key Man said.

"Thank you, dear Key Man. And thank you, too, *soooo* much for my little room. It's adorable."

"I know it's all frills and lace, and you're all sort of plaids. But I just couldn't help myself. I will never have a little girl of my own, and once started on the frills, I couldn't seem to stop."

Heart went over to Key Man, leaned down and hugged him, then kissed him on the cheek. "You are the dearest dear. I love the room more than words can say. It's filled with love. It's the best room I've ever had in my life!"

It was true—really, truly, true. She'd made her room at The Darling Undesirables Residence of Long Prairie to her liking, but it was still an industrial type of room, in a building where all the rooms were the same. The particular exception in her room being the star window.

Rendered to shyness, Key Man turned his back on the gathering and mumbled, "I'm glad you like it."

"Okay, let's get on with the business at hand," Peter said, officiously.

"Now what?" Heart exclaimed, frustrated. "Please, not another thousand things before getting to the Gear Horse."

"That's precisely where we're headed," Peter answered.

"*YES!!*" Heart moved past them down the hall to the showcase where the Gear Horse had been when she first saw him. But he was not there. She looked back at the odd collection of beings following her, feeling like tapping her foot, exasperated. "Where … is … he?"

"I'm here," she heard in her head.

She whirled around in a complete circle but did not see the amazing clockwork creature.

"Where?…." She looked again at her companions, wondering why they must make this so difficult for her.

What was the game now? But she followed their gaze above her head. From the top of the foyer entryway, the Gear Horse looked down at her, hovering, massive, majestic wings spread nearly thirty feet.

"I am here, dear Heart," he said as he floated in a smooth glide down to stand before her. He folded his clockwork wings to his sides, where they became invisible. "I've been so impatient to see you, Key Man let me out so I could work off some of my restlessness."

Heart flung her arms around his neck. "Finally!" was all she could utter. His feelings poured into her— love, patience, impatience, devotion, joy, happiness, and, under it all, a pushing, pulsing sense of urgency.

*　　*

The small band of observers gave the two of them a few moments together, but Heart was distracted and irritated by their presence.

She found herself wondering, "When can I be alone with the Gear Horse?" and immediately got the reply in her head from him, "Soon, Heart soon! And now, it is time you stopped referring to me as 'the Gear Horse.' My name is Equuleus."

"Equuleus! But that has always been one of my favorite constellations. Small and far away, but still, I always look in on it and think it might be a wonderful place to go. No bright stars from here. I think, I feel, I believe—it has a planet not too different from ours."

"I agree. As does Father Inventor."

"Father Inventor? ...."

Peter interrupted their telepathic conversation. "Sorry to intrude. Oh, Heart, what a look you give me! Sorry, really, sorry. But we must get a slew of things accomplished in what remains of this night. The other employees and the public will be at the door before long."

"What do we have to do?" Heart kept one arm around Equuleus' neck, for fear he might disappear as she turned to Peter.

"The most important thing is seeing how close you are to fitting the Gear Horse …."

"Equuleus," she corrected.

"He introduced himself already? Good! Yes. Equuleus."

"What do you mean, 'fit?'"

The others gathered around Heart and Equuleus. Heart looked at Swen, hoping to catch his eye and shrug to him about all the nonsense and melodrama, but she couldn't catch his eye. He looked strangely sad. Well, she would ask him later what that was all about. She hoped he wasn't jealous of Equuleus.

"If you would kindly get on him, we can see how well the fit is coming along."

"Again, what do you mean, 'fit?'"

One of the Wondermen came over to Equuleus and knelt down by his side. He extended his upturned palm to Heart.

"Is it all right, Equuleus?" she asked aloud.

He nodded his head. "I have waited long for this moment," he told her privately.

She put one foot on the Wonderman's knee and as she rose to mount Equuleus, the room swirled and expanded around her.

Her band of friends instantly shrank away to little specks. A golden glow filled the foyer, and the moment she came in full contact with Equuleus, she felt her body shift and she even experienced several clicking sensations. But something was not quite right. Not. Quite. Right.

She saw Peter came beside her, and, by force, pulled her off Equuleus, helping her to her feet.

He kept repeating something. She saw his mouth move and, slowly, sound came out, but it didn't make sense. Finally, she heard him say, "Are you all right?" With that, the foyer snapped back to its proper size and shape. The golden glow around everything and everyone lingered, however.

She nodded. "I'm fine. Fine. Fine." She fell backwards and the Wonderman caught her. "No. I'm not entirely fine. Dizzy. Very dizzy. Thank you Wonderman." She tried to stand, but, oddly, could not find her feet. "Well, all right, what's wrong with me?"

Martha came up to her and patted her hand. "Just take a few deep breaths." She breathed deeply.

Heart imitated her, breathing deeply. She gradually felt steady. "I can stand now." She wobbled to her feet, moving away from the Wonderman and Equuleus.

"That reaction cannot be good."

"It was very good," Key Man said, coming to stand by Martha. "We were prepared for worse."

"Oh, really? What did you think I'd do, fall off and break my neck?"

Swen actually barked in alarm.

"No, no of course not. It's just—Equuleus is a powerful combination of mechanical, bio and dark energy. You need to take your transition in small steps, but that was good. You'll be adjusted in short order." Peter nodded happily.

"Good thing, too, " Key Man added, discomfort showing on his face.

"But, why could I hug Equuleus around the neck, yet practically pass out when I get on him?"

"Equuleus is designed, was constructed, to repel anyone who attempted to climb on him, with one exception."

"Me," Heart said.

"Yes. You. But the you that you will be when you've completed your transition."

"This all has something to do with my growth spurt."

"Yes," Martha said. "You know the twin birthmarks you have about 6 inches above your knees?"

"Yes. I do. But how do you?"

"They are not birthmarks. If you look at your new plaid pants, you'll see eyelets in the inner seam."

Heart looked at the inner seam of her plaid pants, and, above the knee, there was a large, shiny eyelet. "Oh!" she exclaimed.

Those need to line up with your birthmarks before you're ready. As you can see, they're close, but not quite there yet."

"In other words, I need to grow another inch."

"That's what it looks like."

"And then what?"

"Equuleus," Key Man said, "show Heart the connects."

A soft whirring and clicking followed his command, and a pin shot out from Equuleus' side.

"There's one on the other side as well. These pins will fit into your 'birthmarks' when you're ready to mount and ride Equuleus. "But they are not actual birthmarks, they are the means by which you become one with Equuleus."

"So now ... we wait?"

"Now, we wait," Peter said. "We'll have a little dinner," he looked at his watch, "I mean, breakfast, and then, Heart, you must rest. Sleep, if you can."

"I can't imagine being able to fall asleep. Anyway, I don't need much."

"You've not had much. You've been going for days."

"Don't care."

"It'll contribute to the last bit of shifting your body needs to go through in order to fit Equuleus."

Well, that's different. I'm off to my room. I suppose Equuleus will go back in his glass cage so everyone can gawk at him."

Equuleus nodded, then took himself to his case and Key Man locked the door.

Heart put her hand on the glass and looked deep into his eyes as she watched him go into the inert mode he maintained in the confined space.

She followed Martha, Peter, Key Man, and the Wondermen down yet another hall she'd not noticed before, and Swen trailed along by her side.

"You're awful quiet," she observed.

"True."

"And reflective."

"Also true."

"You seem sad."

"I cannot argue with your endless accuracies of observation," Swen said.

The group in front stopped to unlock a door, then turned and waited for Heart and Swen to came up to them.

"To be continued," Heart said.

Swen gave his doggie shrug.

They entered what turned out to be Peter's apartment. It was modest in its appointments, yet warm and inviting. He brought forth an unpretentious breakfast of cheese, bread, fruit, and tea. Much to Heart's surprise, she ate with fervor.

After eating more than she thought possible, she recalled the charming bed awaiting her down another long, dark hall. "I'm ready for bed. I really think I'm going to sleep." She stood.

"I'll walk with you." Key Man took his plates and Heart's as well and put them in the insta-clean, then the three of them, Key Man, Heart, and Swen, walked up one hall and down another to Recent & New Acquisitions to the Antiquities Clockwork Collection. He unlocked the outer door and followed Heart to the inner wall door, making sure that she successfully operated the strange cubical, mechanical key.

The wall door swung open, and with it, the cozy lights inside came on.

"Very good," Key Man said. "I must go on my rounds, so sleep well. Have little dreams of great things."

"I will. Thank you for the blessing! Come on, Swen."

"I think I'll go with Key Man."

"Oh! All right...." Heart felt a stab of sadness and separation as she turned and watched Swen at Key Man's side, walking away from her, his long ears flopping slowly to and fro, in step with the little, clanking man.

*　　*

Heart awoke with a start a few hours later in the midst of a terrible dream of battle, watching the monster Lolly had become, totally encompass Molly. She couldn't remember where she was. Then she slowly realized she was not in the battle, but, instead, in her lovely frilly room in The Museum of Scientific Improbabilities and Unpredictable Oddities.

That did not calm the pain she felt, seeing again the terrible, blood-red creature totally enveloping Molly. Heart was raked by huge, deep sobs, unaccompanied by tears, feeling great, insufferable pain over the sweet little donkey who had faithfully trotted long and hard, day and night, to save her.

She'd left the door ajar, hoping Swen would come in when he returned from Key Man's rounds, and now both Swen and Key Man rushed to her side.

"What's wrong?" Key Man asked.

"*Molly!*" was all she could gasp, so shaken by her own emotional upheaval. "*Molly!*"

"Zack's donkey?" Swen asked.

Heart nodded. "That horrible … thing that Lolly became and … jumped on her. Completely covered her in one gigantic leap. Terrible sight. I haven't had one single minute to think about it, now, in my sleep, the image came up. That … terrible … sight."

Key Man pulled the little yellow rocking chair up right beside Heart, and Swen put his muzzle on her knee.

"Molly is fine, Molly is all right."

"What do you mean?"

"Molly is pure bio. Lolly is her daughter, but she is bio-mechanical. Zack made her from Molly's bio material and a mechanical pattern that he altered from one of Father Inventor's patterns.

"If anyone did not make it, it might be Lolly, because she will give her life to save her mother, in a trice."

"Zack is truly brilliant, and you … you've seen something I'd give much to have the privilege to have seen. Lolly transitioning. Oh, my, amazing!

"What was the last you saw of them?"

"The last I saw was Zack herding this awful creature into the shed. Now that I reconsider what I saw—which was so brief, because Jackson wouldn't let me look—but what I saw, the terrible creature did seem very docile and obedient. Zack waved at it and it went right in the shed."

"Well then," Key Man patted Heart's hand, "They're fine. The shed is shielded. Bots can't see anything that is in the shed."

Heart nodded. "Zack did try to tell me that. But I was such a mess from everything that was going on, it didn't register at the time. I was trying to save Molly."

Key Man chuckled his dry little laugh. "And probably caused more trouble than help."

Chagrined, Heart nodded. Still, she wasn't entirely convinced. Key Man was so sweet, perhaps he only meant to make her feel better. "Will Lolly change back to her donkey form?"

"Sure. As soon as Zack saw that all the bots were either gone or down, he would have her revert. And harnessed them up and gone back home, too!"

"I wonder if there's a picture or any way of seeing them?"

"As you probably know, it's very hard to get images back and forth across The Periphery. In addition, it's against the law, but we can try." He went to his desk in the other room, which Heart had already noted as piled high, almost to the ceiling, and she wondered how he possibly found anything in the muddle. But he came back in a couple of moments.

"Think about Molly, now. The imager is intelligent and will receive your mental image. You can help it find her to send back an image."

"How will we know it's a current image? It could be something from the past."

"No. I'm putting in this minute for the time component we want."

It only took a few moments for a sketchy, scratchy image of Molly and Lolly to come through, munching hay in their little stall at The Mystic's cottage. Right at that moment, Zack came into view. He stopped and looked around.

"Oh!" Heart gasped. "It's Zack!"

"So it is," Key Man agreed.

Zack patted the backs of the two donkeys, but while doing so, he raised his head and looked around again.

"It's almost as if he knows we see him."

"Right. He's a sensitive and we're both –" Key Man looked at Swen, with his muzzle affectionately on Heart's knee, "we're all three concentrating on making this image, so he may very well feel us."

As if on cue, he turned and smiled broadly at them, then, instantly, the image disappeared.

"I guess The Wall sensed us too. No matter. You saw Molly, munching her meal, and Lolly and Zack too. Big bonus. Are you all right now?"

Heart nodded. "Sorry to be so—emotional. I really do not prefer to be that way."

"I think it's just fine if you're that way. Be kind to yourself. You've had an unprecedented few days. I believe emotional release is called for."

"You are *sooo* sweet!" She squeezed his hand and closed her eyes. "I didn't know that when I first saw you. You were all clanking and business, and letting those clockwork creations out. I was so stunned to see them." She felt sleep washing over her again. "Those beautiful clockwork beings … while I hid on the wall and watched them … and you … and then, the Gear Horse … You didn't even know I was there."

"But indeed, I did know you were there," Key Man whispered to the apparently asleep Heart.

Her eyes flew open and she sat bolt upright. "You knew I was there?"

"Of course. Just so you know, nothing gets by me here. I saw you the minute I turned the corner to go to the lock wall, and I thought, well, it's only the moon's night to come out, but here is Heart, big as life, brazenly left the Darling Undesirables. They'll be after her soon, but in the meantime, let's show her some beautiful clockworks. So I brought out the moon, and the little lady pianist and …."

"And the gorgeous, tall, dancing couple," Heart said.

"And the gorgeous, tall, dancing couple." Key Man nodded. "But not Equuleus. It must pass that the two of you meet of your own accord."

"And we did!"

"And you did."

Chapter 16

Heart slept deeply, after the reassurance of Molly and Lolly's—and Zack's!—survival. She had to be awakened by Swen upon the request of the others. He did so with caution, having never seen Heart sleep so long nor so deep. As he suspected, she woke up thrashing. He moved to the corner of the room.

"Whoa, sorry, Swen. Did you wake me?"

"I must confess that I did, but at the bidding of the others."

"I thought they wanted me to lie low during the day."

"They do and you did. The museum has been closed for over an hour, and everyone is standing around counting the minutes."

"I … it's … you can't be serious …."

"I'm serious."

Heart jumped out of the bed and fussed around with making herself presentable in the tiny bathroom. "I don't think I've ever slept all day. Even when I was sick."

"When were you ever sick?"

"Good point. Let's go, they can take me as I am."

"I'm happy with that."

They left the little room. Heart locked her wall door, and the Recent & New Acquisitions to the Antiquities Clockwork Collection door locked itself after them. Then she and Swen trotted down the dark hall, which seemed, to Heart, strangely like home already. She'd never felt as welcome or comfortable in The Darling Undesirables Residence of Long Prairie in all the years she'd lived there, as she felt here after only one day.

She saw the Wondermen at the end of the hall, carrying something long and heavy, but by the time she and Swen got there, they were out of sight. She had no idea what they were up to. She could hear the others chatting animatedly in the neighboring hall. Before turning down it to join them, she went to Equuleus' showcase.

It was empty!

She made a sharp left to move toward the voices, about to demand the whereabouts of Equuleus, when she saw him standing before her in a soft light.

He turned to her as she came running up to the group. "Sorry I slept so long!"

"It's good that you did, I think you'll soon notice something ...." Peter said.

Even as he said it, she noticed that all three of them were yet shorter than the day before.

"I see. You all shrank!"

Swen chuckled. "I don't think so."

"No, I don't think so either," Martha agreed.

Heart looked down at the eyelets in her plaid pants. Her birthmarks lined up perfectly with them.

"I grew an inch in my sleep."

Everyone, including Equuleus, nodded.

"And now ....?"

"And now we get serious." Key Man looked around. "Where are those Wondermen when you need them?"

"I just saw them at the end of the hall, carrying something long and apparently heavy," Heart said.

"The tent," Peter said.

"Oh yes. I told them to get it ready. Right. Well, we need one of them now."

"She can use me. She's done it before," Swen said.

"Oh, no, Swen, I'm bigger now. I don't want to step on you. I don't think I would have stepped on you the first time if I'd known what I was doing."

"Just because you're taller doesn't mean you weigh more."

A giant form blocked the light at the end of the hall, and one of the Wondermen came limbering up to them.

"Good job," Peter said. "That was quick."

"You called him somehow?" Heart asked.

"Right. I have a button in my wrist implant that calls them. I don't like to use it, it seems humiliating. But it's effective when necessary. I hope you didn't leave your partner in an awkward position?"

The Wonderman shook his head. "No," his mechanical voice intoned. "We were starting to spread the tent out on the ground. He can continue with that on his own quite tidily."

Heart giggled at the incongruity of the quaint language in the flat machine voice.

"Quite tidily," she repeated.

"Yes," The Wonderman agreed.

"Let's move into the foyer, where we have more light and room." Peter led the way as they trooped to the front of the building, then waited with edgy anticipation as the Wonderman knelt and extended his hand. Heart stepped up on his knee, then settled on Equuleus' back, relaxing into place. The room did not waver.

"Ready?" Equuleus asked silently.

"As ready as I can be," she said aloud. "Will it be painful?"

"No, Heart," Key Man said, "You will feel no pain."

"All right. Let's see what all the fuss is about." She held her breath, she didn't move a muscle as the pins came out of Equuleus' sides, through the eyelets and into her thighs.

It was a peculiar sensation, but Key Man was right, it didn't hurt. The hook up sent whirrings through her body, radiating down to her toes and up to the top of her head. Maybe even out through her crown, she thought.

A matching humming and whirring passed through Equuleus' body as well. Suddenly there resounded a *CRACK!* as if lightning had struck the building. Heart's ears rang, but she felt no other side effect. Something had fused between Equuleus and herself. The thought crossed her mind that she might be welded to him, never able to leave his back.

"I didn't expect that!" She heard Martha say. Heart wanted to say, "Neither did I!" but discovered she could not speak.

"Are we all right?" she wondered.

"We're fine. Just had to clear an electrical block you'd built up, probably from crossing back and forth through The Periphery."

"Why can't I speak?"

"You will. Be calm, everything will sort out. Want to go for a bit of a ride?"

"Sure!"

Equuleus turned and walked in a stately fashion down the hall, the ring of his metal hooves against the marble floors reverberating through the halls.

"Is this all the faster you can go?"

"I can go very fast. And, remember, I can fly. But walking on these marble floors faster than this is not safe. Key Man would be very upset if another clockwork got injured."

"Indeed! Especially if it were you. Tell me about the accident I heard him mention."

"Several clockwork creatures thought it would be fun to have a race and they begged Key Man to let them. Finally, he gave in. I shan't go into the sad and ugly details, but there was a pile up when the rabbit lost his footing, and, as I recall, half-a-dozen clockwork creatures became piles of junk. He's never gotten over it."

"Of course he wouldn't." Heart felt Key Man's pain, imagining the sad event. "He loves the clockworks like they're his family."

"And we are! It's my good fortune that he feels that way."

"How so?"

"I was a sad, rusted, pile of junk when he first saw me."

"Hard to imagine."

'Don't even try! Key Man rebuilt me, from the bottom of my shiny hooves to the tips of my gear wings. He's simply brilliant."

"And sweet and sensitive as well," Heart added.

"Yes."

Heart brought to mind the picture of Molly, Lolly, and Zack. "I was so grieved thinking Molly had been destroyed in the battle in The Periphery. So he brought a picture of her up for me."

"The First Turning Point Battle," Equuleus said.

"You know about it?"

"Martha often sits in the foyer reading *Ourbook* aloud for hours in the evening, after the museum closes. There are passages I can quote from beginning to end, I've heard them so many times."

"Do you believe in the book's so-called prophecy?"

"It appears that it is so …."

"It doesn't seem logical—things written in a book who-knows-how-long ago ...."

"Two hundred years ...."

"Two hundred years ago are now coming true. That's just weird."

"You don't need to believe it. There's enough of us who do to keep you headed toward your destination."

"My destination is for you to take me to Eye, so we can take him away, and then he and you and Swen, and I find a place to live where we'll never be foun,d, never have to face another Keeper, never again be a Media Pet, or any such thing. That's my destination ...."

"Lovely dream," Equuleus thought.

"Soon a lovely reality."

"I believe your plans will need to shift."

"No. That's my plan. You do intend to come with me, don't you?"

"Of course. From now on, wherever you go, there I'll be. It's just ... where you'll soon be going is different from what you have in mind."

"Tell me ...."

"I cannot."

"Who will, then?"

"Perhaps Key Man."

"I'll ask him. But in the meantime, since you can't run on the marble floors, why don't you fly?"

"Not just yet. You're not ready."

"I want to feel the wind in my hair!"

"Don't worry, dear Heart. You will feel tremendous amounts of wind in your hair before long."

Equuleus turned and, moving slowly, head high, hooves high, returned to the foyer. Heart saw Martha, Peter and Key Man waiting for them with impatience.

"Why are they so edgy?"

"Things are moving fast, Heart, and we have a lot to do in an ever-shorter time."

"What's moving fast?"

"Come along," Peter called as they approached. "Lots to do and I need to get Wonderman back on the tent project."

"Hold your horses," Heart burst out audibly. "Oh! My voice is back! Sorry, I didn't mean for you all to hear that."

Everyone, including Swen and Equuleus, chuckled.

"You hold your horses, little miss," Peter said good-naturedly, winking at her.

Oh, that winking! It made her giddy.

The Wonderman knelt down as Equuleus came up to him.

"Wait. Let me get down on my own. I'll have to, won't I? The Wonderman certainly cannot ride on Equuleus' back everywhere I go."

"True," Key Man agreed. "Stand, Wonderman Two."

He stood, but remained by Equuleus' side.

"I'm ready, Equuleus." She felt the pins in her thighs retract. Then she slid to the ground neatly, as if she'd been doing it every day of her life.

"Excellent!" Key Man said.

"Agreed." Peter nodded, beaming with delight.

Martha came up to Heart and hugged her. "My amazing little Heart."

*　　*

Equuleus went with the Wonderman, while Key Man took Heart to the Recent & New Acquisitions to the Antiquities Clockwork Collection.

She watched Equuleus walk alongside the Wonderman's giant stride down the long Clockworks hall until they disappeared around a corner. She felt odd and at odds. Empty. Slightly confused. Lonely.

Ever since Eye had come into her life, she'd never been lonely. Now she felt guilty—it seemed like betraying Eye to long for Equuleus.

"Come along," Key Man said. "You have volumes to learn. You'll be with Equuleus again soon enough."

Heart fell into step beside Key Man. For a person who only came up to her diaphragm, he could move surprisingly rapidly. Then she remembered his conversation with Keeper A—he was, at least in part, made of Dark Matter.

"You move very fast."

"Oh, this is nothing to what I can do."

"Is that because you are, in part, Dark Matter?"

"Yes, my dearest Heart, it is."

"So … you are made of bio material and Dark Matter …."

"Mostly."

"Mostly?"

"Mostly."

"And ….?"

"A few mechanicals, for convenience."

"Oh. So you are mostly Dark Matter and some bio and some mechanical. And Keeper A is mostly bio and some Dark Matter."

"That's accurate."

"What's it like, being made of Dark Matter?"

"You … you … I … I …." Key Man stuttered.

"That's not very informative."

"No. It's not. We'll continue this conversation after you've learned some of the things you'll be studying the next few days. But as you noticed in the tension between myself and Keeper A, there's generally a clash between Bio Dark Matter people and Dark Matter Bios. An apparently hard-wired antagonism between us that, even as we speak, is not understood. It makes it difficult for society to achieve the advances it could, if not for this incessant conflict."

"Add to that the problem with the people who are pure bio, the Purists, who don't like anybody else, I guess," Heart said.

"Excellent! That's one of our lessons, and you already understand it."

"I can't say that I understand it …."

"Well, you understand it as well as anyone does."

*   *

Inside the Recent & New Acquisitions to the Antiquities Clockwork Collection Key Man led Heart to a far corner of the vast room, and, much to her surprise, there was a desk equipped with a 3-D terminal, set up and waiting for her studies to begin.

The only thing that made life worth living, besides Eye, at The Darling Undesirables Residence of Long Prairie was her studies. She could never understand why the other Darling Undesirables resisted staying in class. They'd often stand up and wander off while the teachers taught. Sometimes Heart and Eye were the only students in a classroom. After a teacher had been hired specifically to teach Eye, she'd be the only student in a class.

And so it was again. She and her instructor, the amazing little Key Man, alone together in a cocoon of learning.

He dimmed the lights and brought up a 3-D video of Pink.

"I've studied Pink," Heart said.

"Did you?" Key Man asked. "Did you enjoy that?"

"I loved it! I love Pink, but I don't really know why. I know Father Inventor constructed Pink, and that during the time of the launch, so many things went wrong. It was around that time that his beloved wife died."

Key Man nodded. "Did they teach you that at The Darling Undesirables Residence?" He sounded surprised.

"Not exactly." Heart looked at her hands in her lap. "I know I'm not supposed to, but I've often studied on my own. I learned quite a few things that I wasn't taught."

Key Man stirred about, clearly agitated, his keys jangling softly in his irritation. Heart was afraid he was going to scold her for studying without permission. "Around here," he said quietly, "you are welcome to study as much as you want. Any subject you want. We do have to make sure you concentrate on your specific studies, but other than that, you are free to roam the halls, the 3-D library, or anything else that you find interesting."

"*Really?!*" What would it be like to take in any 3-D, to ask anyone a question and get an answer?

"Goodness!" Key Man fell to muttering for a few moments, expressing his disgust of the Darling Undesirable residences and everything that had anything to do with running them, which Heart heard only imperfectly. It made her want to smile right down to her toes.

While Key Man muttered, Heart watched Pink in the 3-D time-lapse vid, shot from the earth, with the camera staying on Pink, so it was held steadily in the center of the 3-D, throughout a day and a night. The colors of the day, the clouds passing over it, the reflection of the natural moon, and the night clouds passed over little Pink as if she was a palate for the universe to paint its majesty upon.

Pink's own rotation showed low hills and valleys, and the "light spot" everyone always liked to speculate about. Key Man's muttering, and everything else passed away from Heart's attention as she became immersed in the dream of Pink, suspended before her eyes in the glassy translucence of the darkened room.

She'd always adored Pink, but now, strangely similar to the experience she'd had on Equuleus' back, she felt a soft whirring, deep inside, in her bones. Gradually the 3-D faded.

"So beautiful," she whispered, looking around for Key Man. But he seemed to have stepped from the room. She stood, wondering what she ought to be about now.

"Did you like that?" He popped up from behind a pile of clockworks.

"Oh!" Heart jumped, startled. "It was lovely. But what am I to study?"

"That was your studies for today. Tomorrow we'll study Pink some more."

"But I didn't learn anything about Pink today!"

"Didn't you?"

"You didn't lecture, I didn't read, there wasn't any commentary on the 3-D."

"But—did you learn anything about Pink?"

Heart thought. Indeed, she had learned quite a lot! Watching Pink in its sky, seeing the lay of its land in its rotation made it real as never before. "I did. I learned a lot about Pink."

"So I thought. Now, go find some mischief to get into. But just don't let any patrons see you."

"I'm invisible!" Heart laughed, heading for the door. She paused and turned to Key Man. "I thought I had so much to learn."

"You do. You will. You are."

"I do. I will. I am!" Heart intoned. It reminded her of the ritual chants she and Eye used to come up with.

And then, she became sober. She did not like hearing—even in her mind—the phrase "used to" about Eye. Everything she did was for Eye. And Equuleus. Swen, too of course. But Swen was good at taking care of himself, and Eye was not.

About Equuleus? It was not a question of whether he could care for himself or not. It was the knowledge that Equuleus and she were, together, one being, complete.

But right now, she must learn everything she could wrap her mind around, and quickly, so that one day, she and Eye would be at peace in a home of their own.

Chapter 17

That's when Heart's studies began in earnest. She learned about the rotation of natural and synthetic satellites around Earth and other heavenly bodies. She learned about flight with wings, and then, in particular, flight with Equuleus' wings, which, although mechanical, were also made in part of Dark Matter and driven by Dark Energy—an entirely different sort of flight from other forms.

She learned how to grow plants from seeds on worlds without a plant-supporting environment. She learned how to understand colors when they were shifted on worlds other than Earth.

She studied her own ability to shapeshift, and how to refine and improve it. Fascinated, she studied the history of shapeshifting, and discovered that, previously it had been a fantasy, found only in fiction. But then a few children had shapeshifted after the advent of the use of dark energy.

It was noted that dark energy appeared to produce an unusual electrical field among a small population of children who discovered when they visualized their surroundings they blended to look like it.

This had been quite disconcerting for parents, teachers, and nannies who called the authorities to report their missing children, soon discovered playing right where they'd been last seen.

Heart was surprised to see a reference to herself, accompanied by a funny little holo of her, with a captioned that read, "the only Darling Undesirable to date known to be able to shapeshift."

Shocked, she wondered when had it become common knowledge that she could shapeshift? The author was someone she'd never heard of: Marchand Matthews. Who was this person?

She searched for other works by him and became more and more surprised and uncomfortable when she discovered that the only subject of this writer was herself. He'd written about her star window, about her love of plants and her ability to make anything grow. Most disconcerting of all, he wrote about her affection for Eye in a horrible way, trying to suggest something between them that was not true.

"What do Heart and Eye do, all of that time when they are alone together?" the narrator said, showing a snippet of 3-D with Eye and Heart holding hands, cropping out the surrounding image of them at the dinner table, where Eye was holding Loruza's hand with his right hand, and Heart was holding another Darling Undesirable's hand with her left hand.

Fury rose in her. If they had to talk about her, she could endure it. But saying anything negative about Eye—intolerable.

She slammed her ID code into the system, preparing to remove all of the articles by Marchand Matthews that referenced her, by the authority of being the person written about. But first, she must prove her identity.

As the query form appeared and Heart began to fill it out, Key Man burst through the door. "Stop what you're doing!" he yelled.

"I'm removing these scandalous articles about me, by this, this 'Marchand Matthews.'"

"Undo!" Key Man commanded. But the incomplete form hung in 3-D space, unmoving.

"Undo it, Heart. Quickly, quickly!"

"No."

"It's a trap."

A tumbling series of thoughts ran through Heart's mind like a ball rolling down a hill gathering momentum. She gasped. "Undo form!" she ordered.

The form disappeared. The line where she'd put her ID appeared with her number on it.

"Undo ID entry," she commanded.

Her ID disappeared from view.

"Undo Marchand Matthews search."

A flurry of activity ensued in the space before her as the system backed up to the image of Eye and herself in the dinner hall, holding hands, while the commentary accompanying it started to drone again. Silently, Heart gestured to the image.

"Right," Key Man said. I understand. But undo."

"Undo. Erase entire search and off." Heart and Key Man watched in silence until the 3-D blinked off.

"I was studying shapeshifting. To become better at it, you know. And up came this article about me. I wanted to know who knew so much about me—it just got worse and worse. So much about me that only someone who practically lives in my plaid pocket could know.

"And then that bit about Eye came up, suggesting that we ... we ... we're ... not ... he's like ... he's my brother. I don't have any family. I'm a broken Darling

Undesirable. I have no one. It's just Eye. And I will not let anyone say anything about him that, you know, defames him. This Marchand Matthews knew things about me that only someone who was literally physically close to me could know. I searched for biographical information about him. But there's nothing!

"It made me furious. And it frightened me, especially about Eye. It made me want to run, to fly to The Darling Undesirables Residence of Long Prairie and grab him this very moment. And disappear. Somewhere, anywhere."

Key Man nodded sympathetically. "But where?" He sat down beside her. "You're not ready yet. You are not ready yet! I know you miss Eye, but you dare not get in contact with him."

"But ever since I first crossed over into The Periphery, I've not been able to feel him. Why can't I reach him? What's going on?"

"Quite a lot, Heart. But you must build up a tough skin. This is nothing to what you may see in the future. They're trying to flush you out. We've worked hard to hide you, we need them to believe you're still in The Periphery. But now, I don't know. We have to move as if they know you're here. It was a trick, Heart. To get you to do exactly what you did."

Heart shook her head in dismay. "I should have known. I stopped thinking rationally. They can get me though Eye. That's what started the whole chain of events in the first place when Keeper A punished Eye because I stayed here. I must keep my wits about me."

"Yes. You must," Key Man agreed.

"How did you know what I was doing?"

Key Man turned over his wrist. "This button, as you've seen before, calls the Wondermen. This little plate beside it tells me if you're doing anything—and I mean *anything*—that potentially endangers you. If you code anything into the system that could be traced to you, if you step one inch out of the perimeter of the museum, if someone we don't know is anywhere near you—I get a holo projection from my wrist, showing where you are, and what's happening."

"So—I'm completely protected?"

"As protected as we can make you."

"And I couldn't run away?"

"Again, as impossible as we could make it."

"So—I've gone from The Darling Undesirables Residence of Long Prairie prison, to a prison in The Museum of Scientific Improbabilities and Unpredictable Oddities."

"Well—yes," Key Man said simply. "We're trying to keep you safe, but it's true that you are not free to leave at will."

"I ought to have stayed in The Periphery."

"You would not have succeeded for even one more day. And you'd have caused the termination of many kind and useful beings, both human and nonhuman."

"I see," she said in a quiet, saddened voice, while inside, she cried her mantra, "I want to be free! I want to be free!

*　　*

Ħeart and Key Man joined the others for a small meal and to recap the day. General consternation fell over everyone when Key Man informed them of Heart's foolish behavior.

"I'm sorry," Heart said. And she was. She looked into the eyes of each of her dear protectors. Key Man, Peter, Martha, Equuleus, Swen, and even the two Wondermen, with spinning meshing cogs for eyes, which, nonetheless, managed to communicate their matched emotions of concern clearly.

She understood now that every one of them was endangered, as well as herself, by her foolish reaction.

Much to Heart's dismay, Martha launched into a reprimand. "We must all learn to temper our reactions," she said, the lovely round smile gone from her face, her brow wrinkled into a smidgen of a frown. "Response, thoughtful response, is necessary from each of us.

"If anyone is tempted to take any sort of action, you must run it by at least one other member of our group." She nodded around the somber circle. "We have a larger cause, don't we? We have something bigger than our selves to consider."

Martha's serious tone, and her solemn, earnest message stirred Heart. She asked herself how she could have been so asleep, so oblivious to all that was going on until this moment.

And in that moment, she woke up.

"But—wait …" Heart said, continuing to think through all the connections that fell into place, and the larger picture became more and more clear. "My intention has been, simply, to leave with Equuleus, taking Swen with me, get Eye and disappear. All I've wanted to do is to find quiet lives of our own. And for some reason, I thought you were helping me do that. But you're not.

"I didn't even wonder why you all would devote yourselves to my running away. I just—thought you were! What a stunning, mind-boggling ego I have. What have I been thinking? How poorly I've been socialized at The Darling Undesirables Residence of Long Prairie. My thinking is just—skewed.

"I've been completely wrong. Wrong. Wrong. Wrong. There's something huge going on, and somehow, I'm part of it." Heart took a deep breath, ratcheted up her courage and continued. "The time has come for you to tell me the truth."

Peter nodded, moving to sit by Heart. Key Man moved over. "You're right on every single point you make, darling Heart. We've known your intention, your drive has been to 'rescue' Eye from The Darling Undesirables Residence of Long Prairie. But the truth is, Eye is fine and, other than missing you, he's content with his life. In fact ...."

"Oh!" Martha interrupted, "I don't think you need to tell her that!"

"Don't need to tell me what?" A dark mood washed over Heart. "Don't tell me what?"

"We've kept one bit of news from you because we didn't want it to distract you. But I feel it's important that you know. Eye has established a close relationship with your little peer, Butterfly."

Heart felt a stab of jealousy but refused to allow it to take root. "Well, that's not the worst thing. That's all right. In fact, it makes perfect sense. If he's close to Butterfly, that's better than being close with any of the Keepers, who cannot be trusted. He has to be close to someone, rather than stumbling about, all alone. Butterfly is perfect, so kind and sweet. But if I was there, and I told Eye to come with me, he'd come with me."

Everyone remained silent, and the silence was more upsetting than the news she'd just been told. Perhaps there was more. But she didn't want to hear any more from them about Eye right now. None of them knew the lives they had lived together. No one.

Not even Butterfly knew the life she and Eye had lived together.

But—she didn't want to think it—perhaps this was why she couldn't connect with him. Perhaps it wasn't the distance.

Perhaps it was, simply, that he'd stopped thinking of her.

Everyone remained very quiet. Then Peter turned on the holo. Before Heart appeared Eye. She gasped. Her friend! Her family!

The holo captured Eye bending over a patch of delicate primroses in Butterfly's little rock garden, tending them with his sure movements that always captivated Heart, watching his beautiful flow of movement, uninhibited by the constraints of eyesight.

"Eye!" she whispered.

Then Butterfly appeared in the frame. She knelt next to Eye. Heart watched as their hands moved in concert among the brightly colored flowers, as if their hands and the flowers had rehearsed a lovely dance, privately, for themselves.

It was obvious. Eye and Butterfly had become quite close. Heart turned, confused. Vexed. Relieved. Angry. A deeply haunting sense of utter aloneness. She wanted to leave the room. She didn't want to be around anyone right now, not even Equuleus.

But … as she turned, she saw Eye stand up. She watched over her shoulder as he moved from Butterfly's Fairy Garden to the path beyond. He stooped over and plucked a few blades of grass from one side of the path and then he crossed to the other side and stooped over to pluck a few blades of grass from there as well. Then he turned, and with uncanny awareness of where the camera was, held up each of the few blades of grass in turn, inhaling their aroma deeply.

That was all Heart needed. He remembered—and she remembered—their walk and talk about the grass on the fateful day before her departure. Eye took a chance, or maybe he felt her, that the cameras would be on him, that either live or at another time, she would see this bit of holo. She would know he was still her family.

That was all she needed. She could go on with everything asked of her. She was not alone. Her little brother still loved her, missed her, needed her.

"Wait, Heart," Martha said, coming over and taking Heart's hand. "I know this is a lot to think about, but, because you may have alerted the Purists of your whereabouts, we really must—*must*—discuss some important details. We dare not hesitate."

"Yes." Heart said calmly, sitting back down. Both Swen and Equuleus came near her. She'd hardly seen Swen of late, but now he put his muzzle in her lap.

"You all know something that I don't know. I don't think I can process more right now. My brain feels muddled."

"You'll sort it out," Peter said, resuming his talk. "You'll sort it out because your brain isn't like any other brain on the entire planet."

"What do you mean?"

"Have you wondered, at all, why everyone is after you?"

"Yes! As I've said to some of you …."

"The Purists want you. The scientists want you. And we want to protect you. As of this moment, we've won. We intend to keep it that way."

"The Purists want me? Why? They're only interested in … things … that … are … not …." She slowed as insight took shape in her mind.

"I'm not completely bio …."

"No. You're not," Peter agreed.

"But I look bio."

"Indeed you do. That's where the scientists come in. They're itching to take you apart and see how you've been … been …."

"Hooked together, sewn together, patched together, like Swen or Equuleus." Heart looked down at Swen. "Sorry, Swen. No offense."

"Plenty taken," Swen said, bristling, raising his muzzle off her lap.

Heart heard nothing from Equuleus. An empty nothing. She seemed perversely intent upon alienating herself from everyone in her life.

"You're unique, Heart. The one and only such creature anywhere. You are made of bio material, and a few, but not many, mechanicals, Dark matter, and, here's the compelling, mysterious part of your composition. You are, in part, dark energy!"

"*Dark energy!*" Heart exclaimed. I can't be dark energy. Dark energy flows, it cannot be contained in a bio entity. It will destroy the host and escape."

"You've learned your school lessons well. And what you say is true, everywhere in the world, except with you. Somehow, most mysterious fact, your body is a container that holds dark energy."

"I can't believe you. But—even if you're right, how could it come to be? Darling Undesirables are grown in test tubes. I couldn't have been grown in a test tube if dark energy was involved."

"You weren't."

"The only one who could have put together dark energy and bio matter is … I was made by Father Inventor?"

"Now you have it!" Key Man actually clapped.

"No," Heart protested. "I could not have been made by Father Inventor."

"Why not?" One of the Wondermen asked.

"Yes. Why not?" The other joined in.

"Because he would have kept me. Why wouldn't he keep me?"

"We don't know the answer to that most interesting question," Peter said. "We just know that you were created by Father inventor. And that the time has come for you to save yourself, Equuleus and, we hope, Father Inventor and Pink, as well."

"Oh!" Heart said in a small, whisper. "Nothing too demanding for a small, insignificant creature such as myself."

"Small, perhaps, despite how much you've grown. Insignificant, decidedly not!" Key Man said.

"But, to give you the best answer to your question that we can come up with," Martha added, "we believe that Father Inventor, knowing how precious you are, determined that, as an infant the best care for you would be to hide you in plain sight, at a Darling Undesirables Residence.

"He disappeared over twenty years ago, as you know. We're certain he lives on Pink. But we also believe he sneaked down to Earth about fifteen years ago when he figured out how to contain dark energy in a bio form, which we believe he'd begun years before and had hidden away, before he went to live on Pink. That would be your own, darling, self.

"Because of the Purists, who, as everyone knows, will not touch a Darling Undesirable, he left you, in the traditional fashion, on the doorstep of The Darling Undesirables Residence of Long Prairie, which is the Darling Undesirables Residence closest to the Museum of Scientific Improbabilities and Unpredictable Oddities. Initially, no doubt, standing close by and ready to spring if it looked like any harm might befall you.

"But you were taken in. You lived tolerably well until a timed device went off in both you and Equuleus, each calling to the other."

"Was that what the Mechanical Aurora Borealis was doing the day I came with the Darling Undesirables?"

"No! That light show was a surprise to all of us, including Equuleus, who saw it with your eyes. That light show was Father Inventor acknowledging your presence here.

"We were so excited because we knew that the dramatic behavior of the aurora meant he was watching. It meant that all the preparations we've been doing for years were not in vain. It meant that our understanding of many of the confusing passages in *Ourbook* were starting to make sense."

"But why was there a device that called me to Equuleus? Why?"

"Because you and Equuleus need to go home."

"To go home?"

"Remember when you first saw Equuleus?" Key Man asked.

"I do. I could never forget."

"Remember you saw a red pulsing light, and how it felt like it pulsed in you too?"

"I do remember. But how do you know?"

"Equuleus told me. Equuleus has always known all your thoughts, all your feelings. This is, in part, because the two of you share a bit of brain matter. But that's not the most important point."

"Equuleus and I share actual brain matter?"

"Yes," Key Man said.

"But, as Key Man says, that's not the most important point," Martha said, taking over the conversation. "This is what we learned, over time, piecing all the bits of information together. Father Inventor's beloved wife died of heart failure. He'd been working on an indestructible heart for her because of her weak heart, trying to save her. But it was not to be.

"When she died, he went a bit insane, creating prototypes of humans without hearts, but they all failed. The Life Force would not let him get around the fact that a living being must have a heart.

"So, what he did with you was, he placed your heart in Equuleus. Every beat of the heart in him has sustained your life, through the flow of dark energy that connects you to him."

Heart took in everything Key Man and Martha said, but was there one iota of truth to it? Incomprehensible, beyond fantastic.

"I ..." Heart stood in agitation, "I'm done now for a while. No more. I can take no more just now." She walked out of the room, relieved that no one followed her or called after her. As she strode down the hall, she heard Equuleus a short distance behind.

He joined her, and silently together they walked the darkened halls, the rhythmic, gentle clang of Equuleus' hooves soothing Heart's upheaval.

"Is any part of what they said even possible, let alone true?" she finally asked.

"It's all improbable. It's all true," Equuleus answered.

"But how do you know? They can lie to you just as easily as to me."

"No."

"No, they can't lie to you?"

"No, they haven't lied to me. I remember when Father Inventor, who had made me years before, gave me the heart. Your heart. I remember."

Heart stopped, feeling breathless. "Tell me. Every detail, tell me." She leaned against the wall.

"Father Inventor built me long, long before he did any work with dark matter. Before he did any work with dark energy. He created amazing clockworks, run by gears that were very nearly perpetual motion machines.

"I was his greatest achievement. Or so they said at the time. He had discovered how to make a clockwork creation actually fly. There was considerable contemplation in the media, and among scientists as well, about how his feat of genius could be put to good use for humanity.

"And then, he figured out how to 'show' dark matter."

"Yes," Heart interjected. "Showing that which could not be seen. Like roping an invisible mustang."

"Great image," Equuleus nodded and Heart could have sworn she saw a flash of his beautiful metal teeth in a horsey smile. "And accurate. He not only discovered how to see invisible matter, he demonstrated how it could be used.

"Clockworks, and pretty much everything else that provided energy at that time, became history almost overnight. He put dark matter in his clockworks, and the world went from virtual perpetual motion machines to actual perpetual motion machines.

"At my center—and yours too, Heart—is the equivalent of a small but massively powerful furnace of dark matter, which never gets used up. What it burns for energy is what it eats to survive. Endlessly regenerating and self-manifesting."

"Now you're getting to something I've never quite understood. How is dark energy different from dark matter?" Heart asked.

"You've asked the perennial question. In simplest terms, dark matter regenerates itself from its own by-product. But dark energy actually produces energy from, apparently, nothing. It pulls nothing from nothing and makes something. And once that something is brought into being, it cannot be destroyed nor be contained.

"Until you. You, somehow, contain dark energy. But … it's as if he made you, then broke the mold."

"Why?"

"That, my dearest Heart, I do not know. I have thoughts about it, but I don't know what he had in mind."

"What are your thoughts?"

"I'm thinking that he wanted to see how one eternal being turned out—what she would do, how she'd live—before he ever went near it again."

"Oh!" Heart whispered. Words failed her. "E … eternal being …."

*   *

They continued walking the halls in complete silence. Heart did her best not to have a single new thought. Her head was so filled with thoughts, it seemed certain if even one more came in, her head would split open and everything it contained would spill out and roll across the floor. That wouldn't be all bad, she decided, a head filled with emptiness.

Equuleus kept his thoughts to himself. She appreciated the wisdom of his silence. However, she finally turned and headed back to the group. She didn't want to. She didn't want to talk. She didn't want to listen. But she knew she must.

Of course, the notion that Father Inventor had made her, or that she was pegged together of four components, was preposterous! She was, simply, a human girl, a Darling Undesirable. But even in the midst of all of these thoughts, there was one tiny little candle flame of thought that she fought and fought against, and tried to make go away. Because none of this was real, so that little thought had no place in her, just as it never had any place in any Darling Undesirable. And that thought was ….

I have a father. I am not an orphan ….

She stepped back into Peter's living room finding everyone in a heated discussion. She quickly brushed away the first tears she'd ever shed in her life, that came, much to her shock, at the thought of having a father. Impossible. Impossible. It couldn't be true.

Equuleus nuzzled her cheek where she'd brushed away the tears. The room fell silent, everyone looking at her.

Martha hurried over and hugged her. "What's wrong?"

"No-nothing. Nothing happened. I'm just—working hard not to believe in something I know is not true."

"Nonsense!" Peter exclaimed. "Do you think we have time to tell crazy untrue stories?"

"Gently," Martha said, giving Peter a rare look of disapproval.

He made an unintelligible response then returned his attention to the 3-D hovering over him. "We have more immediate problems. The Purists have succeeded in making a reverse dark energy bomb, which, our infiltrators have learned, they intend to point at Pink to destroy it—and Father Inventor as well."

"No!" Heart whispered. Was it possible for fate to be so cruel, to let her imagine she had a father in one breath, and take him away in the next? "What can I do?"

"We're trying to sort that out. Wondermen, how long before the tent is up?"

"It's rising as we speak," the Wondermen said in unison.

"When will it be ready?"

"Tonight."

"Good. We must pray that it'll take the Purists time to get organized and positioned. Key Man, come with me. We have to come up with a neutralizing device, and a means of deployment."

"You know the method of deployment. That's one place *Ourbook* is not ambiguous," Key Man answered.

"She's not ready."

"She will be."

"Is the 'she' me?" Heart asked.

The room fell silent. Heart knew the silence meant "yes."

Chapter 18

The tent!
Why did "the tent" command so much of their time and attention? Heart wondered.

Why did "the tent" command so much of their time and attention? Heart wondered.

Until this evening, her own attention had been taken with her studies, bonding with Equuleus, wondering why Swen hardly spoke to her and, last but not least, dealing with the dull pain of missing Eye. She swung—moment by moment—between being happy that he had Butterfly to keep him company, to walk with him to the dining hall, to tend to their flowers, and being miserable that her best friend had become so close to someone else.

So the talk about the tent was just another buzz going with all the other buzzing. But tonight she would find out about the tent. Thinking about it distracted her from her studies.

She finally gave up and turned on the 3-D security camera around the museum to check out her surroundings. At the front door, Martha ushered out the last group of school children. As Martha turned, the camera caught an unusual expression of relief and urgency on her face that Heart had never seen.

Then Heart watched as Martha hurried down the hall toward the Recent & New Acquisitions to the Antiquities Clockwork Collection room. In the background Heart saw Peter lock the front doors while Key Man clanked down the hall, Swen at his side, to the wall panel by the doors, ready to bring the grates down over the front doors.

Heart stepped into the doorway as Martha came up.

"You're ready?" Martha asked.

Heart nodded. "Ready and utterly curious. Where's Equuleus?"

"Probably at the tent. Let's go. Peter, Key Man and Swen will join us."

They met in the foyer. Peter led the way to the farthest hall from the Recent & New Acquisitions to the Antiquities Clockwork Collection hall. No one spoke. Strange, Heart thought, given how they had babbled incessantly about the tent—until this moment. There was considerable tension among them.

At the end of the very long hall, Key Man inserted three keys, sequentially, into three locks. A vacuum sound whispered from the lock after the third key, and the heavy door swung open of its own accord. A wall of white loomed up before Heart's eyes.

"What? ...." she exclaimed.

"There!" Peter exclaimed. "That looks good!"

"It does, indeed," Key Man said.

"Indeed," Martha echoed.

"What am I looking at?" Heart asked.

"The tent!" The three of them exclaimed.

"I don't—see—a ..." She looked back and forth and up and down, and finally, she realized that everything before her was the gigantic wall of a tent. "Ohhhhh! *THE TENT!*"

"Looks like it's fully up," Peter said.

Key Man nodded in agreement.

The two of them stepped out and disappeared around the side of the wall. Martha followed.

Heart, still trying to take in the overwhelming size of the wall before her, had not moved.

"Come on, Heart," she heard Martha's muffled voice.

She stepped through the doorway and the door swooshed! shut behind her. As she came around the corner of the massive tent, she saw her three friends waiting for her before its entrance. But she couldn't resist stepping back several yards to try to take in the dimensions of the tent.

It was nearly as big as the museum, pristine white, glowing in the backlight of the setting sun. It rose to three peaks, two shorter ones on either side of one that towered above the museum's rotunda. It billowed gently in the evening breeze and all but beckoned to her to come within. But—the sight of its unanticipated gargantuan size made her feel breathless and overwhelmed. She wanted to step back.

"What's the matter?" Peter asked.

"It's a shock," Martha said. "Let her take it in for a minute."

Heart nodded wordlessly. Slowly she gathered herself and walked toward them.

"In we go, then!" Key Man said, unzipping the tent flap. They stepped inside. Beautiful, soft pastel lights rotated around the interior of the gigantic tent. Other than the soft lights, the space was entirely empty.

"What is the tent for?" Heart asked, finally finding her voice.

"You're going to learn to fly!" Equuleus said, swooping down from above, his glorious wings finally fully spread—a sight she'd not seen before.

No one had told her the full expanse of his wings was half again what she'd seen during his brief flight in the museum's rotunda, and she stepped back from him in awe. All of his glinting gears churned smoothly as if on bands of silk with the sound of a soft melody.

"Oh! The music!" Heart said, reaching out her hands instinctively toward Equuleus.

"Do you hear music?" Key Man asked.

"Beautiful music. Don't you?"

Key Man shook his head. "The sound of Equuleus' gears is gentle and almost inaudible, but I've never heard music."

She turned to Martha, Peter, and Swen, and they all shook their heads.

"*Ourbook* says, 'she shall hear the music of the gears,'" One of the Wondermen said, approaching them.

"Thank you Wonderman, you're right," Peter agreed. "More fulfilled prophecy. "You did an excellent job getting the tent up, Wonderman One."

"Thank you. But dark energy does the real work."

"The tent is held up by dark energy?" Heart asked, feeling anxious.

"A little bit. But then, a little bit goes a long way."

"That must be why I'm not having a reaction."

"Very good, Heart." Peter grinned approvingly. "We did a lot of computations around the amount of dark energy you contain, how much is in The Wall to sustain it, how much it takes to inflate the tent, and learned that at most, you might experience a slight bit of euphoria after an accumulation of a few hours, but otherwise you should not be affected negatively."

All the while, Heart had not taken her eyes off Equuleus, who flew high and low, clearly filled with a joy she'd not seen in him before.

Now she understood that he longed to be free as much as she did.

Finally, he landed with soft precision before them, and, neatly folding his glorious wings, cantered up to Heart.

The Wonderman kneeled beside Equuleus. Heart stepped up and onto Equuleus' back, silently promising herself that this would be the last time she'd depend on assistance to mount.

"I believe you," Equuleus thought in return.

Heart sat still while the pins came out of Equuleus' sides and into her thighs. Once again, she felt the shift through her body and Equuleus beneath her. But this time there was no startling crack of electrical charge. They simply settled into their united state as if it was the most natural thing for horse and rider to do.

Equuleus trotted, then cantered around the circumference of the tent. Peter, Key Man, Martha, and even Swen grinned like proud parents every time Heart and Equuleus glided by the little group of onlookers.

"I want to run," Heart thought to Equuleus.

Heart felt a shift in Equuleus. Energy shot through his body and up into her. His hooves barely touched the ground, and the white walls, bathed in pastel colors, blurred into a delicate lavender-peach-turquoise. Nothing in life felt anything like this complete freedom. They could run like this forever and ever. The faces of her little band of friends blurred into one loooong horizontal, smiling face.

And for once in her life, she was really, truly, completely and deeply, joyous.

"Here—we—go!" Equuleus intoned in her mind over the delicate music of his gears, over the joy in her center, over all the loneliness and searching and hopefulness of her life. Equuleus left the ground. Heart looked down to see her friends, and they looked up at her and the amazing one-and-only winged horse in all of creation.

Equuleus gradually flew higher and higher, near the peaks in the gargantuan tent. His wings glinted out to the edges of her peripheral vision, the flow of air around her soothing as a spring breeze.

"This is easy! Why has everyone been talking about lessons! I'm not doing anything. You're doing it. All I have to do is sit."

"Now we begin the learning part," Equuleus answered. "You must give in to any movement I make, setting aside your natural instinct to resist. Relax into sudden or unexpected movements. Let's try a few ...."

Equuleus made a sharp left turn, Heart leaned hard to the right.

"You must not do that," Equuleus said. "You're behaving like a separate body, but you're not. You and I are one. Picture yourself as a part of my body. If one part of me turns left, all of me turns left."

"I understand, Equuleus. I will do it. Try again!"

For the next hour, Equuleus flew high and flew low, making sharp and unexpected turns, and Heart rapidly became more intuitive about his movements. "I feel you now. I know what you're going to do."

"Excellent! Now to advanced moves."

"There's more?"

"Indeed, there's much more." Without warning, Equuleus folded his wings, plunging from the top of the tent almost to the floor. Heart let out a yell as the ground rose rapidly toward them. She felt her body separate from Equuleus. If not for the pins, she would have flown off.

Heart's indignation was only exceeded by her embarrassment at having yelled. She was even less amused by the chuckling observers.

"You might have warned me!"

"If I'm in the midst of life-saving maneuvers, I'll not be able to call out the moves."

"Lifesaving maneuvers—"

"Yes. Lifesaving maneuvers."

This information sobered Heart. "Oh … forward, then. Continue with the lifesaving maneuvers."

Neither of them seemed to tire as Equuleus engaged in ever-more intricate patterns, including flying upside down for two circuits of the tent.

"And what is the point of flying upside down?" Heart asked, her arms wrapped around Equuleus's neck.

"To save you. Always to save you. If you get injured, I can do little to repair you, but if I get injured, there are better odds that you can repair me."

"Very practical," she said, with a sigh of relief when he righted himself. "But I still prefer heads up."

"Me too!"

After a while, Heart noticed that the only watchers were the Wondermen, standing on either side of the entryway like sentries.

"It looks like we wore everyone out, just watching us."

"They all have things to do. But you're right, none of them are made like we are, Heart. Not even Swen or Key Man."

Heart and Equuleus continued to practice numerous flighted maneuvers for several hours. Finally, they came to the ground and both stretched out on the grass to silently commune.

But before they even relaxed, the tent flap unzipped and Peter stepped in. "I'm glad to see you on terra firma. It's time to go inside. The museum will open before long."

"How secure do you feel on Equuleus' back?" Peter asked as they walked into the museum.

"Completely secure. Like I've always been there. Like it's where I belong."

"That's exactly what I hoped to hear, dear Heart."

If that was what he wanted to hear, Heart wondered, why was there such a great sadness in his voice?

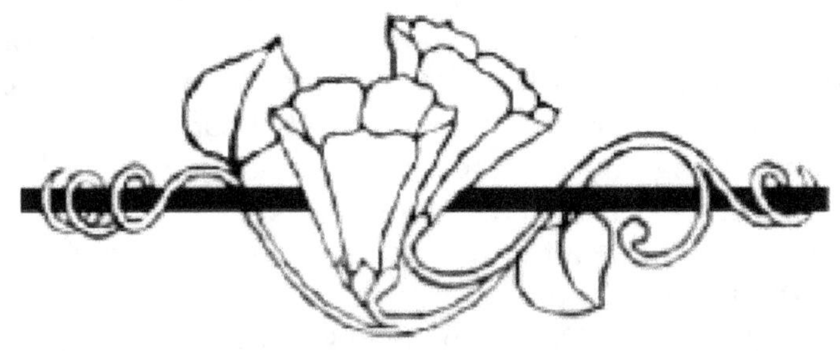

Chapter 19

"**I** *think you ought to read Ourbook,*" *Jackson said.*
"*Why?*" *Heart asked.*
"*It has important information.*"
"*I don't want to read it. I've got enough to think about.*"

Heart jerked up out of her little bed, turned on the light and looked around. No Jackson. *Of course not!* It was a dream, but so strange, so real. As if Jackson was right here, in front of her. She could even see the green flecks in his dark brown eyes.

Agitated, she paced up and down her little room, which, only being four strides, soon frustrated her even more. She sat on the edge of the bed contemplating the plaid of her sleeve, a bit surprised at the same time that she'd not needed to contemplate a plaid to find her way out of irritation since arriving in The Museum of Scientific Improbabilities and Unpredictable Oddities. Until this moment.

And another weird thing—contemplating the plaid because of her frustration over the appearance of Jackson didn't help one little bit! She needed to move. She jumped up and left her room, closing the door behind her.

Standing in the middle of the Recent & New Acquisitions to the Antiquities Clockwork Collection Room, she studied the maze of clockworks around her. What had she in mind? Perambulating among these delicate broken and half-repaired works of art in her agitation? No.

Step outside, although it was mid-afternoon and potentially hundreds of people might see her? No. Having to shapeshift into the wall would not allow her to sort out her agitation. It'd only add to it. Standing in the middle of the room, among the faint illumination from several passive, dark matter lights, she asked herself why she felt so disconcertingly unsettled by Jackson's dream advice to read *Ourbook*.

She didn't want to. But she did, deep down, suspect that the phantom Jackson was right. She wondered if she ought to have been reading it all along. If that were true, wouldn't everyone around her have been trying to get her to read it? No one even suggested it.

She'd noticed that everyone seemed to have a different idea about what was relevant in the book. Heart had less than zero interest in entering into the fray of argument over things she knew nothing about.

Was she upset by having someone—even in a dream—tell her what to do when she could figure out such things for herself, thank you very much! No. That didn't seem logical. People—real people! not figures in dreams—had been telling her what to do right and left over the past few days and she'd happily gone along with everything.

All this thinking, and she still felt as agitated as when she woke up. Why did Jackson's comment cause her this much distress?

But wait! She had an insight. It wasn't what Jackson said that irritated her. It was Jackson. Himself. His presence—his appearance—had irritated the sleep right out of her. Why? Yes, he'd been rude and pushy and exasperating in person, but that was all about his single-minded focus on making sure she got to her destination.

Quite frankly, she thought, he was really not much different from her. She had single-mindedly driven herself to her present circumstances. So what was it about him ....

There was a scrabbling at the door. She paused in her silent argument with herself, listening closely. More scrabbling then a click and a whir.

Someone had a key, and it was not Key Man!

Not only was Key Man at work in the far wing, but even if he'd come around to grab some tool he needed, he'd never scrabble at the door. He'd unlock and open it smoothly.

The door opened a crack. Heart stepped back to the little carousel and watched as the door opened just enough to let a tiny person into the room, then close the door.

As Heart shapeshifted into the carousel, the diminutive woman moved aggressively to the center of the room, which movement turned on the bright overhead lights, transforming all the lumbering shadows of clockwork forms into their cohesive shapes.

She moved around the room, touching this, looking at that, her movements jerky and jutting. It reminded Heart of something, and then it came to mind—she was like an insect, a wasp, poking and peering. Her wee little feet, jammed into ridiculously tall shoes with tiny pointed heels and tiny pointed toes, clicking rapidly across the floor added to the effect.

What was she looking for? Heart still only had a view of her back, Her orange-ish frizzy hair sticking out around a stylish and expensive dark blue hat did not improve the hat in the least, while the hat was entirely at a loss to improve the appearance of the hair.

She wore a blue suit from which knobby, too-skinny legs and ropey, angular forearms protruded. Finally, she came around one of the clockworks near Heart, and Heart could finally see her face. Her first thought was that it was about the homeliest woman she'd ever seen in her life.

Her second thought almost caused her to fall out of shapeshift.

The woman before her was not in the least a woman. It was Keeper B! Heart could never mistake that nasty face. Here. With a key. In the Recent & New Acquisitions to the Antiquities Clockwork Collection. Touching everything. Heart wanted to shudder.

Keeper B went to Key Man's work table and began to touch everything there as well. Heart realized he was trying to figure out how to turn on the 3-D. She wanted to scream at her—at him—at it.

Then she heard a key slide into the door. Key Man! Heart heard him hesitate. Of course, because the door was unlocked. As she watched, Keeper B took a ring that belonged to a tiny clockwork dancer Key Man was rebuilding. Heart had noticed the dancer's charming little rings, six altogether, each set with a different precious stone. Keeper B put the tiny ring on the end of his itsy-bitsy little finger. It went down to the first joint. As the door opened, Keeper B turned to it, putting on a fake smile, his too-small teeth lined up like small grayish bits of chalk.

Heart waited for the explosion of anger from Key Man as he entered and looked around. But the anger did not come. Instead, he smiled at Keeper B. "Ah, clever, naughty girl, breaking into a locked room." He moved over to his work table, giving it a glance. Heart was amazed that he didn't see that the freakish trespasser had stolen the ring right off his table.

Keeper B looked down at Key Man. "I knew you wouldn't mind, given how fascinated I am in the clockworks. And how much I admire your stellar talents in reconstructing them."

"Why, thank you, Miss Madigan. You're too kind, I'm sure." Key Man poked around on his work surface. "I have something here I was going to give you the next time I saw you. Let me see, where did I put it. Ah, here! Look, blue and yellow, perfect with your outfit." He handed her a beautiful blue and yellow glass and silver antique brooch.

"Oh, you pin it on for me, Pookie." Keeper B leaned down.

Pookie?! *Blaugh!* Heart wanted to squirm.

"All right." Key Man reached up and discretely pinned the brooch on the collar of the suit.

"Such a gentleman," Keeper B exclaimed in her ridiculous imitation of a woman's voice.

"Always," Key Man replied, reaching up to take her elbow and lead her out of the room. "Let's see what's going on in the observatory, shall we? I believe there are some delightful festivities in motion ...." He closed the door and the lights shut off. Heart heard the key inserted, and the lock click and whir into place.

She pulled herself from the carousel, at first furious, then hurt, then frightened, and back to fury again. Her irritation over a phantom appearance of Jackson was nothing—*nothing!*—to what she felt now.

Key Man—*a traitor!* Here she slept in his very domain, she'd trusted him with her life, with Equuleus' life, with Swen's life. And he was fraternizing with Keeper B!

Furthermore, not only was he a traitor, but he wasn't very smart if he didn't see through Keeper B's unpleasant disguise.

And—*ugh!*—what was there to be attracted to? Goodness, Keeper B made a singularly ugly woman, by anyone's standards. Just those ropy calves and forearms alone were … *ick!* She didn't want to think about it. Anyway, she had to concentrate on what to do now.

It was all the last straw. She was through. The first chance she saw that she could get on Equuleus and get out, she would get out!

But what about Swen? He spent all his time, now, with Key Man. Maybe Swen was a part of the problem. Under the circumstances, she decided, she could not trust Swen. His claim to having bonded with her, when they were in The Periphery flashed through her mind. But it looked like now he'd bonded with Key Man instead. Apparently, his mechanical part dominated his bio-dog part.

She couldn't think about it. More losses! More sadness! Now it was just herself and Equuleus. Not that she had him until they escaped.

He might not go with her either.

Oh! It had all become too unbearable. In but a few moments, everything fell apart. She went into her room, locked the door from the inside, leaving the key in the lock, which she hoped kept it from being unlocked from the outside. But to be sure, she moved all the furniture in the room, including the bed, in front of the door.

The only being she'd be willing to open her door to would be Equuleus, and he could not fit through the outside door, let alone the little door to her little room.

She sent Equuleus a picture of them leaving the museum, with the idea that details would develop when they were together.

She thought she'd never sleep again, and was surprised when she awakened to tapping at her little door.

"Heart," Martha said softly, "are you awake? We have a lot of work yet to do. And … there's a lovely surprise for you."

More surprises she did not need. Her anger and fear welled up again as she tried to figure out what she'd do in the worst scenario, that being that she opened the door and they all pounced on her and sent her back to The Darling Undesirables Residence of Long Prairie—or maybe even worse. Whatever that might be. Maybe trading her to the Purists.

Martha kept chirping away at her to open the door until Heart thought she would lose what remained of her sanity. She could see them all standing there, letting Martha do the talking.

"I'm not coming out tonight."

She heard a sputter from Peter.

"*Shh!*" Martha said. "But why, Heart? Why won't you come out?"

"You know. And if you don't know, ask Key Man."

"I know what you're thinking, my dear Heart," Key Man answered, "but you're wrong."

She'd always loved to hear him call her his "dear Heart," but now it only caused her pain and fury.

"I'm not your 'dear Heart.'"

There was a bit of shuffling on the other side of the wall, then Martha said, "Oh no, don't do that. It won't help matters."

"I will if I have to," a new voice growled. "Come on now Heart, you're either coming out, or I'm coming in, but we absolutely cannot waste any more time on your princess histrionics."

Jackson!

Oh! Now she was mad. Or something. Maybe—glad. No, that didn't seem right.

She didn't know what she felt.

She began to move the furniture away from the door. Slowly she unlocked it and opened it a crack. Jackson's hand reached in and grabbed her wrist before she even saw it. In a flash, he was in the room, pinning her arms to her sides, looking down at her with those dark brown, green-flecked eyes that she'd seen only a few hours before in a dream.

"What's the matter with you?" he asked in a terrible voice.

"It's great to see you again, too!" She struggled to free herself. "It's not necessary to truss me up, I'm not going anywhere."

He relaxed his hold on her but didn't release her. He looked around the disarrayed room. "Nice job of decorating."

"*Do! Be! Quiet!*" She pulled away from him and he let her move across the room. The others, including Swen, slipped in through the partially open door.

She gave Martha a look filled with frustration and waved at Jackson. "This is the 'lovely surprise?' Where did you get such an idea?"

Martha looked truly wounded. "When you first came through the tunnel, you seemed distressed when he didn't come through, too!"

"You were?" Jackson asked.

"No. Yes. I mean, you said you were coming, and then you didn't. Like everyone and everything around here. Someone says something, but it's not true. You're told that things are one way, but they're quite a lot some other way."

"Sit down, Heart," Key Man said. "In fact, let's all sit down and sort this muddle out."

"As if I'm to trust you to 'sorta muddle out,' when in fact, you'll fabricate a story that makes you look completely innocent, no doubt."

"No doubt," Key Man agreed. "I know you're angry with me for appearing to fraternize with that bizarre piece of work, the so-called Miss Madigan."

"I am. You don't even know who that person is."

"I do know who that person is."

"You do not!"

"That 'person,'" Key Man said, holding Heart's gaze, "is Keeper B, of The Darling Undesirables Residence of Long Prairie. That person is not a woman, thank goodness, as I think we'd all agree that he makes the ugliest woman one would ever hope not to see."

"Precisely what I said to myself!" Heart exclaimed. "You knew? This afternoon, you knew it was Keeper B?"

"I've known since the first time he stepped foot in The Museum of Scientific Improbabilities and Unpredictable Oddities, several years ago. That is to say, I did a careful check on him and discovered his true identity after the very first thing he stole. He is also Marchand Matthews, your news reporting nemesis."

"*Really!?*" Heart exclaimed.

"Really. But we mustn't go into that right now. It's a story all by itself and we don't have time for it.

"Getting back to today, I knew he'd broken in. My wrist implant showed me his every move. Remember, if anyone gets near you, a holo manifests. I let him prowl around—I wanted to see what he was looking for. I saw you shapeshift onto the carousel. Excellent job, by the way. Keeper B didn't have the least suspicion you were there."

"That's good," Heart said.

"When he got a bit too close to accessing my 3-D, I came in. I haven't figured out yet how he got a key, but everything else, I'm pretty clear on.

"Keeper B is a Purist. He's a spy for the Purists, devoted to their cause."

"I suppose Keeper A is a spy for the Purists, too."

"No, Heart, she's not. She's a tough Keeper, I won't argue that. But she truly means to have the Darling Undesirables well cared for. She sometimes does a lousy job of it, however, because, unfortunately, she doesn't understand children. Other than that, she's excellent at running an institution."

"Understanding children would seem to be an important part of the job," Heart said, unable to contain her sarcasm.

"You'd think, but not necessarily so. She does her best to hire people she can handle, who are tolerable Keepers. But she tends to hire people like herself, unfortunately. A bit cold and overly pragmatic."

"As if abusing Eye to hurt me is pragmatic."

"In her thinking, yes."

"And Keeper B?"

"Keeper B got in like he always gets in everywhere, by relentless pushiness, and a cleverness often mistaken for intelligence. Of course, it's not."

"No, it's not. It's sheer, ugly meanness."

"No argument, Heart. But the important question of the moment is, do you believe me? With all that is about to transpire in our extremely near future, you must trust me. If you don't trust me … candidly, Heart, we can all end up dead."

"All end up dead!" Heart jumped up, but with everything and everyone in the room, there was nowhere to move. She sat back down again. "That's not a sentence I ever imagined hearing.

"But I must be honest and say, no, right at this moment, my trust in you, Key Man, has been damaged. I believe you knew 'Miss Madigan' was Keeper B, but that doesn't mean that you're not in cahoots with him. You might be a double spy. Why did you pin that beautiful brooch on his suit? Why would you give him something so beautiful, and not yours to give, if you knew who he was?"

"First of all, Heart, it was mine to give. I've been working on it for some while, expressly to give to him. Secondly … well, let's go to my workbench, so I can show you something."

They all exited Heart's room and lined up around Key Man's workbench. He turned on his 3-D.

Heart shuddered at the sight of Keeper A's pale green inner office.

"They're a bunch of idiots," she heard Keeper B say, clearly still wearing the antique pin. He turned to Keeper A, who sat behind her desk on her throne-like, green brocade wing-backed chair, in all her stunning glory.

"Now who are you droning on about?" Keeper A said, unmistakably bored to her toes.

"The Purists. A bunch of idiots. They're no help to us at all."

"Why should they be? They have their own agenda."

"Sure, sure," Keeper B said in a placating tone. "They have their own focus."

Key Man shut off the 3-D. "And on and on he'll continue, until Keeper A tells him to be quiet, or leave, or something else happens. I'll watch it later for relevant information, but most likely it'll be like everything else I've ever heard from him. Boring diatribe about subjects he doesn't care about, and, frankly, knows little about." Key Man waved and the room lights came on. "That's why I let him in—to give him the spy camera."

Heart glanced down at Key Man's work table to look at the five remaining rings of the clockwork dancer. There were six rings.

"Six rings!" she exclaimed.

"Yes. Six rings."

"But … how?"

"You think things get by me, Heart, but nothing gets by me. I saw the missing ring the moment I walked into the room. I knew it would fit only down to the first joint on Keeper B's scrawny little finger. As I walked him down the hall to the observatory, I took the ring back, without him having the least idea that I'd done so. He'll just think it fell off."

Heart sighed deeply, releasing everything she'd held, pent up, for the last several hours. "I trust you now," she said to Key Man, taking his hand.

"Thank you, my dear Heart. You are my dear Heart, yes?"

"Yes," she answered simply. "I am your dear Heart." Then she teased, "Keeper B called you 'Pookie.'"

"Don't remind me."

"Pookie!" Jackson scoffed. "Now that's damning!"

Heart's agitation over Jackson in her dream rose to the surface. "This whole event happened because of you. Because you came to me in a dream, and I never dream. I was sooo frustrated, I couldn't sleep, I couldn't relax. So I stepped out of my room, then Keeper B broke in …."

"That wasn't a dream, Heart. I was trying to get your attention."

"Why were you trying to get her attention?" Martha asked.

"He told me to read *Ourbook*."

"There'd be little point of that at this juncture. Why, Jackson? We need her to stay focused on the concerns at hand, not try to understand an ancient tome, when people who have spent their lives studying it can't agree on what it says."

"That's what I said to him—sort of—in the dream. Or whatever it was."

"I realized that," Jackson said. "Which is why I came across the wall. Martha has been trying to get me to come over, but I couldn't see how I could be helpful. However, with everything that's going on, and with how fast the prophecies are being fulfilled, I decided I might be more useful with you here than over there."

"How's Molly?" Heart asked.

"'How's Molly?' All you have to say is 'how's Molly?'"

"Yes."

Jackson shook his head in disbelief. "The last I knew, Molly was fine."

"Good."

There was a knock at the outside door. Everyone fell silent.

Heart cocked her head towards the door. "Equuleus," she said. "Wondering what we're all up to."

They filed out into the hall. "Sorry, my friend," Key Man said, patting Equuleus's muzzle." A bit of a glitch that needed smoothing out."

"Do you know Jackson?" Heart asked, smoothly jumping up onto Equuleus' back.

"I know of him," Equuleus told her, looking Jackson up and down.

"Equuleus knows of you, Jackson," Heart said. "I guess your reputation precedes you."

Jackson gave Equuleus a small bow. "It means more than I can say to meet you in a conscious state, Equuleus. The first time I saw you was when I was a small child, with a group of school children. Before I was sent to The Periphery. Like so many children, I was mesmerized by you in your showcase. It's breathtaking to see you in motion."

"Wait until you see them fly," Peter said proudly as if it was his own accomplishment. "It'll take your breath away. Why don't you go with them to the tent and oversee their maneuvers? That'll be helpful as the three of us have much work to do."

"Excellent," Jackson agreed.

Equuleus, Heart, and Jackson turned down the far hallway, heading for the tent. Heart looked back over her shoulder at Swen, wondering if he would come with them. She watched as he stopped at the apex of the halls, looking after Martha, Peter and Key Man, and then take a longing look after Equuleus, Jackson and herself.

But in the end, he turned and followed Key Man. To Heart, it felt like the final time he would be torn. She felt it, a hard, sad loss, in the center of her chest.

Chapter 20

Heart and Equuleus worked on perfecting their moves through much of the night. Heart couldn't understand her strange urge to show off in front of Jackson. She'd never felt an emotion like this. She didn't like it. It seemed petty, but she just couldn't help herself.

Then, even worse, she injured herself, dismounting in a flurry of showing off before the pins had fully retracted.

"Oh, no!" she whispered as she fell to her knees.

"What did you do?" Equuleus asked.

"I don't know." She looked down at her thigh and was surprised to see actual blood, soaking into her beautiful plaid leggings.

Jackson rushed up to her. "What were you thinking? Even I could see the pins weren't retracted," he yelled.

Heart said nothing. Not only had she never seen her blood in her entire life, but from what everyone had said about her "components," she didn't even know she had blood.

She looked up into his angry face, then back at her thigh, feeling weak at the sight of the blood. "What have I done?" she whispered faintly.

Jackson quickly knelt at her side. "This can't be good." He picked her up and carried her to the tent flap.

Who would know how to fix her, she wondered. Key Man? His field was mechanical parts. This was clearly not mechanical. She was shocked when the Wondermen, rather than opening the door as was their job, blocked their passage.

"Not to leave, Heart and Jackson," they said.

"But, Wondermen, I've injured myself. I must get help."

"We heal."

"You—heal?" Jackson asked, incredulous.

"Yes." The Wonderman gestured to Jackson to lay Heart on the ground.

She studied the confused expression on Jackson's face. She could never have imagined Jackson would come to any point in his life where he was unsure about what to do.

"Put me down. Let's see what they do. We can't get out anyway."

Jackson nodded, then gently laid Heart on the soft grass. Even this gentle movement caused stabs of pain to radiate from her thigh throughout her body. Awful, but also, fascinating. She'd never experienced physical pain.

Wonderman One opened his chest cavity and pulled out a small wand-like device. An intense blue light came on when he turned it end for end. Then he waved the light over Heart's wound. The blood stopped flowing, and the blood that soaked her leggings dried up instantly. "Part one, stop further damage."

Then Wonderman Two pulled a wand from his chest, turned it end for end and a lavender light came on. He waved it over Heart's wound. The pain ceased immediately, and the dried blood on her leg and even on her leggings flaked off, leaving not a trace of the injury. "Part two, repair damage," Wonderman Two said.

"No more riding tonight," they said together. "Rest and rebuild injured area."

Heart and Jackson looked at the Wondermen, speechless, in awe.

"Good job, Wondermen!" Jackson finally said when he stopped gaping.

"Thank you," Heart said in a small and ashamed voice. She felt deeply grateful. And humble. She'd just learned perhaps the greatest lesson of all. She must keep her mind focused. She must not allow herself to be distracted by an attractive man.

An attractive man? Is that what she thought, she wondered. Is that what distracted her? Made her show off? And the frustration in the middle of the night when Jackson interrupted her sleep—was it because she found him … attractive?

At that moment, Peter burst through the tent flap and almost tripped over all of them, bent over Heart.

"What happened?" He cried, distressed.

"Small injury," Wonderman Two said.

"We healed," Wonderman One said.

"What did you do, Heart? How could you injure yourself?"

"I dismounted before the pins were fully retracted."

"Why would you do that?"

"Distracted. Don't worry, I learned my lesson. I must keep my focus at all times."

"More now than ever. The Purists are on the move. Fortunately, Keeper B wears that brooch everywhere. We're working furiously on a device that will neutralize their bomb, but we must all be in standby mode. How are your math skills, Jackson?"

"Spotty."

"Good enough. Come with me. Wondermen, I need you, too. We have to do some mighty fast inventing. Heart, Equuleus, take a break and recharge."

They left in a flurry, Equuleus standing over Heart, still sitting on the grass.

"What do you think?" Heart asked.

"I think the time has come to fulfill our destiny. And so, we must relax." He lay down beside her, and she moved over to cuddle up next to his side.

"You're surprisingly warm and comfortable, given that you're all gears and metal."

"It's not about gears and metal, dear Heart. It's about love and affection. That's what one really feels when close to someone they love."

"I believe you're right." She closed her eyes. "What do you suppose is about to happen?"

"The greatest adventure of our lives."

"What do you think of Jackson?"

"What do I think of Jackson?"

"Ummm …."

"Smart. Brave. Hot-tempered. Devoted."

"Yes. Is he attractive?"

"Attractive? Let's see, fine skeletal structure. Well-developed muscles, symmetrical face. Clear, intelligent eyes. Honest mouth. Yes, I'd say he's a beautiful specimen of the human figure."

"Well, I didn't ask if he was beautiful. I just wanted to understand if he seemed attractive."

"What do you think, Heart?"

"Oh … I agree with you, nice form. I particularly like what you say about his eyes and mouth."

They fell into silence. Heart felt unusually worn out with all the emotional and physical upheaval of the last few hours. Soon, curled up next to Equuleus, she fell into a deep asleep.

*   *

Equuleus stirred and Heart woke up. Something was happening, she could feel it.

"The time has arrived." Equuleus stood. Heart stood too. They went through the tent flap. Just as they came to the museum door, it opened to Martha and Jackson on the other side.

"The Purists have arrived," Martha said softly, her round, sweet face somber.

"With their device to destroy Pink—and Father Inventor?"

"Yes," Jackson said.

"The single most important thing that has happened at this moment is Jackson coming to this side when he did. With his mathematical genius …." Martha began.

"Oh, now, that's overstating it," Jackson protested.

"I'm not overstating it! Because of his mathematical genius, the five of them, Peter, Key Man the Wondermen and Jackson—have come up with a counter invention to the Reverse Dark Energy bomb. It appears to work. In a 3-D model, that is. But we can only know if it'll work in the real world by trying it." They all hurried down the hall. "And we must be prepared to do so very soon."

Jackson stopped and turned Heart to face him. "This band of—whatever you'd call them—are perfectly willing to sacrifice you. But I'm telling you, Heart, you do not have to do this."

"Do what, exactly? Could someone at least tell me that?"

Martha came back to her. "We need you to fly into the Mechanical Aurora Borealis on Equuleus, to release the device Peter and Jackson developed, which will neutralize the Reverse Dark Energy bomb.

"Once you are in the Mechanical Aurora Borealis, you will be carried to Pink. And your dream of living a life of peace will come true."

"Just … right now? Right now I'm to leave and not look back? What about Eye?"

"We'll have to consider that later. We'd hoped to have time to work it out before you left. But, now, there's no time …."

Heart heard shouting outside. How many people there must be, to be able to hear their angry, frightening voices deep within the shelter of The Museum of Scientific Improbabilities and Unpredictable Oddities!

"Jackson is right. You don't have to do it, Heart," Martha said.

Heart looked at her, praying for anything that resembled choice. "What will happen if I don't?"

"There is an extremely high probability that The Purists' device will be successful because they've figured out that the Mechanical Aurora Borealis is a direct channel to Pink and to Father Inventor.

"Further, we've kept from you the intensity with which the whole world has been looking for you. You will not be safe here. Nor will Equuleus, because the connection between the two of you is all over the news. Of course, our lives will be as good as over as well.

"If they destroy the Mechanical Aurora Borealis, this building is just a building, they'll destroy it in quick order, given that it's filled with precious inventions that they hate. As you know, we'll all go down defending it.

"The Mechanical Aurora makes The Museum of Scientific Improbabilities and Unpredictable Oddities impenetrable, which the Purists out there don't even know, as they've never gathered enough force to try to storm it.

"But if you successfully detonate the neutralizing device, the museum will be saved as the neutralizing will become a permanent part of the Aurora."

"But I might fail, or the device might fail …."

"Yes. Those are possibilities."

"Come with me back to The Periphery," Jackson pled. "They ask too much of a girl."

"Jackson," Martha had a reprimand in her voice Heart had never heard from the sweet woman, "you know *Ourbook*. You know it's a girl that saves Father Inventor and his works. If she is successful."

"If she's successful. *Ourbook* is not clear on the outcome."

"Such is the way with free will and fate," Martha answered.

Heart turned to Equuleus. She put her forehead to his forehead. "What do you think? What do you feel?"

"Father Inventor gave me my life. It's a privilege to protect him. Other thoughts are superfluous."

She turned to Jackson and Martha. "He's very clear. There's only one choice, I don't know why I even hesitate. We must do what we were made to do, and that is to save our father if we can. This is my family, isn't it? Father Inventor and Equuleus. Why are we wasting time?"

Heart jumped onto Equuleus and for the first and only time, he ran on the marble floors of The Museum of Scientific Improbabilities and Unpredictable Oddities.

Chapter 21

At the front of the museum stood Key Man, Peter and the two Wondermen. They were but a tiny band of protectors against the horror developing outside, which they watched in consternation on the 3-D.

As Heart and Equuleus approached Key Man and Peter, she watched them study her with mixed expressions of relief and anxiety. Between them was a soft-looking form draped in velvety, multi-colored material.

"Did Martha explain …?" Peter asked.

"She did. And, before you waste time on more questions, Equuleus and I know our destiny—to save our father, if we can."

A terrible crash clanged against the door. On the 3-D they could see that the Purists had a battering ram, smashing it into the door.

"Well, there's a waste of energy and time," Peter said. Even though Heart had been told the museum was protected by the Aurora, she was surprised to see that the huge battering ram didn't even dent the filigree or break one bit of glass.

"That's got to be a surprise," Jackson said. "It'll cool their heels. Maybe they'll give up."

"No," Key Man said, it will only make them angrier."

It appeared he was right, as several hundred more joined their ranks, furious and shouting.

A gigantic, heavy, hovering craft came slowly to the front of the museum. The Purists swarmed over the craft when it landed, everyone clearly knowing what to do.

This event had been rehearsed.

A tarp flew off the object on the flatbed, revealing a huge, terrifying, spiked object.

"*What … is … that?*" Heart asked, knowing the answer.

"I'm sorry you had to see it, Heart. But understand that a large part of the Purists' method is drama. The actual component that is the reverse dark energy bomb is the size of your fist, inside that ridiculous monster. But that part, I will not lie, is something to fear.

"Be brave, dear Heart. Let us prepare."

Peter and Key Man, with a reluctant Jackson, positioned the velvet-covered container they had constructed, under Equuleus. It fit neatly under him and seemed to weigh very little.

Peter handed her a small button. "All you have to do is push this button when it glows pink. It will be an extremely vibrant glow, you will not miss it. When the button glows pink, that means the reverse dark energy bomb is within range, and you can destroy it. You will release the neutralizing force. The bomb will become inert and fall, so much metal and nothing else, back to Earth.

"Then you'll be propelled through the Mechanical Aurora Borealis to Pink. When you reach her weak atmosphere, we'll know you've arrived by a lavender blossom of light as you and Equuleus enter her atmosphere."

Heart held tightly to the button, then she raised her eyes to look around her. All the clockworks had gathered in the foyer and surrounded her! Key Man had energized each and every one of them, and they waited with vibrant anticipation for the flight of their peer, Equuleus, and Heart, their most adored Darling Undesirable.

She felt such compassion from every single being around her, regardless of their composition, that she feared she may shed more impossible tears.

Peter reached up and gave her an awkward hug.

"Release," she said, and the pins pulled in from her thighs. She slid off Equuleus and hugged Peter back, giving him the wink she had practiced and practiced, almost as much as she'd practiced flying.

He winked back, but around tears he did not try to hide.

Martha rushed up to her and gave her a big hug, forcing her face into all its sweet round smile with her little crescent moon eyes.

Key Man took her hand, and kissed her fingers. She put her arms around him, hugging him tightly, which he returned, wordlessly.

When she reluctantly pulled away, she looked about frantically for Swen. How could she ever say good-by to her protector, her dear friend? But he was no where in sight. Was it possible he wouldn't be here now, at this moment? She dared not waste another second.

Then, she saw him, behind Equuleus' empty showcase, head hanging as hangdog as ever she had seen him. She hurried to him, kneeled on the floor, flinging her arms around his neck and burying her face in his fur.

"I love you, my best friend and valiant protector. I love you, dearly!" She could feel his head nodding, but he could not say a word.

She leapt up. "Send me images!" She called back to Swen.

With a flying leap, she landed squarely on Equuleus' back, the pins reinserted into her thighs. She was ready to fly.

Jackson stepped away from making the last check on the device suspended under Equuleus. "It's all in your hands now, strange girl!" He reached up to hand her the button, and, as she leaned over to take it, he put his arm around her shoulders, reaching up to kiss her cheek. Much to her own surprise, she turned her face and kissed him on his irritating and sweet mouth.

His surprise mirrored her own, as Key Man threw switches that opened the rotunda to the Mechanical Aurora Borealis.

A universal gasp went up from both inside and outside the museum. The aurora shifted into a gigantic lavender arch, with a clear golden path below. Equuleus took two steps, then, extending his wings, flew up through the rotunda and into the golden aurora path. Immediately, Heart felt the tug she'd felt when first she came to The Museum of Scientific Improbabilities and Unpredictable Oddities.

Glorious! Glorious! The sensation of being pulled forward, and flying in an element that was home for both herself and Equuleus.

"*Glorious!*" she sang, the music of Equuleus' gears coming into full force. "Glorious," she sang back down into the rotunda to her friends rapidly becoming so small she could not distinguish them.

So enthralled by the flight, by the aurora pouring lavender and gold around her that she forgot, for the moment, the assignment at hand.

But finally she heard Equuleus through her rapture. "The button, Heart, the button."

That's when she noticed the pink glow in her hand, and a dark spot in the Aurora below, growing rapidly toward them.

She closed her eyes and pushed the button. Equuleus buoyed up as the weight of the velvet encased device beneath him released.

She gathered her courage, and looked down. A translucent purple projectile curved around and down, around and down the edges of the aurora as if riding the banister of a winding stairway, while the black spot grew into an expanding hole in the middle of the aurora. Heart felt herself grow weak, and it seemed Equuleus was losing altitude.

Are we all right?
Doesn't feel like it.
My fault?
Doesn't matter. Keep focus.
What should I focus on?
Going up. Not down.
Yes. Up. Up. Up.

Heart continued to picture flying up into the beautiful Aurora, yet it became weak and more and more translucent.

LOOK! Equuleus tilted sideways and they both watched the projectile they dropped contact the growing black hole, and disappear.

Nothing happened other than the hole continued to grow rapidly towards them. Equuleus flew around the aurora, trying to gain altitude, but failing. Heart couldn't tell if they were sinking toward the hole or if it was coming at them, or both. Little matter, she could almost feel its blackness licking at Equuleus' heels. Guilt and rage overcame her.

"NO!" She yelled with a volume beyond any she had ever heard issue from her lungs.

At that moment, a brilliant lavender light cracked open the black hole. The hole tried to continue to climb, but rapidly lost altitude. A delayed repercussion knocked Equuleus and Heart to the edges of the Aurora, then sent them zinging back and forth within it. Equuleus tried valiantly to maintain his flight around the edge of the Aurora, but Heart could see that his right wing had been damaged.

You're injured.
Jammed, is more like it.

He pulled his left wing in to match the restricted extension of his right wing. His flight evened out, but he could not gain altitude.

Suddenly the turmoil below stilled. A remarkable lavender bubble rose up from the mayhem and popped right around them, enclosing them in its beauty. It continued to rise like a bubble caught on a breeze, up and up inside the Mechanical Aurora Borealis.

They rose further and further, with beautiful little Pink above, and lovely Earth home below. Out here, through the Aurora, Heart could see the other moons, Yellow in the near distance, and the two little Blues, far away, in the sky of the southern hemisphere.

Heart relaxed, Equuleus relaxed. In silent communion, they delighted in the wondrous universe around them, pulsing with dark energy and dark matter.

Eventually—Heart had no idea how long it took— Pink filled their field of vision. The little moon was as pink and delightful close up as it was from a distance. There appeared to be no vegetation, but small hills and valleys made the terrain interesting.

And then the tug of the gravity of the sphere took over, and Equuleus flew around in the lavender bubble, preparing for touching down. As his feet touched the surface of the moon, the giant lavender bubble protecting them burst, and Heart was certain that she heard a cheer rise up.

Did you hear that?

Yes. It seems our friends were watching our arrival.

They must have planted an audio receptor on us so we could hear them—so we would know we are not alone.

So it seems.

Chapter 22

All Heart saw when she looked around were rolling hills with a pinkish hue. She and Equuleus wandered for hours—or perhaps it was days. She wasn't sure, as there was no way to tell time, or even sense it. The thought that they had no supplies of any sort began to weigh heavily upon her, and she came to the conclusion that the two of them would expire, or slowly grind to a stop, out here, alone, on Pink.

At that very moment, on the horizon, Heart saw a fabulous, glowing, lavender castle.

No one had ever mentioned this structure on Pink. Heart suspected it was because no one knew it existed. It sat on the edge of the far side of the moon, the part that never rotated to Earth's visibility.

"This must be Father Inventor's home. Why hasn't he come to greet us?"

Equuleus kept silent, but Heart felt his tension growing as they approached. She felt ill-at-ease as the castle loomed larger and larger. Everything about it was unnaturally still.

Heart slid off Equuleus when they came to the front door. Cautiously, she knocked on the door. It slowly swung open.

"Come in, come in!" She heard from all around.

She hesitated, but Equuleus pushed past her and stepped inside. Heart decided she had little choice but to follow. As she came fully into the great entrance, the door shut behind her with a solid slunk! accompanied by the whir of locks.

"Come along," the all around voice said pleasantly. "Please follow the lavender carpets."

Heart watched as Equuleus trotted forward on the plush lavender runners, down a long, brightly-lit, hall. She followed, but with hesitation.

At the end of the hall, a door stood open, and she watched as Equuleus hurried though it. What would cause him to behave so strangely?

She followed, her curiosity now outweighing her caution. As she stepped through the doorway, the door behind her closed softly with a soft sigh, like a lid sealing a jar. All around were gorgeous floor-to-ceiling mahogany shelves, every one filled with real books. She'd never seen anything like it! She fell instantly in love with the room.

"Wonderful, wonderful!" A short, portly, slightly balding, unassuming-appearing man stepped from a neighboring room and rushed up to Equuleus. "Equuleus, my beauty, how are you? How are you?"

Much to Heart's shock, the man threw his arms around the gear horse's neck and hugged him tightly. Even more surprising, Equuleus let him, when the only person besides herself she'd even seen Equuleus let touch him was Key Man.

But that shock paled when she saw tears spring from her beloved gear horse's eyes.

Then she heard Equuleus say, "I am well, Father, I am well. I'm … so … happy! I've missed you very, very much."

"And I, you, my beloved Equuleus."

Equuleus nodded toward Heart.

The man turned to her, took a few steps toward her, then stopped.

"Heart."

"Yes."

He extended his hand. "I'm Raymond Thompson."

"Mr. Thompson? Father Inventor?"

"Well, some say so, yes."

Heart didn't know what or who she had expected, but this nice, smiling—so-very-human—man was not a picture she'd ever had of Father Inventor.

He chuckled, reading her thoughts. "Tales of my impressiveness are greatly exaggerated. I agree."

He smiled at her with an endearing shyness.

Then he winked.

And everything was all right then. *Everything would be all right.*

"You … you are my father. My family."

"Yes Heart. And I must say, you've come to look so much like your mother, you fairly take my breath away. Let me show you."

He led Heart and Equuleus into the next room where a cozy fire played in the fireplace, while light sconces on the walls cast gentle golden dancing lights across the room.

Father Inventor walked up to the mantle. Heart followed him. He pushed a button. A 3-D image appeared of a stunningly beautiful young woman, dressed in old-fashioned clothing, a high collar with a brooch at her neck. She had a captivating, joyful smile in her eyes. It even seemed that a faint scent of roses came from the image.

"You see? See how like her you've become."

"Oh, no. I look nothing like that!" Heart couldn't believe he'd even suggest she had anything at all like the look of this wondrous woman.

"I disagree. Look here." He gestured to the mirror on the mantle.

Heart stepped back as she came to the mirror, as somehow, another woman had entered the room. She looked around.

There was no one.

She returned her gaze to the mirror. The reflection was even more golden and remarkable than the young woman who had greeted her in the Mystic's hearth mirror.

"*Oh! My!*" She whispered, then looked at Father Inventor, quizzically. "How I have changed!"

"You've always been beautiful, my darling daughter."

"*No!*" she exclaimed, stepping away from him. "You must not call me 'daughter.' I'm not bio. I can think of you as father because you've created many things, you are father to many inventions. But I cannot be your daughter, because I'm not bio."

"You are partially bio. But even if you weren't, you are still my daughter."

"I don't deserve to be called daughter. I'm pegged together with all these components that real people are not."

Father Inventor took her hand and led her to a large, golden velvet overstuffed sofa, gestured for her to sit, then sat beside her. "My precious girl, it's not what anyone is made of that makes them worthy. It's what they make of themselves that's important.

"No father has ever been more proud of a child than I've been of you. Following your heart. Not the physical one, but the one made of soul, intelligence, kindness, loyalty. You have the grandest heart as has ever been.

"And now that you're here—safely here—you can make anything of yourself you desire."

Heart looked away from him. "My greatest desire is to make a home with Eye."

Father Inventor sighed deeply, taking both of her hands in his. "Except that, my dearest. I'm sure you noticed all the doors sealing closed as your walked to this room. That's because I'm fully bio. I cannot live outside of the castle on my own little pink moon that I made. I'm all right with that, because, well, it's my life, and I made it.

"But we can't expect Eye, who is fully bio like me, to live in this way. It would be cruel and selfish to expect him to be captive in this building and never leave.

"You and Equuleus with your non-bio components, can range freely all over lovely Pink. Your life will be rich with experience—you'll discover many wonderful places to explore on our little moon home. I've developed so much here that no one on earth even knows about. I trusted one day you would come, with Equuleus. But no fully bio creature can live on Pink.

"Don't worry, dear Heart! We'll take care of Eye. We'll take care of all the darlings. Oh yes!" Father Inventor leapt up from the sofa, enthusiasm in his voice, in his step. "I know about your deepest desire, my sweet girl. To make it right for Eye. And I have many plans to make it right for him—and all the Darlings. But I need help. I simply cannot do everything without assistance. You won't mind assisting me, will you?"

"Of course not," Heart answered emphatically. "Of course I want to help you." Her mind raced through all she'd experienced, all she'd been called to do. The delusion that she'd taken her destiny into her own hands to be with Equuleus.

But all along, from the instant she stepped off the air bus at The Museum of Scientific Improbabilities and Unpredictable Oddities—maybe even before that—this future was unfolding. This moment, when she found herself far from the life she knew, and even the life she'd imagined. Impossibly far from Eye.

Yet, somehow she would be able, from this remote place, to make Eye's life all she'd ever dreamed of for him. Minus herself.

She would have to give up her own desires.

The pain she felt as she tried to imagine never again being with Eye cut deep.

But … she gazed around herself again, taking in, yet more fully, the beautiful, luxurious surroundings. The deep, rich wood. The gorgeous books, the dancing lights. Equuleus.

Her … *father!* There was much to love here.

And—Eye did have Butterfly. She knew Butterfly—intelligent, and intuitive—would never abandon Eye.

Heart looked up at Father Inventor, smiling warmly, affectionately, at her. She and her father would make a wonderful life for Eye—and for all the Darling Undesirables.

And that's all she had ever intended to do.

*　*

Later that evening, Heart stepped outside with Equuleus to look at Earth, like a giant moon in her sky, beautiful in radiant blues and greens. Though she had arrived at a place of peace with her life, she couldn't

help but wonder, with a lonely tug at her soul, what
Eye and Swen were doing at that very moment on the
glowing beautiful planet, so far, far away.

The End

Continue Heart's Adventure in the Twilight World of Pink in the next book, *Moons Rising*. Following are the opening pages ....

Before the Beginning

Keeper A kept her eyes on the 3-D projection of a brilliant lavender light jetting upward in the night sky. She leaned forward slightly, back ramrod straight, her perfectly manicured fingers curled around the arms of her enormous chair. The ceiling-tall metal shutters, locked tight, made her massive office even darker than the nearly moonless night.

As she watched, the brilliant light within the beam of the Aurora Borealis advanced faster and faster. A funnel of ballooning darkness appeared below, hurtling toward the glowing pastel light. Keeper A couldn't see what transpired inside the funnel when the darkness encountered the light, but she knew a fierce battle raged.

An explosion suddenly disrupted the funnel. She held her breath. As the dark smoke cleared, the brilliant lavender light burst through. Eventually, the horizon of the little satellite moon, Pink, filled the view of the 3-D projection. The bright lavender light landed on Pink's surface in a radiant bubble. She heard a faint cheer rise up, as if the very sound followed the enthralling light.

The door to Keeper A's office flung open, and a nervous, wiry, tiny man, dressed in a bright yellow body suit, came into her office. As he focused on getting to the desk in the room's darkness, he blurted out, "Did you see .....?"

"*Get out!*" Keeper A commanded in a low, dangerous voice.

The tiny man raised his eyes to the 3-D, watching the lavender bubble burst upon the surface of Pink. "*Oh! How* do you have this view on Pink before even the news bots?"

"*Get out!*" Keeper A's voice rose a notch.

"Right." The intruder retreated as he'd come, daring to glance again at the glowing lights above Keeper A, pulling the door shut with a solid thud as he exited.

"*Idiot!*" Keeper A whispered. She returned her attention to Heart, the runaway Darling Undesirable, secure upon her stunning, intrepid, winged clockworks horse, Equuleus, as they moved from the midst of the ballooning lavender light. Alive.

Instantly, the feed went black, the few minutes of her exorbitantly expensive space bot's near view of Pink, drained. She sat in the darkness, pegging together many bits of information that would have shocked almost everyone who knew her.

Chapter 1

Heart tried to adjust to the endlessly pink environment, to the profound stillness, to the lack of responsibilities. She tried to adjust to the eternal twilight, with no true daylight, no real night. But she missed her garden, her flowers. She missed her precious friend, Eye. If she just knew she'd see him again, she could endure anything. But what was the likelihood of that? It appeared she'd remain on this small moon forever, while Earth loomed overhead in the sky.

She loved Equuleus devotedly, and she came more and more to adore Father Inventor—*her father!*—but she'd never been so isolated. Coupled with nothing meaningful to do—such as care for crippled and broken children, as she'd done at the Darling Undesirables Facility at Long Prairie—began to wear on her.

She sat with these brooding thoughts, book open, staring out at the pink and lavender hills. Equuleus nuzzled her shoulder.

"Enough of this dark reflection, Heart. Let's explore!"

She reached up and patted him. "Explore? To find what? Pink upon pink—and then we'll find—more pink."

"You never know. We might find a flower, or—something."

"Or something."

"Well then, humor me. I need to stretch my wings."

Heart plopped the book without ceremony on the little mahogany side table. "Why didn't you say so? That's something else altogether. Let's go!"

She didn't bother to tell her father they were going out. He'd been relentlessly busy, rarely uttering a full sentence to her. He seemed unable to focus on her whenever she tried to talk with him. She feared he regretted bringing her here, and, politely as possible, ignored her.

Equuleus started off in a lazy canter after they exited through the double airlock of the front door.

"What about the wing stretching?" Heart asked.

"Ah, if it's flying you want, it's flying you shall have!" Equuleus broke into a full run and lifted off the pink terrain.

"*Yes!*" Heart's mood rose from the doldrums as they flew into Pink's sky. "This is exactly what I need!"

"*Me too!*" Equuleus banked and spun, pulled in his wings and dropped, then turned over and over in a series of cartwheels. Heart stuck like a burr.

Exhilarated, they finally came to the ground. Heart jumped off Equuleus and they wandered to a small hillock, sinking down to rest. She leaned against him, contemplating Earth overhead. "Do you ever … do you ever miss Earth? I mean, do you ever miss being on Earth?"

"For myself? Not really, Heart. Through you, yes, I feel it through you. But for myself, all I need is you, and I'm happy. And being here with Father …."

"Yes. But …" Heart paused.

"But what?"

"I feel he doesn't—it seems he wishes—I mean, he's always acting like he's impossibly busy. As if I'm …."

"No, Heart! You're not in his way. He loves you. But he's working diligently on something of great importance."

"You know about this?"

"Sort of."

Stunned, Heart sat up and faced Equuleus. "You know something I don't know? I didn't think you even *could* keep secrets from me."

"Ordinarily, I can't. But Father has needed to engage certain of my integrated bio dark matter components, that are unique to me. Although I'm aware of the project in general terms, I *cannot* tell you. He has it locked away from even my access."

"Oh! That doesn't sound right. Why would he hide things from us? From me? Why? If you're certain he's not regretting that I'm here …."

"He's not! What he's doing is for you. And for all the mechanical, clockwork, and bio beings."

"But, will you promise to tell me anything if you become aware of it?"

"I will, Heart."

"Hey!"

Heart and Equuleus leapt up from the ground.

"What was that?" Heart whispered.

"Hey!" a squeaky, high-pitched voice demanded, "under your feet."

Heart and Equuleus looked down, where, right between Heart's feet, the furry long ears of a lavender rabbit peeked from a rabbit hole.

"A *rabbit!"* Heart stepped back. "Where'd *you* come from?"

"I *live* here. A more relevant question would be, where did you come from?"

Heart pointed to the sky. "Earth," she said simply.

The little lavender rabbit looked skyward. "Earth! Ah … *soooooooo* beautiful! I love Earth. Truly, truly."

The little rabbit's hyperbole made Heart and Equuleus chuckle.

"Is there something funny about Earth?" the rabbit asked, indignant.

"No," Heart tried to stifle her giggle, but failed.

"Then logical extrapolation would only leave the probability that you're *laughing at me!"*

Equuleus snorted, the last straw for Heart, and she burst out in an unseemly guffaw. "No. Sorry. I mean, yes. Yes, we're laughing—not *at* you, just, you know, you're so cute! And so indignant, and—you're, *ahm,* well, you're a rabbit! We're charmed."

"Oh, well then," the rabbit's tone calmed, "that's all right." Her little lavender front paws appeared at the edge of the hole and she pulled herself out, brushing off a couple bits of pink with her long ears. She extended her paw to Heart, "I'm Violet. I'm very pleased to meet you, Heart."

Heart took the offered paw. "I'm delighted to meet you, as well, Violet. But—how do you know my name?"

"You two have been sitting over my head jabbering away …."

"True," Heart agreed.

"I'm not a dummy …."

"Clearly not! I imagine you're the smartest rabbit anywhere."

Violet bowed slightly. "Thank you. Much appreciated. Though I suspect on Earth there are other brilliant rabbits."

"Why would you say that?"

"It seems logical."

"Ah, well, though you may be right, I can tell you that from my experience, I've never seen another rabbit such as yourself."

Violet hung her head, her ears flopped forward, dramatizing her sadness.

"Oh dear, now what?" Heart asked.

"I know," Violet sat on the ground and crossed her furry, lavender legs, "I know I can be very contrary at times. Although it's lovely to hear I'm the most brilliant rabbit anywhere, it's also very sad to imagine I'm the *only* one."

Heart sat next to Violet, and Equuleus joined them. "I understand. I know what it's like to be one of a kind. It's the same for me."

Then Equuleus quietly whispered, "And the same for me, too, as long as we're making confessions."

"*Equuleus!*" Heart exclaimed, "I didn't know you were lonely …."

"Well, now that you've come into my life, I'm not. But, there *are* those times when one thinks, *ummmm*, it'd be glorious to fly with another winged gear horse."

"*Oh!*" Heart put her arm around his neck and hugged him.

"All those years in that showcase, waiting for you to come, Heart," Equuleus continued, "now and then I'd dream of flying with another creature such as myself."

"Well," Heart said softly, "That's a lovely dream, I trust you still have it."

"Mixed feelings. A poignant pleasure."

Violet hopped closer. "Yes. I have dreams of digging tunnels with other rabbits. Sometimes it seems so real. But when I wake up, this is my reality." She waved her paw about. "Don't get me wrong, I love my home—I love Pink. But those dreams of being with other rabbits …."

Heart patted Violet, nodding. "I have truly strange dreams—I can never fully remember them—of flying through the Universe, and feeling so, *so* un-alone."

They reflected upon their private dreams until Heart broke the spell. "But, we're not alone—we have each other!"

"*Yes!*" Violet hopped up and down. "We have each other."

A beeping sound issued from Equuleus.

"What's that?" Heart asked, frowning.

"Father installed a communication module on me." He paused, listening. "He's calling us back to the castle. That's what we get for not telling him we were leaving."

"We'd better go." Heart stood. "It's been wonderful meeting you, Violet. We'll come visit you now and then, if you'd like."

"*Like?* I await the moment. Time will drag without meaning until I hear your dulcet voices again," Violet's squeaky-sweet voice trilled.

Laughter overtook Heart and Equuleus again.

"Really!" Violet demanded. "*What. Is. So. Funny?*"

"Hmmm, it's hard to explain." Heart leaned down and gave Violet a big hug. "You're just so adorable!"

"Good enough, I guess. As long as you're not laughing at me. I have my pride, you know."

"Of course!" Heart jumped on Equuleus. "Good-bye, dear Violet, until we meet again!"

Equuleus took a running leap and left the surface of Pink, then he circled above Violet three times before heading back to the castle. Far below, Violet waved her paw and ears, calling after them something they couldn't hear in that comical little pontificating tone of voice, making them smile all the way to the castle.

Chapter 2

"Father's message says he has dinner waiting for us." Equuleus landed with a soft *"swoosh!"* at the front door.

"That's unusual."

"Rather."

As they entered the dining hall, Heart noticed the light from the wall sconces muted into a mellow gold. Two places on the side of the table near the fireplace were set with muted golden plates and cups and dinnerware.

Everything glowed in a mist of gold.

"*Oh! My!*" Heart sighed, drinking in the beauty.

The door behind them slid open and her father came up to them. "Do you like it?"

"It's stunning," Heart said. "What's the occasion? Ought I to have changed into something more formal?"

"No, dear Heart, not at all." Her father led her around to the two place settings. The fire crackled, adding its golden flowing light to the room.

He patted Equuleus on the forehead, who settled down in his place by the fire, relaxed but attentive. Then her father pulled a chair out for Heart. He sat beside her, then rang a little golden bell. A clockworks butler appeared from the kitchen, carrying serving dishes.

"Oh! Father, a clockworks friend, how lovely!" She turned to him. "Hello," she said as he dished up green beans for the two of them.

The butler didn't say anything.

Heart looked at her father, bemused.

"I'm sorry, Heart, he's only clockworks. He has no dark matter or bios."

"Oh!" Heart said, disappointed. "What a pity. I'm not used to clockworks that are only clockworks. But he seems to be quite intelligent, coming when you call, and gracefully serving us food."

"His computer program makes him quite clever in his specific duties, but he's limited beyond that."

"What's his name?"

"Why, I haven't named him," Father Inventor said, acting surprised. "I think you'll have to name him!"

"You've done that on purpose."

Her father smiled at her warmly. "Perhaps."

"So … *hmmm* … what's his name? Let … me … think."

The butler stopped and turned to look at Heart, his clockwork eyes making direct eye contact with her. A frisson rushed through her, and the strangely familiar look they exchanged stopped her breath. *"Ohhhh!"*

His gear eyes sparkled. He knows more than he's letting on, Heart thought. "I am going to name you, *HelperFriend*." She paused, feeling quite pleased with herself. "Yes, it's HelperFriend!"

The clockworks man's mechanical eyes twirled in a twinkling dance, catching the firelight, and reflecting the sprinkling, golden light about the room like tiny fairies.

"Well, I like that very much, and apparently, Mr. Butler likes it as well," her father said.

Equuleus made a soft neighing sound.

"Yes, and Equuleus," he added.

HelperFriend returned to the kitchen.

"Oh, Father! The dinner, the clockworks man—everything is so, *so* lovely. You've made me very happy!"

"Mission accomplished! Shall I pour you some tea?"

"Yes, please."

Heart watched as her father made a small ceremony of pouring her tea. A cozy warmth rose up in her. "But—Father, this feels like an occasion."

"No occasion, Just … being in the moment. I know I've been neglecting you. I have too many projects, too much to do. I've been planning to have this dinner for some time, with poor Mr. HelperFriend hidden away in a closet, waiting for me to bring him out and put him to good use.

"Every day, which, of course, is rather metaphorical here as there are no days, but, as every metaphorical day flew by, I'd say to myself, I'll do it soon.

"When I discovered that you and Equuleus left the castle without even telling me, without even a note, I realized I've neglected you so badly you felt I wouldn't even miss you, and that you ought not bother me."

"That's true," Heart said softly, looking down.

Her father patted her hand affectionately. "So! The time had long passed for me to give you some undivided attention. And to bring a helper onboard for you to direct as you please—to reach books off the top shelf in the library, to help you plant a garden, or what-have-you. Anything you might wish you had another pair of hands to accomplish."

"*Plant a garden!!*" Heart flung her arms around him. "*Oh, Father!*"

He giggled a shy, schoolboy giggle.

"Is it possible? Is it at all possible that I could have a flower garden here?"

"Indeed. You and HelperFriend can build a greenhouse, anywhere you want it."

"Wouldn't it be lovely to have flowers along the walkway to the front door?"

"It would, Heart, very lovely. But please promise me you won't be sad and depressed any more. I know it seems like I'm off in my own space, without hardly knowing you're here, but that's not true. Yes, I'm working furiously on several projects, but you are always on my mind."

"I believe you. I believe you now, anyway. I thought you regretted my coming here."

"*NEVER!*" He appeared to surprise himself with the force of his denial. "Never," he said again, tenderly. "You are the reason behind everything I do."

"Equuleus said something like that."

He turned to Equuleus, "Really?"

"Only because I told him," Heart went on, "that I thought you regretted my being here. He said that much of what you're doing is *because of me.*" She paused, then probed, "Whatever it is that you're doing. I'd be most interested to know."

HelperFriend returned with steaming bowls of vegetables, disrupting the moment.

"Not to worry, my own Heart. It's nothing other than boring math and the like." He changed the subject. "So, Mr. HelperFriend, big day for you! You've been named, and are likely to help plant a flower garden on a synthetic, plant-less moon, off world from one of the most verdant planets in the Universe. I guess I'll have to increase your programming."

HelperFriend seemed to understand exactly what Father Inventor told him, and, much to everyone's surprise, he carefully set down the bowls, then danced and twirled up and down along the far side of the table.

"Where did that come from?" Father Inventor, asked, clearly shocked.

HelperFriend snapped his metallic fingers, and fabulous music came on from everywhere and nowhere.

"Amazing! Let us be in the moment!" Heart's father stood and extended his hand to Heart.

"Yes! Let's!"

They joined HelperFriend, twirling and whirling about the room. Equuleus rose from his cozy space and flew straight up to the ceiling, adding the sparkling glimmer from his wings to the golden glow below, while HelperFriend spun faster and faster, until he looked as though his dazzling, twirling gear eyes wound completely around his head.

*   *   *

*You can find **Moons Rising** at your favorite store as an ebook, paperback, or hardbound.*

DEAR READER ....

Thank you for reading *The Darling Undesirables* – don't miss any of Heart's saga!— *The Darling Undesirables, Moons Rising, The Inventor's Clone, and Heart's Quest* are available wherever books are sold.

And be sure to request your free copy of *The Heart of Leo*, the novella prequel to Heart's entire story.

P.S.: You'll make Heart very happy if you leave a few kind words in a review.

Books & Audio by Blythe Ayne

Fiction:
The Darling Undesirables Series:
The Heart of Leo - short story prequel
The Darling Undesirables
Moons Rising
The Inventor's Clone
Heart's Quest

Short Story Collections:
5 Minute Stories
Lovely Frights for Lonely Nights

Children's Illustrated Books:
The Rat Who Didn't Like Rats
The Rat Who Didn't Like Christmas

Nonfiction:
Love Is The Answer
45 Ways To Excellent Life
Horn of Plenty–The Cornucopia of Your Life
Finding Your Path, Engaging Your Purpose

How to Save Your Life Series:
Save Your Life With The Power Of pH Balance
Save Your Life With The Phenomenal Lemon
Save Your Life with Stupendous Spices
Save Your Life with the Elixir of Water

Absolute Beginner Series:
Bed Yoga – Easy, Healing, Yoga Moves You Can Do in Bed
Write Your Book! Publish Your Book! Market Your Book!

Poetry, Photography, & Art:
Life Flows on the River of Love
Home & the Surrounding Territory

Audio:
The Power of pH Balance –
Dr. Blythe Ayne Interviews Steven Acuff

About the Author

I live on ten acres of forest in the Pacific NW with a few domestic and numerous wild creatures. Along with creating an ever-growing inventory of books, my writing has appeared in hundreds of publications.

As an insatiable student of the human condition, I earned my doctorate in in Social Psychology and Ethnography from the University of California, Irvine.

The next book in *The Darling Undesirables* series is *Moons Rising,* where Heart's adventures continue to escalate. The third book is *The Inventor's Clone,* and the fourth book is *Heart's Quest.*

The Heart of Leo is a novella prequel to Heart's story. I'll send you the ebook as a gift if you would like—just send me an email requesting *The Heart of Leo,* and I'll send it right along.

Visit my website: *BlytheAyne.com* to see my other books, and to learn about my appearances and other writerly activities.

Blythe@BlytheAyne.com